C

W9-ADH-208

BLOODY FABULOUS PRAISE FOR
MARIO ACEVEDO'S

THE NYMPHOS OF ROCKY FLATS

"My built-in garlic factor usually puts me off vampire
books, but Mario Acevedo has come up with such a
fascinating character—Iraq war veteran Felix Gomez, who
is a private detective as well as a vampire—that I was won
over. . . . Acevedo, a former Desert Storm infantry officer
and helicopter pilot, has shrewdly sucked up enough inside
details to make the plot of his first novel (which includes
outbreaks of nymphomania and murder at a secret
government facility) a jaunty and even touching experience."
Chicago Tribune

"A witty, fast-paced, detective tale that also manages to
update vampire lore in clever and imaginative ways."
El Paso Times

"Warning: The author of this book must be a vampire,
because he had me hypnotized from page one. I defy
anyone to read the first chapter of Acevedo's *The Nymphos
of Rocky Flats* and not fall under its spell. Vampire P.I.
Felix Gomez is irresistibly entertaining."
Rick Riordan, Edgar® Award-winning
author of *Mission Road*

"[A book] deserving of fanfare and a wider audience. . . .
A comedic approach to vampirism."
Baltimore Sun

"*The Nymphos of Rocky Flats* is a sassy, fast, fun read."
Boulder Daily Camera (CO)

By Mario Acevedo

The Adventures of Felix Gomez

THE NYMPHOS OF ROCKY FLATS
X-RATED BLOODSUCKERS
THE UNDEAD KAMA SUTRA
JAILBAIT ZOMBIE

Department of Energy
Washington, DC 20585

JUN 2 1 2004

Mr. Mario Acevedo

SUBJECT: Response to Review Request (04SA20B000117-JA)

Dear Mr. Acevedo:

This responds to your request dated April 28, 2004.

This is a:

XX   Complete Response

___   Partial Response

___   Final Partial Response

Findings/Instructions:

XX   We indicated the result(s) of our review on the first page of the document(s) at enclosure(s) 1 (see stamp[s]).

___   **Special considerations apply to this request. See important details at enclosure ___.**

___   Note that we changed the category of some material to **Restricted Data**.

___   Note that we changed the category of some material to **Formerly Restricted Data**.

___   The document(s) at enclosure(s) ___ is/are denied in its/their entirety.

___   We bracketed in ___ the Department of Energy (DOE) classified information and/or Unclassified Controlled Nuclear Information (UCNI) that must be deleted from the document(s) at enclosure(s) ___ prior to release.

___   We indicated next to each bracket the appropriate Freedom of Information Act or Mandatory (Executive Order 12958) exemptions.

_____ The document(s) at enclosure(s) _____ do/does not/no longer contain(s) DOE classified information and/or UCNI, and therefore, we have no objection to its/their declassification and release.

XX The document(s) at enclosure(s) 1 is/are Unclassified and does/do not contain UCNI; therefore, we have no objection to its/their release.

_____ We declassified the document(s) at enclosure(s) _____.

_____ Where applicable, we indicated the name(s) of other agency(ies) and/or office(s) that we recommend review the document(s) prior to its/their release.

_____ Details and appeal procedures for the requester are at enclosure _____.

Sincerely,

Gregory J. Gannon
Acting Program Manager
Statutory Reviews Program
Document Reviews Division
Office of Classification and Information Control
Office of Safeguards and Security Policy
    and Classification Management
Office of Security

Enclosure
Manuscript, dtd 4/28/04 (U)

the NYMPHOS of ROCKY FLATS

Mario Acevedo

An Imprint of HarperCollinsPublishers

EOS
An Imprint of HarperCollins*Publishers*
10 East 53rd Street
New York, New York 10022-5299

Copyright © 2006 by Mario Acevedo
Excerpt from *The Undead Kama Sutra* copyright © 2008 by Mario Acevedo
Cover art by Danny O'Leary
ISBN: 978-0-06-143888-2
www.eosbooks.com

First Eos paperback printing: January 2008
First Rayo trade paperback printing: March 2006

Printed in the U.S.A.

10 9 8 7 6 5 4

Para mi hermana Sylvia,
por sus años de apoyo y fe

Many thanks to Diana Gill at HarperCollins, and to her diligent assistant, Will Hinton. A special note of gratitude to my agent, Scott Hoffman of PMA Literary and Film Management, Inc. for listening to my elevator pitch—while in an elevator—and then agreeing to give my manuscript a read. And to his colleague, Peter Miller, for his support. I couldn't have gotten this far without the wisdom and camaraderie offered by my friends in the Rocky Mountain Fiction Writers. I owe much to my fellow critique members—many of whom have come and gone over the years—with special thanks to Jeanne Stein, Tom and Margie Lawson, Sandy Meckstroth, Jeff Shelby, Heidi Kuhn, and Jim Cole. *Mil gracias* to Tanya Mote and Anthony García of El Centro Su Teatro for their encouragement and *amistad*. To my family who has always stood beside me: my Tía Angélica; siblings Sylvia (and her partner Janet), Armando; my late sister Laura; and my sons, Alex and Emil.

CHAPTER
1

·

I DON'T LIKE WHAT Operation Iraqi Freedom has done to me. I went to the war a soldier; I came back a vampire.

Two weeks after President Bush stood on the deck of the aircraft carrier *Abraham Lincoln* and declared "Mission Accomplished"—victory over Saddam Hussein—we in the Third Infantry Division were still ass-deep in combat along the Euphrates valley. Tonight we were after *fedayeen* guerrillas in a village south of Karbala.

My fire team hunkered inside the troop compartment of our Bradley fighting vehicle. Dirt sifted through the open hatches above. Each of us wore forty pounds of gear like a hide—armor vest, helmet, radios, protective mask, lots and lots of ammo and grenades—under which we marinated in a greasy funk. Days of grinding mechanized combat saddled us with a fatigue as thick as the grime caking our weary bodies.

Each of us had bloodshot eyes and was queasy from bombardments delivered danger-close. Our artillery, the air force, and the navy demolished entire city blocks while we waited across the street. Our officers joked that we were smiting the enemy with an ass-kicking of biblical proportions.

We'd get the warning, drop low, cover our ears, and open our mouths to equalize the pressure. The blasts bounced us off the ground. Our eyeballs rattled in their orbits. Dust smothered us. Concussion from the bombs would slam into my belly, and I felt like I'd gotten run over by a parade of Buicks.

A painful spasm twisted my insides. I didn't tell anyone that I had started pissing blood. If I were evacuated, who would take care of my men? It was my duty to get them out of this shit-hole alive and in one piece.

Our Bradley veered sharply to the left and right as if following a rat through a maze. The abrupt movements jostled us in the darkness of the troop compartment.

Machine-gun fire rattled along the steel-armored skirt. My jaw clenched. The worst part of war was that everyone played for keeps.

Our Bradley clanged to a stop. The turret basket swiveled to the left. The 25mm cannon answered the enemy with a comforting *wham, wham, wham*.

Staff Sergeant Kowtowski dropped from his seat in the turret basket. He flicked on the flashlight clipped to his armor vest and a blue-green glow illuminated my team's anxious, dirty faces. Kowtowski pulled aside the boom mike of his crewman's helmet and yelled. "Gomez, when you un-ass, lead your team to the left. There's a Humvee with the lieutenant."

"Roger," I yelled back. He could have told me this through my radio but I think he wanted to look at his men one last time in case he never saw us alive again. Softhearted bastard.

"Good luck," Kowtowski shouted and turned off the flashlight. He climbed back into his seat. The Bradley groaned forward. The turret machine gun let loose and joined the chorus of staccato blasts from the Bradleys flanking us.

I knelt against the ramp and held a strap to steady myself. Private O'Brien readied his M249 machine gun and looped the belt of ammunition over his left arm. The other men in the team crowded next to me, all of us a tight, warm ball of fear.

The Bradley halted. My shoulder banged against the hull. The ramp winched open. We ran out, our heads scrunched into the neck wells of our armor vests. My index finger reached across the trigger guard of my carbine.

Our Bradley was parked close to a long mud-brick wall, the front of a lopsided row of houses that stretched across the block. The other Bradleys from our platoon blocked the intersections before and behind us, standing guard like immense war elephants. Garbage littered the street. The night air was filmy with dust. Slivers of light escaped from shuttered windows.

We stayed behind cover, squeezing between the Bradley and a flaking plaster wall as we moved toward the Humvee.

From the top of the Humvee, the machine gunner behind an armor shield aimed a searchlight at the front door of a home. In the cone of light, the lieutenant and a gaunt Iraqi interpreter banged on the wooden door. The harsh light reduced their forms to broken silhouettes.

The interpreter twisted the doorknob and beat the door harder as he yelled frantically in Arabic. His tense voice revealed fear, not anger.

"Enough," the lieutenant shouted, "we're not here to sell Avon." He drew his pistol and pushed the interpreter aside. The lieutenant aimed his automatic at the keyhole below the doorknob.

O'Brien and I crouched beside the lieutenant like a pair of twitching junkyard dogs waiting to attack.

The lieutenant fired once. The knob flew away in a shower of splinters. He reared back and kicked the door open to the shrieks of female voices.

We sprang forward and panned the room with our weapons.

Three Iraqi women huddled like frightened birds in one corner. Their ashen faces hovered above trembling hands. They clutched black shawls to their throats. Were they a mother and her daughters? They eyed us fearfully, their gazes fixed on the night-vision goggles clipped to the front of our helmets. Rumor was the Iraqis thought the goggles gave us X-ray vision and we could see through their clothing.

A swaying electric bulb lit the room. Shadows danced across the walls. Broken furniture, loose plaster, and paper lay scattered over a threadbare carpet.

The interpreter entered and was followed by the lieutenant. Pistol in hand, he yelled at the interpreter and the women. "Why didn't you open the door? Where are your men?"

The interpreter turned to the women. When they heard his Arabic, they surrounded him, gesturing and screaming angry questions. The oldest woman gave the best performance, repeatedly pressing a hand to her forehead and swooping her other arm at the ruin in her home.

An explosion shook the house. We ducked against the closest wall. The women dropped to the floor with practiced agility. Dust trickled from the ceiling.

The lieutenant answered his radio and then hollered. "Sergeant Gomez, we got contact. Get around back ASAP."

No shit, we got contact. My team dashed into the next room, tramping over unmade beds and knocking over dressers. There was a flimsy wooden door along the back wall that I busted open.

We emerged into an alley—barren and spooky. Reaching to the front of my helmet, I flipped the night-vision goggles down over my eyes. A greenish image materialized inside the lenses, a fuzzy picture of a dark background cluttered with bright abstract shapes.

Hustling to what remained of a brick wall, I lay prone amid the rubble while my team took positions alongside.

The lieutenant whispered excitedly over the tiny earpiece of my radio. "Four, maybe six *fedayeen* dropped into a canal about fifty meters past the alley." He ordered me to take my men to the berm overlooking the canal while another team flushed the *fedayeen* toward us.

We crept down the slope to the canal bank, our reflexes primed as we expected the enemy to open up at any second. I went up the berm first and snaked on my belly to the top. My heart thumped so loud I was afraid the enemy would hear it.

O'Brien startled me when he groped at the dirt to lie down behind his M249. His eyes reflected the dim green light coming from the back lenses of his night-vision goggles. The rest of my team joined us on the berm.

"How many of these guys do you think we gotta kill before we can go home?" O'Brien whispered.

"I'm pretty sure it's all of them," I answered.

"Too bad they don't stay in one place. This war would be over that much sooner if everyone cooperated."

From the depths of the image in my lenses appeared four figures, moving like specters along the muddy bank of the canal. My breath quickened.

The enemy was close enough to see that they carried equipment over their shoulders. Explosives perhaps? Rocket-propelled grenades—RPGs? They moved haltingly and whispered in Arabic. Their implements clinked together.

The lieutenant blurted over the radio. "Get ready."

In a quiet voice, I alerted my team. As one, we shouldered our weapons and curled index fingers over triggers.

A machine gun to my left growled, spewing a cascade of red tracers. O'Brien opened up. An M203 barked, lobbing a grenade into the center of the enemy.

We caught the Iraqis in a thick crossfire against the bank of the canal. The four intruders withered under a hail of tracers and the white flash of grenades exploding among them.

I fixed on the falling bodies and fired quick bursts, nailing each one in turn.

The lieutenant's loud voice sang over the roar of our guns. "Cease fire, goddamnit."

We released our triggers, the blasts from our guns ringing in my ears. The spent brass casings still whirling in the air pinged on the ground. An incandescent swirl of smoke rose from the hot, glowing barrel of the M249.

I flipped the goggles up from my eyes. My heart pounded in euphoric victory. The moment was exhilarating, my senses taut as a trip wire.

I could hear the smile in O'Brien's voice as he said, "Damn, that felt nice."

A wail rose from one of the bodies sprawled at the water's edge. Not a man's cry but the shriek of a girl, a horrible noise that told me my life would never be the same again.

The lieutenant and three other men crept around the berm and gathered around the fallen bodies. I pushed up to my feet to join them, the girl's wail tearing at my nerves.

The lieutenant produced a flashlight and swung its blue-green beam over the area.

A girl in a knee-length dress lay face up on the dirt. She looked maybe twelve years old. Screaming, she stared at us, her eyes so wide with fright that her pupils seemed to hover above the whites of her eyeballs. Her thin legs pumped at the ground as she tried to push away from us. Her right hand covered her belly. Blood seeped through her fingers.

Two women in black robes lay beside each other, mouths gaping, arms and legs ragged with ugly wounds. Each woman rested across a pole. Ropes lay twisted from the ends of the poles to plastic jugs.

An Iraqi with mustache, beard, and a checkered head-dress squirmed on his back, wheezing. His eyes were shut in a grimace of pain.

"Oh God, oh God," one of the soldiers sobbed, "what have we done?"

O'Brien kicked the plastic jugs and his voice broke. "They were just *haji*s trying to get water."

Other soldiers had killed civilians by mistake. The bad breaks of war, I'd thought at the time. Now that I'd done it, the earth seemed to heave beneath my boots. I became dizzy and fought the urge to throw up.

The Iraqi man raised an arm and blindly called, "Ani."

The girl pulled herself toward him, crying out.

The man's arm dropped. His face slackened.

The girl shrieked louder, realizing that she was alone, wounded, and surrounded by us, a gang of assassins.

"Ah shit," the lieutenant kept repeating. He took off his helmet and ran a trembling hand over his burr cut. He called the company commander over the radio.

After a brief, tense exchange, the lieutenant released his radio mike. His shoulders drooped as if the world had landed on him. "We gotta evacuate her ASAP."

I yanked open the first-aid pouch attached to my armor vest and snatched the bandage. "Somebody give me a poncho. Now."

I tore open the plastic wrapper, pulled apart the ends of the bandage, and knelt beside the girl. She shrank from me, her face pale with terror.

We unfolded O'Brien's poncho and tried to coax the girl onto it, but she kept scooting away. O'Brien grabbed her hands and held them in a corner of the poncho while another soldier clutched her feet.

I had to expose the wound and drew my bayonet to cut

her blood-soaked dress across the middle. Howling mania-
cally, the girl whipped her body against the poncho before
going limp. She whimpered in Arabic. It wasn't enough that
we had shot her in the belly and slaughtered her family, she
must have thought, now we were going to rape her as well.

Blood flowed from a hole beside her navel. I pressed the
gauze pad against the wound. Her warm blood soaked my
hands. I reached under her tiny waist to tie the ends of the
bandage around her.

How could this have happened? I knew what I had seen
through the goggles. How could I have been so wrong?

We carried the girl away from the canal, her cracking
voice echoing across the desolation. The night disintegrated
into a dismal blur.

O'Brien slowed and tugged at his end of the poncho.
"Hold up."

We shuffled to a halt. A rivulet of blood poured from the
poncho.

We laid the girl on the ground. O'Brien put his fingers on
her throat. "Tell the medics not to bother." He crossed himself.

Grief wracked my body. I felt pain from the bottoms of
my feet to the inside of my skull. The agony squeezed my
heart, compressing so hard I thought it would burst.

White tracers splattered around us. Jolting with terror, we
dove and scattered. The bullets hunted us. One thumped
against my armor vest. Another slapped the carbine from
my hand.

RPGs exploded around me, knocking the helmet from
my head. Dirt pelted my skin. My ears rang from the concussion and for what seemed like an instant, I blacked out.

Dazed, I pushed myself off the ground and staggered
painfully to my feet. The fighting had stopped. I called to
my team but saw that I was alone, surrounded by the bodies
of the Iraqi civilians we had killed.

Where was my unit? Had they left me for dead? With trembling fingers I clutched a grenade. The silence betrayed nothing; even the enemy was gone.

I hobbled to the top of the bank, shivering like a frightened, wounded animal. At the far end of the alley, a ball of fire consumed the Humvee. Flames jumped from the roofs of the houses. Gulping for breath, I tasted ashes and fear.

I turned to my left, as if following a meridian that pointed the way to safety. Picking my way through the rubble of the brick wall, I limped for the closest dwelling.

A strange force pulled me and I stumbled over debris littering the threshold. Smoke clouded the interior, rolling up the walls and escaping through a hole in the ceiling.

I crept to a window. I stayed hidden inside the gloom and glimpsed outside. The canal twisted below like a piece of beaten pewter. On the banks lay the forms of the Iraqis. The girl's dress shimmered against the dark earth.

Her blood glistened on my fingers. Bloody handprints stained my trousers. Confusion and shame coiled around me. I felt as if my uniform were strangling me.

I was no hero.

I was a murderer.

I pulled at my collar. We'd been sent here to kill the enemy in the name of freedom, and instead we had massacred an innocent family. Our great cause was a sham. I didn't want anything more to do with this stupid war.

Smoke drifted through a door leading to another room. The force that had drawn me here led me to the door.

In the next room stood a man tending a flame, poking a long stick at the coals piled on the dirt floor. He wore a tattered vest over a dirty robe. His head turned toward me, a mustache, beard, and bushy hair outlining a drawn face.

His eyes shone like those of a wolf, two red shiny disks. My reflex was to flee, but his gaze held me with a power that reached through my eyes and seized my thoughts. His will became mine.

He commanded, "Come here."

His voice came from inside my head. It was not in Arabic, nor in English, but was a soothing tone that cut through my delirium to promise relief from despair.

"You need no weapon."

I let the grenade drop, not caring if the pin still secured the safety lever. I approached with my hands raised, my fingers mottled with the blood of the Iraqi girl.

The stranger grasped my hands and brought them to his face, smearing my dirty, bloody fingers against his cheeks and nose. "Nothing is as precious as the blood of the innocent." He put a hand on my shoulder and stared into my eyes. "It is this girl's blood that torments you. Why?"

His question pumped more anguish into me. I choked on my words. "I didn't mean to kill her. It was a mistake. I didn't know. I was wrong."

"You are a soldier. You kill. That is your job."

"My job isn't to kill the innocent."

The stranger stroked my neck with the back of his hand as if what he desired was within my throat. I wanted to recoil in revulsion but this strange, hypnotic trance overpowered my instinct to escape.

"Death would end the guilt." The stranger's grin threatened more than it reassured. "You want to die?"

I forced myself to shake my head, since my body no longer felt like my own.

He yanked my armor vest and pulled me off balance. I fell to my knees in front of him. He cradled my head in his rough hands and his thoughts materialized inside my head.

"If not death, then suffering would appease this guilt. Is that what you want?"

I whispered, "We didn't come here to slaughter children

and their mothers. If someone must be punished, then make it me. Hold me accountable."

"Punishment? How noble of you, soldier. Everyone else begs for mercy. I could make this pleasant, but you want to suffer."

His face approached me. His lips parted. An intense creepiness overcame me, a horrid sensation like hundreds of spiders crawling over my skin. But I could do nothing except let him turn my head to expose the left side of my neck. Moist lips touched my skin. Two sharp points punctured my flesh. I clenched my fists to endure the pain.

The drumming of my heartbeat slowed. My muscles relaxed. The maddening distress spinning in my head dissolved into a dreamy, pulsating haze. A coolness crept up my limbs to my torso. My toes and fingers began to tingle. The fog in my brain thickened. The shroud of death brushed over me.

Then the stranger pressed his mouth against mine, and a salty ooze of blood washed over my tongue.

My throat burned as if acid had been poured into me. My guts twisted and writhed like a snake set afire. I tried to retch but he held me tight against him. When I started to convulse, he let go and my body jerked in feverish spasms. I lay on my side and looked up at him. An orange aura—like the glow from hot coals—surrounded him. He wiped blood from his chin.

I gasped for the words. "Who are you?"

"I am the damned son of Nadilla, the undead queen of the Tigris and Euphrates." His answer was drenched in bitterness and self-loathing.

I dragged myself away from him. The orange glow radiated from my hands as well. My insides thrashed in panic. "Undead?"

He nodded. "And I've given you what you wanted. A punishment even worse than death. I've given you immortality. As a vampire."

CHAPTER
2

SOMETIME AFTER MY DISCHARGE from the army, I was driving my '62 Dodge Polara north on Highway 93. The rugged foothills of the Rocky Mountains were to my left, and in the distance to my right stretched the sprawl of the Denver metroplex. Here Highway 93 cuts through a grassy plain littered with cinder-block-sized rocks. Past the intersection with Highway 72, I turned right at the first traffic light and entered the Department of Energy's Rocky Flats Closure Project, formerly known as the Rocky Flats Environmental Technology Site, but always remembered by its original function—the Rocky Flats Nuclear Weapons Plant.

I halted by the shack alongside the entrance road. A guard wearing a gray camouflage uniform and a large black holster cinched to his dumpy waist greeted me. A sign on the guard shack listed prohibited items: guns, explosives, cameras, binoculars, all non-DOE-approved communications devices—whatever those were.

The guard asked for my license. He examined my photo and growled, "Mr. Gomez, please remove your sunglasses."

Despite the fact he had a gun and I didn't, he gave a frightened grimace when I removed my sunglasses. I expected the reaction. The dark rings surrounding my eyes gave me a hungry, predatory appearance. I squinted because of the sun and shielded my face with one hand.

He would've crapped in his pants if I had removed my contacts. These special contacts masked the reflection from the mirror-like *tapetum lucidum* at the back of my eyes, which gave me a threatening, lupine gaze. The *tapetum lucidum* allowed me—and all vampires—both night vision and the ability to see the psychic energy auras that surrounded living things. I wore contacts to keep from spooking the humans.

My vampire sense, a heightened awareness of my five other senses, which my brain processed into an intuitive sixth sense, detected his fear. Instinctively, I ran my tongue across my upper teeth, feeling my incisors start to grow. I smiled at him and replaced my sunglasses.

The guard quickly returned my license. After checking his clipboard, he gave me a pink plastic ID tag stamped VISITOR. A dosimeter was affixed to one corner of the tag.

He pointed to a black Humvee parked beyond the guard shack. "They'll escort you to your destination."

Two more guards in gray camouflage climbed into the Humvee. Besides submachine guns, these guards donned police helmets and carried protective masks strapped to their thighs. The edginess in their manner made me wonder if this had something to do with the reason I had been summoned here.

I followed them for a quarter-mile, taking in the desolate

quality of Rocky Flats. From my reading of public documents about this place and its notorious past, I expected a giant industrial complex. Instead, rows of steel containers lay stacked together on asphalt pads, surrounded by sparse grass, dirt, and the ubiquitous rocks. Boxcars sat on rusted wheels, resting on segments of track leading to nowhere. Ahead of us stood the gray concrete buildings in the Protected Area, where DOE and its contractors used to manufacture plutonium. Rolls of razor wire glittered atop chain-link fencing that marked the perimeter.

I lowered my window and let in the aroma of sagebrush. A mood of apprehension and restrained panic permeated the air. My vampire sense failed to pinpoint the cause, and this should've alerted me, but in my arrogance—I was in the company of blunt-toothed humans, after all—I dismissed any concern.

My college roommate, Gilbert Odin, now the Rocky Flats Assistant Manager for Environmental Restoration, had asked for me. Hearing from him after losing touch for a long time surprised me, but not as much as the twenty-thousand-dollar check he had Fed-Exed as an enticement to consider his proposal. Which was? I didn't know, but the money was enough to tempt any private detective.

The Humvee took the left fork of the road and continued until we ended in a gravel parking lot adjacent to a series of long office trailers.

The guards dismounted, keeping their submachine guns handy, and pointed to the wooden steps of the trailer to my right. Did everyone get so much special attention?

Removing my sunglasses, I climbed the short, creaking steps and entered a tiny, carpeted foyer lit by weak fluorescent lighting. The interior was of modular construction, with upholstered wall panels in alternating beige and gray. Along one wall hung photographs in cheap plastic frames, portraits of the President, the Secretary of the Department of Energy, and all the DOE management flunkies in the hierarchy between Washington, D.C., and Rocky Flats.

The hall emptied into a receptionist's office. No one sat behind the desk. Stacks of papers and binders covered the surface, crowded against framed photos of a smiling middle-aged blonde posing with children and a man about her age. A pile of thick folders lay on the chair.

The door behind the desk opened and Gilbert Odin stepped out. My friend stood as tall as I remembered him, at six foot four. His tie ended three-quarters of the way down his shirt. We hadn't seen each other in years, and while I recognized his thick mustache, the bald pate pushing through a crown of gray and brown hair was new. It was as if his worries had burnished the hair off his head. His gray eyes beamed pleasantly through the rimless glasses perched on a long, narrow nose. He carried a smell of cabbage, as if he'd just finished a plate of sauerkraut.

We made eye contact.

Gilbert's eyes opened wide, and his head tipped back in surprise.

I gave him a practiced smile and offered my hand, ignoring his stare. "Hey, Gilbert, what's it been? Years and years?"

He gave my hand a weak, hesitant shake while he continued to study my appearance. "Yeah, something like that."

We went into his office and he shut the door. The office was what I expected for a mid-level government hack. More modular walls and fluorescent lighting. A desk and matching cabinets, finished in a fake teak veneer. Computer monitor and keyboard on the desk. An in-box overflowing with correspondence.

Gilbert put his hand up, indicating that I should halt. He pulled a black box the size of a cigarette pack from the pocket of his trousers. He pressed a button and red lights flashed along the box that I recognized as an electronic bug detector.

Waving the box from side to side in front of me, Gilbert flicked his gaze from the box to my person. When he pointed at my ID tag, the lights flashed steadily and the box began to chirp.

He retrieved a letter opener from his desk and pried the dosimeter from my ID tag to expose a silver capsule sprouting wires. A listening device.

"Got you, ya bastard." Gilbert dropped the bug on the floor and crunched it under his heel.

He motioned for me to sit in the chair before his desk. My gaze lingered on the broken remains of the miniature transmitter on the carpet. My vampire sense had missed the bug, and I felt uncomfortably naïve and paranoid. I wanted to start with my questions, but Gilbert put his fingers to his lips, so I kept quiet. He picked up the receiver of his phone and hollered into it, a yell so loud I winced.

He returned the phone to its cradle. "Whenever I have a guest, those assholes in Security crank up the sensitivity of their snooper. I love to make their ears ring for the rest of the day."

A black boom box rested on the credenza behind Gilbert's desk. He flicked the on switch and filled the room with the strains of a Metallica concert loud enough to drown the shriek of a turbine engine. How the hell were we going to talk?

He opened the center panel of the credenza and placed both the boom box and his telephone inside. When he shut the panel, it turned the heavy metal guitar whine into a muffled drone.

"Let's see those bastards try to eavesdrop now." He sat in his high-backed chair and folded his hands on his desk, smiling wryly.

As a vampire and private detective, I should be used to the bizarre, but nothing in my experience had ever matched this loony display.

I looked back at the destroyed bug on the floor. "If we're not safe to talk here, why not go off site?"

"If I did that," Gilbert replied, "Security would get suspicious."

"Seems to me they're already suspicious."

"This is nothing. They're just covering their butts. It's the illusion of vigilance that comforts them. In these days after 9/11, any act of paranoia is justified."

Gilbert's eyes shifted from my face to the bottom of my neck. He must have noticed the makeup smeared against the inside of my collar. According to popular lore, vampires aren't supposed to be able to endure sunlight. Thankfully, popular lore doesn't take into account the modern miracles of sunblock, vitamin supplements, and cosmetics.

"If you don't mind me asking, what's with your eyes and the makeup?"

"Gulf War Syndrome," I replied. "The second Gulf War. Operation Iraqi Freedom."

His expression became anxious. "I read that it's not contagious. *Is* it?"

Not unless I bit him. "No," I reassured him. "But I was exposed to every suspected agent. Got the notorious anthrax vaccine. The latest issue of the *Gulf War Review* says that I could have leishmaniasis or mycoplasma. During battle we drove through the smoke of burning enemy tanks that we had destroyed with depleted-uranium penetrators. God knows what we inhaled."

"Try beryllium, americium, and plutonium besides the depleted uranium," he said. "Those rounds were made of U-238 dross from the enriched stuff we processed here."

"So it's ironic that I'm here," I said.

"Irony has nothing to do with it. And neither does depleted uranium, I don't think. I asked for you because of your credentials."

"So I gathered. When you sent a check for twenty grand

and a request for an interview, I figured there was more to it than you asking how I've been. This is about Rocky Flats, right?"

"It is."

"Then I don't understand how you expect a civilian investigator, an outsider, to accomplish anything here, considering your safeguards and security requirements."

"Felix, it's precisely *because* you're an outsider. A known quantity I can trust. For example, three weeks after you took the Blanford case, you traced them to their hideout in St. Lucia and found their stash of embezzled monies on Vanuatu."

"How'd you learn about that?" I asked.

"The Patriot Act," Gilbert replied smugly. "Ask the right questions and it's amazing what can be learned. Your reputation is impressive."

"Okay, so I do a good job," I said. "What does this have to do with me being here?"

Gilbert walked over to a map of Rocky Flats on the wall adjacent to his desk. He pointed with his pen to a collection of black rectangles inside a crooked trapezoid on the map. "This is the Protected Area."

"The 700 series of buildings," I said. "Where you manufactured plutonium detonators from enriched uranium. I did my homework."

"Good. The situation . . ." he drawled, pausing to indicate that by *situation* he meant *problem*, "began here." He tapped his pen against the rectangle labeled Building 707.

"And this situation is?"

Gilbert turned from the map. "We were finishing the final survey of Building 707 for decontamination and demolition when . . ." Gilbert cleared his throat. "We had an outbreak of nymphomania."

Nymphomania? Rocky Flats was getting weirder by the

minute. I cupped my hand behind an ear and tipped my head. "What? Run that by me again."

"It began with rumors of a few of our women employees rushing home to their significant others and leaving them exhausted. After a week or so, more of the women began engaging in coitus with their coworkers—in closets, conference rooms, secure chambers within the protected area. Even the most reticent were affected. My own secretary, a Sunday school teacher, is on administrative leave because of this."

"I hope she's okay." Though I wasn't sure how she could've hurt herself, other than getting a sore vagina.

"She's fine. It's her poor husband who couldn't keep up. Threw his back out."

"My condolences."

"We've worked hard at recruiting women, and damn if it hasn't backfired on us. Half of our guard force is female, and in case you didn't notice, none of them are on duty. It's played hell with our productivity, our morale, and our security. Two, make that three weeks ago, one of our female guards got the itch, which she satisfied at gunpoint with a victim."

"Must've been one hell of a scandal."

"You'd think so," Gilbert said. "But God watches out for drunks, fools, and DOE. Turns out the visitor was a senior auditor from the Office of Management and Budget. He was going to ream us about our property accountability— or lack thereof—when the guard pulled him over and had her way with him. What could have been a disaster for us became instead a delightful encounter for some wonk from OMB. On the street he'd pay five hundred bucks for treatment like that. Here he got it for free." Gilbert sighed. "That was the most extreme example."

"So what'd you do?" I asked. "Let these women screw their brains out on government time?"

"What was the alternative?" Gilbert replied. "Fire fifty percent of our workforce? DOE wants full disclosure of our activities—except for the embarrassing stuff." He fidgeted with the knot of his tie. "At first we thought we'd just let the women get it out of their systems. To accommodate their needs, as it were," he cleared his throat, "we had open purchase orders with every lifestyle store in the metroplex. Vibrators, dildos, lube by the gallon, condoms by the gross. We even had copies of the *Kama Sutra* delivered in bulk."

"Fortunately, we discovered an ally among the pharmaceuticals." Gilbert opened a side drawer to his desk and produced a small plastic bottle. He shook the vial, rattling the green-and-white pills inside. "A daily dose of sixty grams of selective serotin reuptake inhibitors. Fluoxetine hydrochloride. Prozac."

Gilbert put the bottle away. "Now we have plenty of happy women and very few horny ones. Rumor has it the holdouts were tramps to begin with."

"So, is the outbreak, if you want to call it that, contained?"

"Yes." Gilbert unfolded a paper from a folder. "This shows how the outbreak spread." The chart was a spiderweb of lines linked to circles that denoted each affected individual. "Here in the center are the first three women contaminated. Since we didn't know they had been exposed to something transmittable, we didn't have the foresight to quarantine them."

"How was it spread?"

"We're not sure. Perhaps by casual contact, a handshake for example. Maybe by airborne transmission. The outbreak has been contained, meaning no new instances of, er, the nymphomania."

"And the women contaminated now are under medical supervision?" I asked.

"Yes. Fortunately the outbreak seems to have passed.

Most of the women affected are on medical leave or have been transferred."

"Then case closed. What do you need me for?"

"To find the cause."

"Gilbert, this sounds like a job for the Centers for Disease Control. You need teams of viral pathologists and microbiologists—not *me*."

Gilbert returned to the map. He jabbed at Building 707. "Something happened here that triggered the outbreak. On Valentine's Day, no less. The first women infected were part of the survey team."

"So what's keeping you from finding out?" I asked. "You're responsible for the goddamn cleanup. Right?"

"Right. And wrong," Gilbert replied wearily. "The audit trail ends the day before the surveillance."

"What do you mean, ends?"

"The paperwork was done, all right. I just can't find it. All the files from the final phase of the Building 707 reclamation are gone."

"This sounds like more than missing paperwork," I said. "This is a turf battle within DOE, and I've learned to stay out of family fights. If DOE is comfortable with this fabrication, then why do you care?"

Gilbert's fist tightened. The heavy smell of cabbage—almost artificially strong—tainted his perspiration. He either needed to ease up on the *kimchi* or try a better deodorant.

"I didn't come to DOE from a weapons background," he said. "I came from the environmental side. Believe it or not, some of us at DOE do care about the Earth. And besides that, I'm not going to hang for someone else's mistakes."

"Fair enough," I replied. "Now tell me, how far can a private investigator poke into business here?"

"Your cover would be that you're a nuclear health physics consultant."

"Why not up the stakes and pass me off as a two-headed plastic surgeon? What do I know about nuclear health physics?"

"You don't have to know anything. Just talk bullshit and you'll fit right in."

"What about a security clearance?"

Gilbert pulled a form from the folder on his desk. "With your top-secret army clearance, I was able to fast-track you a DOE Q-clearance."

"I only had a secret clearance in the army."

Gilbert shrugged. "Somebody made a typo. By the time the Office of Internal Security finds out, you'll be done and out of here."

"I appreciate the vote of confidence, but the more I hear, the more I think your optimism might be a little misplaced."

"You'd have six weeks."

"Why six?"

"Because in six weeks the first shipment of contaminated material from Building 707 will be trucked to the WIPP site, the Waste Isolation Pilot Project."

"You mean burial deep inside Carlsbad Caverns?" I asked. "If that's the case, why don't you inspect the shipping manifests? I can't believe you don't have the power to do at least that."

"What the manifests declare and what is shipped can be two different things."

"Are you *that* powerless?"

"No, I'm not. I've got resources. You." Gilbert turned to a section in my folder. "Besides the Blanford case, there was another assignment that told me you were the man for this. The Han Cobras."

Chinese heroin smugglers. Ruthless. Maniacal. Killed three Federal Drug Enforcement agents, not to mention dozens of foreign cops. Invincible. Except against a vampire.

Gilbert read from my file. "Felix Gomez survived numerous ambushes . . . entered the most heavily guarded safe houses undetected . . . exhibited almost supernatural powers of stealth and escape."

"Stop it, you're embarrassing me."

"Embarrassing or not, these, quote, supernatural powers, unquote, are what's going to keep you alive. Somebody doesn't want the truth to get out. Remember what happened to Karen Silkwood?"

"She died in a car wreck, or was murdered by thugs from the nuclear power industry, depending on your faith in conspiracy theories. What are you getting at, Gilbert?" My vampire sense blossomed into full alert. "I haven't accepted anything. You want a hero, find someone else. I'll even give back the twenty thousand, less expenses for driving my hairy ass out here from California."

Gilbert closed my file and lowered his gaze. "You could leave now. All you'd prove is how much I misjudged you."

The words cut like broken glass. My *kundalini noir*, the black serpent of energy that resided in every vampire's breast in place of a beating heart, shifted uncomfortably.

Gilbert raised his gaze, his eyes pools of desperation. "Felix, that twenty grand came out of my pocket. And I've got another thirty thousand to hand over when the assignment's done. If you won't do it to help me, then do it for the money."

Anger at Gilbert made my fangs grow. I pressed my lips together to hide my incisors as I forced them to retract. He had set me up. A friend begs for help, and how could I say no without looking like a chicken-shit gumshoe?

After a moment I was composed enough to say, "Okay, I'll take your fifty thousand."

CHAPTER 3

MY HOME WAS MENLO PARK, California. Here in Colorado I needed a base for my investigation, and for that I needed a better place to stay than a motel.

I found an ad for a two-bedroom apartment in Edgewater, a tidy enclave swallowed but not yet digested by the Denver sprawl. Edgewater seemed perfect, right off the interstate, a convenient drive both to Rocky Flats and downtown Denver. It had quiet, short streets crowded with bungalows, a trailer park or two, and a couple of shopping strips. Bars and fast-food joints faced Sloan's Lake, which always had a stream of people jogging along its shore and dog lovers taking their mutts for a walk.

I drove a Ryder rental truck with my Dodge in tow and parked in front of the apartment building. It was small, only eight units. A short, older man, maybe sixty, wearing faded bib overalls, poked a broomstick along a dormant flowerbed.

"I'm looking for the manager," I yelled to him.

He straightened up and walked over, offsetting a limp by bracing against the broomstick. He hadn't done a very good job shaving his wrinkled, dark face. "You the *vato* who called about the vacancy?" His northern–New Mexico lilt told me that he had been raised somewhere between Española and Raton.

Standing beside my truck in his overalls and leaning on the stick, the whiskered old man looked like he'd fallen out of a Norman Rockwell painting. All he needed to complete the folksy picture was a straw hat and a pig under his arm.

"Yeah, that's me. Name's Felix Gomez."

He squinted suspiciously at my face.

"It's a skin condition," I said. "From the Iraq War."

"You a veteran?"

"Sergeant. Third Infantry Division."

"An enlisted man, eh?" He smiled. "*Qué bueno. Soy* Victor Lopez. I had my fill of candy-assed officers when I was in Vietnam. I got a war-related condition, too—commie shrapnel in my ass. Wanna see?"

I smiled back at Lopez. "No thanks."

"Didn't think so. No one ever does." He turned around and limped to the apartment building. "Well, come take a look at the place. Where's your *familia* from, Gomez?"

"Originally? Chihuahua, Mexico. I grew up in Pacoima, part of L.A."

"One of those California Chicanos? A troublemaker." The twinkle in his eyes matched his smile.

"I've been accused of that."

"I was once married to a California *chica,*" he said. "Damn could she cook. In the kitchen and in the bedroom." The old man sighed. "Then some big *negro* came riding on a Harley. She hopped on the back and *adiós mi amor.*"

"Happens. How's the food in Edgewater?"

"Best goddamn pizza in town. And plenty of *comida Mexicana* close by."

"What about meat markets? Butcher shops?"

Lopez pointed south. "Drive down Sheridan or Federal and you'll find your pick of *carnicerías. Tripas* for *menudo. Sesos. Lengua.* You name it."

It wasn't tripe, brains, or tongue that I wanted but fresh animal blood. Any *carnicería* would do.

He showed me the apartment. It was recently repainted and overlooked the lake. The second bedroom would be a perfect office. The place was cable-ready, too.

I inspected the kitchen, looking specifically in the cabinets, to see where I could build a false partition to hide my laptop in case someone broke into the apartment.

I signed the lease and gave him a deposit. We returned to the Ryder truck. I detached the towing dolly and my Dodge, then opened the rear door of the truck.

Lopez watched. "Need help? I know a couple of teenagers down the block who could use the extra money."

With vampire strength I could easily move all of my belongings, but for appearance's sake I said yes.

Lopez pointed into the truck. "What the hell's that?"

"It's a Murphy bed," I replied. "It folds up against the wall."

Actually, it was my coffin. Some legends are true. Vampires are nocturnal creatures, and keeping a regular human schedule wears us out after a few days. And, of course, nothing is as refreshing as a good snooze in a comfortable casket.

Lopez left to find the teenagers. I started to move my belongings inside. The teenagers showed up, a chatty blond kid and his girlfriend. After we emptied the truck, I gave them each a twenty, returned the Ryder truck, and caught a cab back to Edgewater.

I put away my things and took a break to inventory my contact lenses. More than any other accessory, these custom eye covers were the most important item that modern vampires need to blend in with human society. I kept extra sets stashed in my clothes, my car, and about the apartment. Unfortunately, while masking our eyes the contacts also mute night vision and block our ability for hypnosis.

I practiced inserting and then flicking the contacts from my eyes into my hand. I had to be ready to go from friendly human to controlling vampire in an instant. I wished that I could've practiced in front of a mirror, but, well, you know.

There was no formal program in becoming a vampire, not even a correspondence course, and I had learned "on the job," so to speak. I found other vampires and learned the tricks and ways of our culture, always mindful of this warning: "Above all, don't let the humans know we exist."

That evening I ordered delivery of the famed local pizza—pepperoni, black olive, and jalapeño—which I smothered with warmed cow's blood. An hour after sunset I went outside my apartment and removed my contacts. The evening shadows became transparent to my night vision. Every animal shimmered with a red aura. I stepped behind a pine tree where I was hidden from casual view. I set my fingers and toes against the brick wall of the apartment and climbed up, stealthy as a lizard.

Once on the roof, I sat quietly on the warm shingles to catalogue the sights, sounds, and smells of the neighborhood. I needed to know what normal was like so I could detect the abnormal.

While I looked around, I stewed over how Gilbert had suckered me into accepting the assignment. Nymphomaniacs. Conspiracy. Only the federal government could invent such a mess. If I hadn't heard the words from Gilbert's mouth, I wouldn't have believed the cockamamie story. But the offer of fifty thousand bucks did a lot to make me try and see things his way.

Hell, why was I worried? I should solve this case within hours. All I had to do was interrogate the affected women under vampire hypnosis and get to the truth.

A black Ford Crown Victoria cruised down the street. The Ford slowed as it approached my Dodge. The auras of the two occupants brightened, showing that they had an interest in my car. After a moment, the Ford sped up and disappeared down the street.

No cause for concern. My Dodge Polara was a collector's item. I should sell it and drive newer wheels, perhaps a Toyota with an FM radio and a CD player.

I lay flat on the roof and sighed. This trip to Denver was going to be a vacation.

My *kundalini noir* twitched. I sat up and looked in the direction the Ford had gone. My vampire sixth sense nagged at me and whispered danger.

I dismissed my doubts. I was dealing with humans. What could go wrong?

CHAPTER
4

ROBERT CARCANO LIVED ON the left side of a red-brick duplex in north Denver. For vampires in the Denver *nidus*—Latin for nest—he was their patriarch. I'd never met him, though we had traded a few brief emails. He edited *The Hollow Fang*, an Internet magazine for vampire aficionados, and where better for vampires to hide than in the middle of the wanna-bes and pretenders?

An amber bulb in a glass lantern fixture illuminated the steps leading to his porch. The crisp, night air carried smoke drifting from the neighborhood chimneys. Mixed in with the smells of burning pine and cedar was an enticing whiff of blood. My mouth watered.

I rang the doorbell and waited. A shadow darkened the curtain drawn over the door's window. The dead bolt snapped, and the door opened.

A man, shorter than myself, portly, round-faced, and

hawk-nosed, with a sloping forehead retreating into a bald scalp, looked at me from around the door's edge.

I smiled politely and introduced myself, though I knew I was in the presence of one of my own. "Mr. Carcano, I'm Felix Gomez."

He opened the door fully and waved me inside. He wore a blue sweater, khaki pants, and tasseled moccasins. "Good to finally meet you, Felix. Call me Bob."

The foyer was so small that Bob and I bumped into one another. Beside the front door stood a rack of shelves, stacked with mail and packages. Once inside, the aroma of blood became stronger.

He opened an interior door and led me into a sparsely furnished living room. The blood smell grew intense. Tall, black halogen torch lamps shone their illumination upward to the ceiling, spreading a warm glow throughout the room. Along the counter separating the living room from the kitchen sat four blood-transfusion machines. On each machine, a plastic bag filled with blood cycled back and forth on the rocker cradle.

"It's dinner," Bob explained. "In my day job I'm the quality-control supervisor for the Front Range Blood Bank."

"Quite the scam," I said, hiding my anxiety at the prospect of insulting my host when I refused a meal of human blood.

"It's more than that," he replied. "This way I get only safe blood. Can't be too careful these days what with HIV and hepatitis C, among other things. One fellow in Frankfurt contracted Marburg. A ghastly disease, much like Ebola. Poor guy lost most of his lower intestines. Wearing a colostomy bag certainly takes the bloom out of being immortal."

Bob pointed to the two black-leather and chrome-tubing chairs beside a glass-topped table. "Have a seat. Drink?"

"What? Bloody Marys made with real blood?"

Bob frowned. "What do you take me for? Count Chocula? Get real. My specialty is Manhattans."

"Then bottoms up."

He mixed Canadian Club, vermouth, bitters, and ice in a chrome cocktail shaker. As Bob shook the drinks, I popped out my contacts and put them in their plastic container, which I slipped into my trouser pocket. With my unfiltered vampire vision, Bob's orange aura danced over his skin. Bright streaks spiraled over his arms and legs. Each creature's aura was as different as a snowflake and remained as unique and expressive as a face.

He poured my drink into an old-fashioned tumbler with thick, beveled edges, very traditional and reassuring. Bob lifted his glass in a salute. "Cheers."

The Manhattan was sweet, with a good kick to it. Could have used a dash of goat's blood, though.

Bob sipped and smacked his lips. "The Araneum thinks highly of you. Felix Gomez, vampire detective."

Araneum meant spiderweb in Latin, an appropriate name for the worldwide underground network of vampires.

"They did save me. Maybe someday I can repay them."

After I had returned from Iraq, the army isolated me in a special ward of the Walter Reed Army Hospital. I was too weak and disorientated by my new vampire nature to escape. Then a colonel arrived, one of us, sent by the Araneum to keep the authorities from learning what I actually was. The colonel had me immediately discharged from the service as a disabled veteran and sent home. I never heard from the colonel again and learned only later that his mysterious manner was typical of how the Araneum worked.

"How much do you know about the Araneum?" I ventured.

Bob walked into the kitchen and started collecting dishes. "Only that we've been aiding each other to escape the mortals since, well, there were human necks to suck on.

Then in the 1300s the Pope ordered the Knights Templar to seek and exterminate us. Our loose arrangement of vampires wasn't enough. So the Araneum was formed and has been active ever since." He ladled spaghetti from a stockpot into a large ceramic bowl. "I wanted to surprise you with *mole* but my recipe was no good."

"And how does one join the Araneum?" I asked.

"They'll let you know."

"Are you in the Araneum?"

He smirked. "Wouldn't be much of a secret organization if I told you, would it?"

"Okay," I chuckled, "but can you discuss *The Hollow Fang*? Clever way to meet family."

Bob spooned thick beef cutlets into the bowl. "As a printed newsletter it's been around in one form or another since the 1880s. I took it over a few years ago and put it on the Internet."

He came out of the kitchen holding a tray with a basket of bread, a large steaming bowl, and dining ware. After resting the tray on the glass table, he arranged the dishes, silverware, and napkins.

I heaped spaghetti and beef cutlets onto my plate. My fangs grew in anticipation of tasting dinner.

"While on the subject of the *The Hollow Fang*, the local fan club is hosting a 'vampire party' this weekend." Bob handed me an invitation, which I glanced at and tucked into my coat pocket.

"Come by and get acquainted with the local *nidus*," he continued. "They're a fun group. And meet the humans. Mostly posers who get off pretending they're undead. You'll also meet a couple of snaggletoothed plasma guzzlers, real old-timers."

Bob read the temperature display of the closest blood transfusion machine. "One hundred and one degrees. Perfect. I like my victims to be a little feverish."

He turned off the machines, the rhythmic click-clack giving way to the soft buzz of the torch lamps behind us. Grasping the bags by the corners, he placed them in a basket, which he covered with a napkin to trap the heat. "These are all type O-positives. I hope that's okay?"

Now to share my ugly secret. "I'd rather have something else."

Bob stopped in mid-stride. "Oh?"

"I prefer animal blood."

Bob set the basket on the table. "Why? This is premium human juice."

I dislodged the words from my mouth. "I've never dined on human blood. It has to do with the circumstances of how I became a vampire."

Bob frowned. "You're not the first. Does this aversion to human blood have to do with your war service?"

"It does."

"Why must it bother you? Do you think the real perpetrators of the war—Saddam Hussein, President Bush, the oil barons, the arms merchants—lose any sleep over what they've done?"

"They weren't there. I was."

"They use money and power to distance themselves from their crimes."

"That doesn't mitigate my guilt. I pulled the trigger."

He lifted a bag from the basket and placed it in my hand for me to experience the squishy feel of 450 milliliters of warm, whole blood.

"This was donated in the spirit of altruism, to share the gift of life," Bob said. "It wasn't shed in terror or under duress. Enjoy."

Into my mind flashed the image of blood draining from the bullet hole in the Iraqi girl's belly and staining my hands. The bag of blood turned into the girl's heart, and I dropped the bag into the basket in disgust.

Bob sighed. His disappointment skewered me.

Someday I'd find the Iraqi vampire who had forced me into this existence. I'd repay him by chaining his undead carcass to a cement mixer and rolling it into a volcano.

"I wouldn't be a gracious host if I didn't accommodate my guests. There's horse blood in the refrigerator. Let me heat it in the microwave."

I was a poor guest but I couldn't ignore the guilt that festered inside of me like a tumor.

Bob returned from the kitchen with a plastic carafe. I opened the carafe and poured. Steaming red blood flowed over the spaghetti and cutlets. The aroma restored my good mood. I stabbed a cutlet with my fork and smeared it in the blood.

Bob grabbed a bag of human blood and tore the corner. His fangs protruded from under his upper lip. "Not as good as sinking my teeth into an unsuspecting human's neck and drawing a fresh meal. But who gets that opportunity these days?"

He squeezed the bag over his pasta and cutlets. The red fluid spread across his plate like marinara sauce. "I brought these samples from a blood-donor clinic in Colorado Springs. Part of an evangelical Christian workshop for teens where the young women pledged to remain virgins until marriage."

"So that's the blood of innocent maidens?"

"As innocent as you'll find these days." Bob twirled the bloody spaghetti over his fork.

Bob was a good cook, and the meal soothed me. I finished the cutlets, emptied the carafe over my plate, and sponged the blood with bread.

"You have a good appetite," he said. "Vampires shouldn't live on blood alone. The pasty-faced look is the result of an incomplete diet. I spiced the meat with Saint-John's-wort and royal bee jelly." He squinted at me. "Your complexion looks almost human. You use a Dermablend foundation?"

"It's a vampire's best friend," I replied. "That and Maybelline."

"We could talk makeup tips all night like schoolgirls, but I'd prefer to learn why you're in Denver."

Down to business. "You know I'm a private investigator," I said. "I've taken an assignment for the Department of Energy."

Bob put his fork down. His aura brightened several watts. He removed his contacts. The camaraderie disappeared from his eyes, replaced by the angry glow of his *tapetum lucidum*. "What did they hire you for?"

So far I had spurned Bob's main course of human blood and now threw acid on the insult by provoking a reaction as if he'd caught me stealing. If Bob were to have confidence in me, I had to make him understand, so I told him about the nymphomania at Rocky Flats.

He gulped his Manhattan. The Dermablend may have hid the change in Bob's complexion, but the more I spoke the brighter his aura became. "I don't like this. You're in danger."

"How so?"

"Things have changed for us, Felix. Once upon a time, we could live in a castle, guarded by pathetic minions, and swoop out at night to feed on the necks of the local wretches. Now humans have technology. Their computers and DNA testing can track us across continents. They don't need wooden stakes, they have assault rifles. A trail of desiccated corpses was once a monument to our power. Today, just one body with puncture wounds in the neck is enough to send a taskforce of forensic pathologists and district prosecutors on our trail."

"I don't intend to bite anyone at Rocky Flats, so don't worry, Bob."

"How many humans have you fanged?"

"Fanged? You mean converted?"

Bob snapped his fingers impatiently. "Yes, yes."

What business was this of his, anyway? I hesitated to answer. "None."

"And how many necks have you sucked on?"

"I've bitten three people."

"I thought you didn't like human blood."

"I had to subdue them. I didn't feed."

Bob stared pensively. "Your behavior is irrational and unhealthy. Preying on humans and drinking their blood is our nature."

"And if I don't? Am I going to get kicked out of the vampire's union?"

Bob got up from his chair and prepared another Manhattan. "By refusing to drink human blood, you're turning away from your vampire side, the source of your strength. If you don't drink human blood, you'll lose your powers. It's what nourishes the *kundalini noir*."

"Blood, any blood, is all we need."

"As if I don't know what I'm talking about," he said. "Why did you come here tonight?"

"Dinner. To meet you. To learn."

"Then listen and learn. I was fanged in 1694. I haven't done it all, but I've seen enough to know that it takes some effort not to give in to hopeless cynicism about this cycle of betrayal and death between us and humans."

Bob drank from his Manhattan. "It's a restless existence, this life as a vampire. Even if you come to a cordial arrangement with your human neighbors, how long can you stay in one place before they become suspicious as to why you don't age and wither as they do? This gift of immortality becomes a heavy iron yoke. You'll see."

This allusion to the tragic life of a vampire ruined my appetite, and I let the remaining blood congeal on my plate. "Perhaps, but I've got a lot to experience before I become a jaded old bloodsucker."

"Like myself?"

I knew better than to answer.

"We fill a need for humans," Bob said. "This terror of being preyed upon excites them, it breaks the ennui of their dreary lives. That's the mysterious beauty of this symbiotic relationship that binds us. You know the erotic allure of submission. The offering of a bare neck is not much different than opening one's legs. Both are sensual, powerful. I'm sure you've done women. And if you haven't already, you'll get rid of your lingering homophobic reservations and do men, as well."

I looked around Bob's spartan accommodations. "And where are your women, your men?"

"I'm staying celibate this decade. After a hundred years or so, fondling genitalia and plugging orifices for the sake of an orgasm loses its novelty."

"So I've got a while before I get bored with sex?"

"Don't get flip. Because then you'll get complacent. Let me tell you why I fear the Department of Energy. Somebody doesn't want their secrets to get out."

"I've faced worse."

"This isn't some gang of trigger-happy dope smugglers. You'll be dueling with one of the most secretive arms of the federal government."

"You're forgetting that I'm a vampire."

"Don't be too cocky about your powers. Rely on them too often, and they'll give you away. And then"—Bob cupped his hands together—"humans will trap you. An iron cage won't hold us for long, true, but what about a magnetic containment unit, or something more exotic? Look at their prize. A vampire. They'll perform biopsies—no, vivisections—to learn about our immortality and powers of transmutation into other forms, a wolf for example."

Bob touched his eye and then his upper incisors. "They'll

carve out your *tapetum lucidum* and your fangs. You might get into trouble so deep not even the Araneum could help you."

If he had witnessed the paranoid nuttiness at Rocky Flats as I had, perhaps he'd lose this appreciation of DOE's prowess. "You make it seem bleak. I can handle myself."

"I don't understand why you don't quit this assignment. What are you trying to prove?"

"This is my job, for one. Am I supposed to wet my pants and run every time someone yells boo? I'm a vampire, for Christ's sake. Humans are supposed to run away from me. And I agreed to help a friend in trouble."

"A human?"

"Yes, a human."

"Felix, remember who you're dealing with. In the centuries I've been around I've seen humans only get more conniving and cruel. We are supposed to be the evil ones, yet are we worse than a serpent? We are simply predators who dine on human blood. Isn't that how God made us? Look at the real evil in history. The Inquisition, the Holocaust. Vampires didn't highjack airliners and crash them into buildings. Who invented the guillotine? Nerve gas? Humans! And you're working for the very people who massacred hundreds of thousands with the A-bomb in Japan, injected pregnant women with plutonium just to see what would happen, and lied about radioactive fallout poisoning families in Nevada. God knows how much land they contaminated around Denver."

"I'm aware of this."

"Be careful, Felix. If you get caught and the government realizes that they have a vampire, then we as a species are doomed."

CHAPTER
5

DURING MY FIRST OFFICIAL day as a nuclear
health physicist, I spent my time organizing my desk
and learning how to find my way around the maze of office
trailers. Gilbert Odin met with me to pass along the names
of the three women who first exhibited the nymphomania.
All of them were radiological control technicians who had
been on the same survey team for Building 707. And all
three RCTs were still on medical leave. Gilbert cautioned
me not to pry into their records at Rocky Flats or I'd alert
Security about my investigation.

In the afternoon, I left Rocky Flats and returned to my
apartment. First, I had to find the RCTs. Since a private detective deals in information, what better source for that
commodity than the Internet? I sent five hundred bucks a
month to a private mailbox in Kalamazoo, Michigan, and in
return an anonymous freelance hacker offered a keyhole
into almost every database hooked into the Internet. I wrote

an email asking where the RCTs lived, what kind of cars they drove, and their family status.

While I waited for a reply, I warmed up a half-pint of cow's blood in the microwave. I poured the blood over a slab of focaccia and ate dinner.

A little after six in the evening I got my answers. I decided to begin by questioning the team leader, Tamara Squires.

She was married and had three sons. I received the vehicle plate numbers of a late-model Jeep Wrangler registered to her, plus home and cell phone numbers. And two addresses, one to a house in the suburb of Lakewood, and the other to an apartment, also in Lakewood. Tamara had lived in the house for ten years and for only one month in the apartment.

There could be two Tamara Squireses, but I had my doubts. I guessed that the nymphomania had strained her marriage and that she had moved out of the house and into the apartment. I'd look there first.

I waited until well after dusk before setting out. Vampires are nocturnal predators, so it is then that our powers are strongest.

The apartment was in a small complex, a two-story building overlooking the parking lot. A balcony ran along the front of the second floor. Each apartment had a picture window beside the entrance door. Lights above each door and in the stairwells illuminated the complex.

A white Jeep Wrangler sat in the parking lot. The Jeep's plates matched the numbers I had been provided.

I munched on a breath mint, climbed the stairs to the balcony, and walked to apartment 2C. Before knocking, I scanned the area, listened carefully, and took a couple of deep sniffs. I didn't detect anything unexpected.

I rapped on the door. From inside, footsteps approached. The window blinds parted a crack, not enough for me to see who peeked out.

Her voice muffled by the windowpane, a woman asked, "What do you want?"

"My name is Felix Gomez. I'm with DOE." I slipped a badge from my coat pocket and showed it to her.

"And?"

"I need to talk to you."

"Are you from Security?"

"No."

The window blinds closed. The deadbolt clicked, and the door opened. A brass chain stretched at shoulder level.

A woman, easily six feet tall, looked down through the gap between her door and the jamb. She had an oval-shaped, pretty face that tapered to a delicate chin. A mane of loose blond hair hung past her neck. She appeared to be in her early forties.

"Mrs. Tamara Squires?"

"That's me," she replied irritably. "Isn't this kinda late? Is this so goddamn important that you couldn't call me to the Flats instead? I don't like work following me home. It's wrecked my private life enough already."

"That's why I'm here. I want to talk about what's happened to you."

Her eyes narrowed and scrunched the tiny crow's-feet at her temples. "What's your job?"

"I'm a health physicist."

"With Rad Safety? Industrial Hygiene? I've never seen you before."

I thought I'd be asking the questions. I'm not even in the door and this woman was busting my chops.

"I specialize in post-exposure rehabilitation. I'm from the Lawrence Livermore National Lab. California."

"Yeah, I know where that is."

I gave her my most sincere look. "I'd thought you'd be more comfortable talking here in your home than at Rocky Flats. My apologies, I should've called first."

Tamara's frown disappeared. "You're the first from DOE to ask how I'm doing. And the only one to offer an apology for anything." Closing the door, she unlatched the chain. "Come in."

She was a big, well-proportioned woman. A baggy, light-gray sweatshirt covered her torso and clung to the swell of her large breasts. She wore tight, black leggings that came down to the middle of her well-muscled calves. Her toes peeked from under the straps of blue plastic slides.

Tamara lived in a studio apartment. A twin bed with a quilt and pillows stood against the far wall to the right, opposite a television stand with a TV and DVD player. In the middle of the wall hung a framed photograph of three smiling, adolescent boys. A tiny kitchen with a two-burner stove and a small refrigerator was to my left. Empty cartons of Chinese takeout sat by the sink. Separating the living area from the kitchen was a wooden card table surrounded by padded folding chairs. A brown leather purse, a packet of cigarettes, and an ashtray rested on the table.

"Mi casa, su casa, yada, yada." Tamara walked into the kitchen. She moved in a loose gait, and the exaggerated movement of her hips and shoulders emphasized her meaty curves.

I sat in the chair closest to the door.

She reached into an overhead cabinet and pulled down a bottle of tequila. "Drink?"

"No thanks."

Tamara rolled her eyes. "C'mon. With a name like Gomez you're saying no to tequila? What a wuss."

Lady, you're talking to a vampire.

"I'm on duty."

"Like that's ever stopped anyone from drinking at DOE." She picked a lime from inside the refrigerator and started slicing. She brought the tequila and a plastic tray to the table, carrying sections of lime, a saltshaker, and two shot glasses.

She sat in the other chair and uncapped the tequila. Despite my refusal, Tamara set a shot glass in front of each of us and filled them. She licked the top of her fist and sprinkled salt on the moistened flesh. Lifting her glass, she said, "*Salud*," and poured the tequila down her throat. She licked the salt on her hand and bit into a piece of lime. After pursing her lips for a moment, she gasped, "Damn, that was good."

I barely sipped my tequila. The salt-and-lime routine had never worked for me, even before I was a vampire.

Tamara lit one cigarette, took a puff, and exhaled. She twisted her mouth to one side in that curious way that smokers do to pretend that they're not stinking up the air with their habit. "What's with the makeup, Felix? Does it have anything to do with you not wanting to drink tequila?" Her smirk added, "you pussy."

Not only was she insulting my status as a vampire, now she was going after my masculinity as well. I had thought I had done a good job with my makeup but apparently not. "It's medication. I have a skin condition."

Her mouth formed an "O," and she feigned embarrassment to have noticed.

Since I was the investigator, it was time for me to earn my pay. "How are you managing on medical leave?"

Tamara poked at the surroundings with her cigarette. "Take a look. I'm doing like shit. I used to live in a four-bedroom split-level two miles from here. Now this shoe box is home."

"I mean health-wise."

"Mental health? At first I was so freaked out that I bought a gun." Tamara stuck her hand in the purse on the table.

Was she after the gun? I got ready to grab her wrist.

She withdrew a plastic, amber-colored bottle. "You know they put us on Prozac."

I relaxed and smiled inwardly at the false alarm.

She dropped the bottle back into her purse and combed a hand through her hair. "I had to quit taking it. Prozac looks so perfect at first. Everything seems under control. Then you realize that parts of you are missing, I mean parts of your personality. The more you use it, the more it feels like you are dissolving into the air."

I had to fake concern while I steered the conversation to the incident in Building 707. "Are you better now that you don't take it?"

"I feel more complete." She mashed the cigarette into the ashtray. "On the other hand, it's like I'm walking on ice. At any moment something will crack and down I go."

"Go where?"

"Into nympho-land." Tamara hung her head and clutched her fingers. "It sounds funny, doesn't it? Like a joke. A bunch of horny women going out of control." She lifted her head and gave a weak grin. "A man's fantasy, no?"

"For some."

Tamara reached into a pocket of her purse. She opened her hand to show me a gold wedding band. "It cost me my marriage and my family. I couldn't control myself."

This was regrettable for her, but what I needed to know was what had caused the nymphomania. I'd let her volunteer information before I resorted to vampire hypnosis.

Tamara prepared another shot of tequila. Good. The more lubricated she got, the easier my job. She gulped and slammed the empty glass on the table. "But you know what? The truth is, the real goddamn unvarnished truth is that I enjoyed it. I mean, what I can remember."

She closed her eyes and clenched her hands before her face. "It's like you're on fire. You want it."

"It . . . what?"

Tamara gave me an incredulous stare. "Sex. Everything about sex. Regular sex. Oral sex. Butt sex. Period sex. You go and you go," she pumped her hand, flailing her head, shaking her blond tresses, "until you're sizzling with lust, aware of nothing but your pleasure. Then you float back to reality, and it's like you're washed up on a beach after a storm."

Tamara sighed and lit another cigarette. She brushed a strand of hair from her face. "And I don't mean a nasty cold beach, either, I mean one of those beer-commercial beaches where the water is warm and the sun toasts your skin."

She sucked on a lime and remained quiet for a moment. Looking over her shoulder to the picture on the wall, she said wistfully, "I do miss my boys." She turned back toward me. "Can't say I miss my husband, though. He turned into a real asshole about this and kicked me out of my house and then filed for divorce. Just because I nailed his brother, and the minister."

Tamara pushed the sleeves of her sweatshirt over her forearms. She leaned on her elbows and gave an accusing glare. "You know what I learned from all this?"

"No." But keep talking.

"How much you men fear women. I mean this whole sex thing. Women being the fair, weaker gender and all that bullshit. That you men grant us sexual permission. It's a myth so you can control us."

"Okay, guilty as charged," I said. "Put all of man's failures on my shoulders." Now shut up about this and tell me what happened in Building 707.

"All of man's failures?" she laughed. "Who are you now, Jesus Christ?"

"If I'm going to help, you'll have to tell me about the beginning."

"What if I don't need help?"

"You like what happened?"

"Not what it cost me."

"Then I need to know what caused it."

"Read the report."

"What report?"

"If you have to ask that question, I can't tell you. It's classified." Tamara crossed her arms. "I could lose my job. Hell, I could even go to prison for revealing anything."

Time for my vampire powers. This brassy Amazon had no defense. I bowed my head and popped the contacts from my eyes.

"Are you okay?" Tamara asked. "You really can't handle tequila, can you?"

I sat upright and stared at her, shining the full effect of my *tapetum lucidum* into her eyes. My lupine gaze transfixed her. The red aura of a human shimmered around her.

"Holy shit." Tamara jerked her head back in surprise, but only for a second as my hypnotic spell took effect. Her blue eyes dilated. Her face relaxed. Her lips parted slightly and released a curl of smoke. Her arms unfolded, and the cigarette dropped to the carpet. Such a strong-willed woman, and yet such easy prey.

I could turn my vampire gaze away for ten seconds, maybe even a minute, depending on the human, before I lost the hypnotic lock. I snatched the cigarette and snubbed it in the ashtray. Returning to stare into her eyes, I held Tamara's hands in mine and kneaded the flesh between her thumbs and index fingers. Her breathing slowed, and her eyelids fluttered to remain open.

Gently, I raised our hands and, in a quiet voice, commanded her to stand up. I led her to the bed and levered her long body onto the mattress, resting her head on a pillow. The plastic slides fell from her feet. A wave of pheromones rose from her body. My control over her was complete.

The halo of her aura floated on the pillow. Her hair fell away from her neck and exposed the tender skin and tempting veins. The pleasure of erotic domination surged through me. My fangs started to grow, and I lapped my tongue against my dry lips. Blood tastes *much* better than tequila.

But I wouldn't bite her. This investigation was tricky enough without me leaving holes in the necks of the witnesses. Plus, who knew what had contaminated her?

I climbed on the bed and straddled her, careful to put my weight onto my knees and not against her hips. Her pelvis arched aggressively and she pressed her groin against me. Odd. Hypnosis victims have always remained passive.

I laced our fingers together. Now to question her. The complication was that hypnosis opened up a victim's subconscious and there was no telling what could come gushing out. Some blabbed like they were on a psychiatrist's couch, and the trick was to get them to stick to my questions and shut up about everything else.

Staring into her eyes, I said, "Tamara, tell me what happened in Building 707."

Her breathing deepened. The middle of her sweatshirt creased as her breasts rose and sank. She gulped. The focus in her eyes bore into mine, and she stared through me as if I wasn't there.

In a relaxed voice, Tamara explained that as each floor of a building in the Protected Area was torn down, a survey team would go into the next area scheduled for demolition for a final "reconnaissance level characterization."

"We were in the basement of 707, mapping discharge points beneath the foundry and casting modules. It was a real mess. Miles and miles of unmarked pipes. Sofia, Jenny, and I wore coveralls and respirators. We kept following one pipe after another, trying to match the master layout. Then we got lost. Apparently we had walked into a corridor that didn't exist on the original print. We kept going since our TLDs didn't register anything."

"Transluminiscent dosimeters?"

"Yes. We had the new ones that chirp an alarm. About the time we figured we were under the north loading bay, we found a secure door."

"Secure door?"

"It looked like the ones blocking the 'infinity rooms' in Buildings 371 and 776. The rooms that are so crapped up with radiation that the instrument counter goes off the scale to infinity. But this door wasn't marked. It seems the demolition above had shattered the concrete around the door and sprung it open. As many times as we've gone through those buildings to update the placards and warnings, I wondered how anyone missed this one."

"Did you go inside?"

"Not right away. We radioed the RLC coordinator for instructions. He didn't know about the room, either, and told us to investigate. So we entered and looked with our flashlights. There were rows of fifty-five-gallon drums and boxes shaped like caskets."

Caskets? Were there bodies? "What about markings?"

"There weren't any. They looked like they were painted black."

"Had you seen anything like them before?"

"Not the boxes. The drums, yes. They were standard, though usually they're painted gray or white."

Tamara lay quiet, swallowing nervously.

I stared at her, renewing my concentration to coax her to start talking again. "Continue."

"Suddenly, something hissed, like a steam vent. A vapor started swirling from the drums and boxes, rising and surrounding us."

Tamara's hands trembled. I squeezed to reassure her. And strangely enough, she squeezed back.

"Tamara, you're safe here. Go on, tell me what happened."

She bit her lower lip. Her chin quivered.

"Tell me."

"First my TLD started chirping. The three of us backed out of the room. Sofia's TLD went off. Then Jenny's. We shouted for help over the radio and ran like scared dogs. By the time we reached the entry point, our TLDs were showing seventeen rems."

Tamara's eyes watered with distress. "We were crapped up and had to go through rad decon. The other RCTs stripped us naked under the shower and scrubbed us with brushes. Security guards in bunny suits with Tasers and guns escorted us to bioassay."

I knew about rad decontamination. What I needed was more details about the room. "Tell me what you saw."

She closed her eyes and started to weep.

"Shh," I whispered. I tightened my grip on her hands to comfort her.

Tamara turned her head from side to side to wipe her tears against the pillow.

"What about the report?"

"The Tiger Team report?" Tamara gripped my fingers hard. Her aura took a yellow cast.

This alarmed me. Never had a hypnosis subject initiated such physical action, nor had I ever seen an aura change color like this. And to yellow? Was this the nymphomania at work?

"Tell me about the Tiger Team report."

Tamara opened her hands to loosen my grip. "Big Wong has it."

I let go of her fingers. I'd never experienced this. Normally I was in absolute control of the hypnosis. "Dr. Wong?"

Leaning forward, I cradled her head in my hands and raked my fingers through her sweat-damp hair. Her aura clung to my fingers like Saint Elmo's fire. "You mean Bigelow Wong, the head of Radiation Safety?"

"Yes," she moaned. Her lips darkened. Her female scent gushed up at me. The aura lost its yellow hue and turned red.

Now I felt I was in control again. Releasing my hold on

her head, I relaxed, admiring how easily I manipulated her, like I could any other human.

"Tamara, open your eyes and look at me."

Moaning again, she slipped her right hand under the pillow.

I caressed her face. "Tamara, look at me."

Her eyelids popped open, her pupils riveted on me. Her aura turned bright yellow again. Her right hand jerked from under the pillow and she pressed the muzzle of a Browning automatic against my forehead.

CHAPTER
6

MY CONSCIOUSNESS SHRIVELED around the circle of steel where the business end of the pistol barrel pressed into my skin. I couldn't move fast enough to parry the gun without risking a bullet through my skull. Vampires don't fear wooden stakes nearly as much as high-velocity metal-jacketed slugs. Especially to the brain.

My hands still cupped Tamara's head. The yellow aura sparkled over her skin. Her eyes retained that faraway gloss from the hypnosis. Except for her holding a gun to my forehead, I'd have said that she was still under my control.

So as not to startle her, I whispered slowly, "What do you want?"

"Take off your pants," she said in a curious, distant voice.

Ordinarily when a nymphomaniac tells you to undress, her intentions are obvious. But the gun confused the situation. I didn't know whether she wanted to play with my nuts or shoot them off.

Her finger tensed on the trigger of the Browning. "Take off your pants," she repeated. "Let's do it."

At this proximity the pistol looked as big as a howitzer. "Sure, but under the present circumstances I might have performance issues."

"Men. Such babies." Tamara's left hand groped for my waist and fumbled with my belt buckle.

I nudged her hand away. Straightening my legs, I lay flat on top of her and caressed her voluptuous torso. I nuzzled her neck, cognizant of the pistol now pressed to the side of my skull.

The humid scent of her perspiration and natural phero-mones formed an inviting cocktail of aromas. I kissed her neck and nibbled tenderly on the skin beside her jugular. Such temptation. My fangs protruded to their maximum length, and they ached to bite through skin.

Tamara's breathing deepened. Her feet hooked over the back of my ankles, and she tilted her big hips to rub her pubic bone against my groin.

I didn't want to bite but the hypnosis wasn't controlling her. I had no choice but to subdue her the traditional way.

Putting my wet open mouth against her neck, I let my sa-liva deaden her nerves. My fangs hunted for her jugular. I broke the skin and let the blood seep onto my tongue. Hu-man blood was supremely delicious, but I couldn't enjoy it. I let her blood dribble out my lips.

Tamara moaned. Her left hand stroked down my shoul-der and back until she gripped my butt.

Any other vampire would've sucked her blood until she passed out. Instead I worked my spit into the punctures to let the narcotic effects of my saliva sedate her.

Tamara's breathing slowed. Her aura faded to a dull red color. Her muscles relaxed. The Browning clattered to the floor. Her hands dropped to her sides.

Satisfied that she was unconscious, I sat up, pulled a

handkerchief from my coat, and wiped my mouth. A wave of remorse turned into a nauseating dread. What had contaminated her at Rocky Flats? And since the nymphomania had begun, what sexually risky aerobics had she indulged in? I tried not to ingest her blood—even one drop containing a pathogen could be enough to destroy me. If she were infected. I hung my hopes on that doubt.

Tamara lay peacefully on the bed, her serene face pale. Blood trickled from the two small holes in her neck.

I pressed the handkerchief against the wound until the bleeding stopped. Besides its analgesic and sedative effects, vampire saliva also accelerated healing. I had hardly drained any blood, so the bruising would be negligible, and by the time she awoke she'd only have two tiny scabs surrounded by yellow discoloration.

I climbed off her and replaced my contacts. To erase evidence that I'd been here, I washed my shot glass and returned it to the cupboard.

Tamara would suffer amnesia from both my hypnosis and the narcotic chemicals of my saliva. She wouldn't remember anything, starting from the half-hour before I arrived. Tomorrow morning she'd be one very confused woman.

I returned to my apartment and climbed into my coffin to reflect on what had happened. I ran the air conditioner to recreate the cool dankness of a crypt. Incense—Dresden cadaver, my favorite—should have given my bedroom that perfect Old World decaying smell that induced relaxed meditation.

Funny how becoming a vampire changed things. And, no, I don't mean the obvious physical stuff. I was much more of a beer and tacos man, and I still like them, only now I needed to add the rich liquid texture of blood. I couldn't deny my vampire personality and my awareness of the psychic plane we inhabited. In times like this I embraced the gloom to rejuvenate myself.

But this time, the incense and darkness weren't working.

One afternoon years ago, when I was still human, I had discovered that my car was missing from where I had left it. I searched the parking lot, bewildered, wondering if I had even driven to the store at all. I couldn't believe that my car had been stolen. I felt off-center, empty, and confused. Not only had someone taken my property, they had also upset my perception of reality.

Now I had the same feeling of disorientation. I fidgeted against the satin lining of my casket. This incident with Tamara was supposed to have enlightened me. Instead I had stumbled deeper into a labyrinth of questions and shadows. Why hadn't vampire hypnosis worked? Why had her aura changed from red to yellow when she succumbed to nymphomania? What in Building 707 had caused this? I needed to interrogate the other affected RCTs and cut through the confusion surrounding the investigation. This time I wouldn't be so complacent.

The next day I left my apartment to visit the second RCT. To bypass rush-hour traffic, I took a short cut along a quiet road parallel to an abandoned railroad line in the neighborhood.

I drove with the driver's window open. The sun filtered through the trees growing alongside the railroad tracks. My fingertips tingled where they touched the steering wheel. The day was too clear, the air too crisp, the mood too normal to inspire trouble. Concerned that something might be wrong with my car—a wheel out of balance, for example—I let off the gas pedal and listened to the tires rumble over the asphalt.

A whirring sound, like a hornet, buzzed past my ear. Something popped against the right inside of the convertible top. Sunlight instantly beamed through a finger-sized hole in the fabric.

My fingers twitched in alarm. Someone was shooting at me.

I pressed the gas pedal. The Dodge leaped forward, pushing me back against the seat. A second buzzing sound and another hole popped in the convertible top. The shots came from my left.

Yanking off my sunglasses, I turned my head to see where the shooter might be. A car horn blared at me. I faced the front. A stop sign appeared from the center of an overgrown lilac bush and a blue Chevy Impala screeched before me. I stomped on the brakes. My Dodge skidded through the intersection and missed the Chevy by inches. My car slid to the muddy right shoulder and stalled. The Chevy slowed, honked the horn as a curse, then hurried off.

A black Ford Crown Victoria approached in the rearview mirror.

I turned the ignition key, but all the engine did was whine and not start. My vampire sense blaring the danger signal, I opened the door and bolted from the car.

The Ford swerved and presented its passenger side to me. A large man wearing black leaned from the window and panned me with the muzzle of an M16 that had a silencer attached.

I sprang to the left and right as I ran for the cover of the trees along the railroad tracks. Bullets nipped the air close to my head.

I tripped and splashed into a shallow ditch next to the railroad. Scrambling to my feet, I kept running as the bullets pecked at the leaves and branches around me.

The dirty water went from ankle deep to mid-shin. I hurdled over tires and a shopping cart discarded in the ditch. The Ford started up the road to overtake me.

I crashed through a wall of reeds. Here the ditch joined a culvert about as wide as my shoulders. I dropped to my hands and knees and shimmied into the culvert, wallowing in grime and mud. I slid deep into the dark corrugated tube, not waiting to find out if I had lost my pursuers.

I needed to see. Removing my contacts in these conditions would be risky but I had to do it. I whisked my hands through the water to rinse the mud from my fingers. Carefully, I pulled the left contact out, then the right. Grit scratched my eyeballs. I splashed the filthy water into my eyes in an attempt to flush the irritation away.

Minutes passed. I heard nothing and could see little. A human would've been mortified with claustrophobia to be in this tight culvert for so long. But this reminded me of stories of being buried undead and emerging decades later, refreshed by the extended siesta.

Something blurry with a red aura approached to sniff my head. My claws instantly extended to defend me. The thing with the red aura growled and snapped at my face. It was a raccoon.

I bared my fangs and snapped back. The raccoon held its ground. We bitch-slapped each other until I'd had enough and retreated backwards to the ditch. Pausing before exposing my feet, I listened for danger, the quickened breath of my excited pursuer, the scratch of his finger along the rifle trigger, the tires of the Ford scraping over gravel. Nothing.

I backed out to my knees. Still nothing. Then out completely. The sun poured upon me and stung my naked eyes. A crow squawked at me from the concrete embankment of the ditch. The shooter was gone. I sloughed off the mud and rotting leaves from my trousers. Reeking of garbage I stumbled out of the ditch and walked along the shoulder back to my Dodge. Water squished in my shoes.

I inspected my car to see if it had been left alone. It had. Getting a canteen from the trunk, I washed my face, touched up my makeup, and put in a new pair of contacts. I sat on a towel to protect the driver's seat and tried the ignition key.

The engine turned over right away. Before I drove off, I surveyed the area and reflected on the attack.

Who was the shooter? He knew my route. He knew me. I was sure I had seen him and the black Ford before, if only incidentally. I promised myself that in the course of this investigation I'd get even with this shooter. It would be a delightfully hideous revenge.

Back in my apartment, I scrubbed myself clean and decided to continue my interrogation of the RCTs. I headed for the next address, which turned out to be a town house in Littleton, a suburb southwest of Denver. The dwellings were three-story units scrunched together between juniper hedges. I walked up the narrow porch of my destination and rang the doorbell. The lock on the front door clicked and the door opened.

The woman peeked at me from around the door's edge. Neon-blue eyes were inset within her pretty, square-shaped face, matched in intensity by her crimson lipstick. A terry-cloth headband kept her wavy dark hair from spilling over her forehead. My libido piqued with the scent of her perspiration.

Showing my ID, I introduced myself and recited my credentials. "I'm from the Flats. You are a friend of Tamara Squires?"

"Tamara? Is this about the outbreak?"

"It is. And are you Sofia Martinez?"

"Yes I am." She politely agreed to let me in. Tugging at her moistened T-shirt, worn braless over smallish breasts, she said, "I just got back from the gym. Hope you don't mind me smelling like a mare."

"I hadn't noticed."

"Don't bullshit me, Mr. Gomez. I saw your nose wrinkle." Black spandex shorts clung to her substantial, inviting butt.

I followed her into the modest living room, where I sat

on the sofa and she plopped in the stuffed armchair. A snowboard rested in the corner. Softball and soccer trophies on the mantel crowded around a figurine of the Madonna and Child.

Sofia slipped loose her cross-trainers, peeled off her socks, and folded her bare, muscular legs underneath her hips. Suddenly, she sprang from the chair and headed for the kitchen. "Oh gosh, where are my manners? Coffee?"

I needed to ask questions and not waste time. "None for me. But thanks."

"Too late. Since I'm having some, so are you." She yelled from the kitchen. "Are you here to talk about the nympho thing?"

I hadn't mentioned anything about that. "How did you know?"

"Because you asked about Tamara and then you come to see me. That was a no-brainer. Her life really went into the poopster over this, didn't it?"

"According to her, yeah."

Sofia returned with a serving tray with two delicate china cups filled with coffee. "I take mine with cream and a dash of sugar. I put the same in yours."

She set a cup and saucer in front of me on the coffee table. "Let me tell you a secret about myself"—Sofia took her cup and curled into the stuffed chair—"I was a goddamn nympho *before* all this crap happened at the Flats."

"So it had no effect on you?"

Sofia scrunched her lips together and wobbled her head as if deciding what to say. "I wouldn't say that. It did make me lower my standards on occasion." She set the cup on an end table. Clasping her hands, she shoved them between her knees and rocked forward. "I shouldn't have said that, it was stupid. Sorry. For me, it couldn't have come at a worse time." With a flourish of her left arm, she looked up at the ceiling. "Here I am, in my mid-thirties, divorced, my goddam biological clock ringing so loud that I'm surprised the neighbors can't hear it, and I can't find someone to give me a kid. And then, to make me a certified sexual basket case, I get nymphomania for real."

"No Prozac?"

"Prozac? What the hell do I need that for? My only problem with sex is this." She snatched an envelope from the corner of the coffee table. "Here's another invitation from one of my sisters to yet another baby shower." She shook the envelope at me. Her cheeks darkened to the shade of her lipstick. "When's *my* baby shower? Huh, Felix? When's mine?"

Sofia sat still, sulking. "Am I a bad person?"

Should've brought rubber boots; I didn't think I'd have to wade this deep through emotional wreckage. "No," I told her.

She aimed those blue eyes at me. "Do you think I'm pretty?"

"Yes, I do." This was true.

"Then what's the problem? Am I too forward? I thought guys didn't like all that prissy bullshit." The words spewed out of her mouth like she had a motor in her throat. "Every guy worth having sex with is either fixed or won't give me a kid. I don't want to marry anybody again or bust his ass over child support, I just want to be able to point out to my baby, 'There's your daddy.' And then I get this goddamn nymphomania and I go through enough condoms to make a zeppelin because I don't want to get pregnant from the wrong dipshit."

"Have you gone to a clinic?" I asked. "For a baby, I mean."

"I'm not doing the turkey-baster thing. I want quality sperm fresh out of the penis."

"Maybe you have to compromise."

"Compromise what? All I want is to get laid and get pregnant by somebody decent," she shouted. "It happens millions of times every day to women on this planet—just not to me."

How sad for her, but I had to steer the conversation back to the nymphomania. I took the last sip of my coffee and set the cup on its saucer. "So your biological clock started ringing before the outbreak?"

"Hello? Didn't I say that? I've been after a baby since I was divorced six years ago."

"Seems like plenty of time."

"You'd think. Casual sex was not the problem. It's that the guys either did the daddy-thing already with their exes or they don't want kids, period. So here are these otherwise perfectly suitable mates and I have to throw them back because"—her voice angered—"they won't give me a baby.

"I'm racing the calendar." She held up three fingers. "This is how many years I got. No woman in my family over forty ever got pregnant."

Her eyes glistened. She wiped a tear. "Sorry to act this way." Her voice trembled. "But I really want a baby. I even have a nursery upstairs. Wanna see?"

God no. This woman had enough problems to keep a platoon of shrinks busy. "That's okay."

Sofia gave a smile so tense I thought her face would break. She finished her coffee. Closing her eyes for a moment, she sighed deeply and her cheeks turned their natural color. "Let's change the subject. What's with you? That makeup?"

"A skin condition. Gulf War Syndrome."

"Yew." She squinted and turned her head to examine me. "Other than that, you're not bad-looking. That syndrome didn't leave you . . . shooting blanks?"

"You mean sterile?"

"That. Impotent."

"There's a difference," I said defensively. Vampires certainly weren't impotent. But we *were* sterile and propagated solely by fanging. "My plumbing works. But I am shooting blanks."

"See what I mean?" Sofia splayed her hands in a gesture of resignation. "Another decent guy who doesn't cut the mustard."

First time I'd ever been called decent. "I thought we had changed the subject. What can you tell me about your contamination in Building 707?"

Sofia crossed her arms. "I can't go into details about that. Why are you asking?"

Time for vampire hypnosis. I bent my head down and dropped the contacts into my hand. I lifted my head and stared at Sofia.

Her rosy face blanched. Her eyes widened. Her lips parted enough for a whisper to escape. "Oh wow."

That I'd never heard from a victim before. Considering my experience with Tamara, I approached Sofia cautiously, lest she kept a pistol jammed between the seat cushions. Her aura surrounded her like an electric cloud.

Sofia's cheeks darkened again while her eyes gazed at mine expectantly. Tendrils from her aura turned yellow. A wave of pheromones smothered all other smells. My fingers tingled in alarm. I started to step back. Her legs reached for mine and her ankles scooped behind my calves. She grasped my wrists and pulled me down on her. "Come on, Felix. Do me."

The yellow in the tendrils migrated into the rest of her aura. My paranoia bordered on panic. It wasn't the threat from her I feared but this unknown reaction to my hypnosis. I wasn't able to easily control her.

As with Tamara, there was only one remedy. I knelt before Sofia and took her head in my hands. She let go of my arms and pulled her T-shirt over her breasts.

"Yeah, Felix," she growled seductively and leaned into me, "I'll bet you have a weapons-grade hard-on for me."

I sank my fangs into her neck and tasted her sweet blood. Thankfully, she nodded off soon and went limp in the chair. I cleaned up and left.

After driving home, I meditated in my coffin and reviewed what little I had learned. This nymphomania didn't seem supernatural in origin or effect, yet that it could cut through vampire hypnosis distressed me. Plus, every time I remembered the taste of Tamara's or Sofia's blood, my bowels weakened in panic from the danger I'd put myself into. It was wishful thinking on my part to imagine that I was safe from contamination. The next time I went into the bathroom I might find myself glowing with radioactivity, or, worse, look down and see that my dick had rotted off.

Still, I had one more chance. I needed to interview the third radiological control technician. Jenny Calhoun.

CHAPTER
7

JENNY CALHOUN LIVED IN Arvada, a bedroom
suburb right smack in the center of the radioactive smoke
plume should Rocky Flats catch fire, like it has twice before. She agreed to meet that afternoon at a coffee shop
next to a supermarket, which suited me. I couldn't easily
hypnotize her in such a public place, but she wouldn't try
to seduce me, either. Plus, the openness should keep the
mysterious assassin from lunging after me again. I hoped.

Over the phone, Jenny described herself as young-
looking—whatever that meant—with wild red hair.

From my background info on her I knew Jenny to be
twenty-six. At a table outside the coffee shop sat a slender
girl with narrow, trendy eyeglasses and a mane the color of
hot copper wire. Young-looking was right. She appeared
sixteen—maybe. On this bright day, it was warm enough for
her to sit slouched with her sweater unbuttoned. A midriff

blouse and black skirt clinging to her lithe frame didn't add one year to her apparent age. Had to be Jenny.

She zeroed in on me as I approached and kept her green eyes fixed on my face. When I got close and removed my sunglasses she said, "You're an interesting-looking specimen."

"I'm Felix Gomez. And you're Jenny?"

She lifted her paper cup in a cardboard sleeve. "The one and only." She shed a flip-flop and with her manicured toes, nudged an empty chair away from the table. "Sit."

The aroma of caramel and coffee rose from her cup. I could do with a good jolt of caffeine, but as I didn't have any blood to spike it with, I'd wait.

I scooted the chair into the shade of the umbrella and sat. "You don't mind talking here?"

"Nope. I ain't gonna say anything I shouldn't."

"I'm going to ask about the outbreak."

Jenny faked a pout. "Shame. You know I can't say anything about that. I was hoping you had read my number on a bathroom wall and wanted a date."

"Sure, we'll go on a date." Anything to get her talking.

"I'm teasing. I'm under medication and wouldn't be much fun."

"Prozac?"

Jenny shook the handbag hanging off the back of her chair. The sound of pills rattling against plastic came from the bag. "It's put a crimp in my social calendar, but then again, when I wake up in the morning I no longer ask where am I and who is the guy snoring next to me."

"Did the outbreak make you that promiscuous?"

"Felix, let me put it this way. Assuming the average penis is six inches long, since the outbreak I've had about twenty-five and a half feet of dick from different men."

Charming calculation. "So if you're not looking for a date," I asked, "why did you agree to see me?"

"Curiosity. To see who else wanted to ask strange questions."

"What kind of questions? Who asked them? Someone from DOE?"

"No." Jenny sat up and curled her fingers around the cup. Her voice turned serious. "This guy didn't show me any credentials. He was a foreigner I'm sure. Spoke with an accent, though his English was good."

"He asked about the outbreak?"

"Not really. He knew about it. Called it the sickness." Jenny looked down to her cup. "But mostly he asked about others talking to me."

The comment triggered my sense of self-protection and heightened my awareness of the surroundings. Our table was closest to the corner of the sidewalk. A few cars drove past the curb as they cruised through the parking lot of the strip mall. Everyone seemed preoccupied with something else, certainly not with us.

"What other people?"

"Not people." Jenny raised her eyes, her features tense. "He asked about vampires."

Her answer was as shocking as a live wire against my nose. Vampires? I held my breath to retain my composure. Since when do humans ask about vampires? We were myths, as fantastic to humans as unicorns and UFOs.

Jenny's gaze darted suspiciously about my face. She pulled her hands from the coffee cup and put them in her lap.

"What's the matter?" I asked.

"It's the make-up," she whispered.

Her concern implied danger and I readied my hand to remove my contacts and hypnotize her.

Her expression grew more apprehensive. "You're not a—"

Smiling, I interrupted her. "A vampire? What do you think?"

Jenny stared for a moment, then gave an apologetic grin.

"Of course not." She extended her arms across the table and held her coffee cup again. "Sorry."

"My skin condition is from the Iraq War, the second one." I touched my face and lowered my hand. "I'm hypersensitive to the sun."

"Like a vampire?"

I laughed. "Sure, like a vampire if you want."

Jenny chuckled with me. "I once slept with someone who wore makeup. Didn't really sleep, as it turned out. He was all into the Goth thing, which didn't bother me, but when he came out of his bathroom sporting an erection, eye shadow, and lingerie, that was my cue to leave, nymphomania or not."

But what about the snoop who came looking for my kind? "The guy who asked about vampires, what did he look like?"

"Older. Way older." Jenny stroked her scalp. "Buzz cut. And a beard. Big cross around his neck. Nerves wound kinda tight. Creepy even."

"Was he alone?"

"No. He came to my house in a van. Somebody else was driving. Couldn't see who it was."

"And he asked about vampires? Just like that?"

"I didn't want to talk to him, especially since details about the outbreak are supposed to be confidential. The vampire question came out of the blue."

"Did you report him, Jenny?"

"No. The vampire question was too weird. I'm under enough scrutiny already, so why draw more attention to myself? DOE acts like I contracted the nymphomania just to embarrass them. The guy left straight away and I didn't see any harm done. So I kept quiet about it."

"When did he visit?"

"Two days ago." Jenny twirled a lock of her hair between her fingers. She stared at me as if she could see through my makeup. Her gaze beamed desire. Was the nymphomania taking hold?

"Has your medication worn off?"

"The hell with my medication." Jenny rubbed her foot up my sock and between my trouser leg and shin. "Wanna make it twenty-six feet? Assuming that you're average, of course."

"Twenty-six feet of what?"

"This." Jenny reached across the table and grabbed my belt buckle. I pulled away, but she kept her grip and caused me to drag her slender body against the table. We knocked over her cup and spilled coffee on the sidewalk.

I needed to subdue her before she started stripping. I turned my face downward and squeezed the contacts into my empty hand.

"Come on, Felix," she cooed. "Don't get shy on me. I hear you combat veterans can get really perverted."

I palmed the sides of Jenny's head.

Her aura burned a hot cadmium yellow. The nymphomania was in control.

"You demented bastard," Jenny sneered, eyes closed. "The rough stuff, huh? Right here in public? I can take it."

With my back to the parking lot, in the reflection of the café window I saw a passing BMW slow down. The driver's window retracted and a woman's anxious face peered out at us.

"What's going on?" she asked.

I kept my back to the BMW, didn't want to subdue that woman as well, and brought my nose against Jenny's.

Her eyes opened and bore into mine. "Holy . . ." She went limp, her tongue drooling over her slack jaw.

Hurriedly I folded Jenny's tongue back into her mouth and shut her jaw. I sat her in my chair and pulled my sunglasses from my coat pocket. Covering my eyes with the glasses, I approached the BMW and explained in my most professional, soothing voice. "There's no trouble, ma'am. My patient's had a seizure. She's okay."

The woman scowled. "Like hell. I know what I saw."

She lifted a cell phone against her cheek. "You can explain it to the police." I was close enough to touch her door when the BMW accelerated away. The woman tossed one look back at me.

I lifted my sunglasses and zapped her.

Her eyebrows rose in astonishment and her lips formed an oval around the gape of her mouth. The BMW zoomed through the pedestrian crossing. Shoppers jumped out of her way. The BMW veered to the right and crunched into a parked Cadillac SUV, spraying the asphalt with the shattered red plastic of the tail lamps. The Cadillac's alarm screamed as if wounded.

Under the cover of this distraction, I gave Jenny another vampire glare to refresh the hypnosis. Jerking her by the arm, I tugged her around to the alley behind the strip mall. She stumbled behind me. Her flip-flops slapped the pavement.

The alley reeked of urine and rotting food. Piles of flattened cardboard boxes stood along the walls. I pulled Jenny toward the Dumpster.

"Uhh, inside the Dumpster—now that's kinky," she whispered excitedly. Pheromones gushed from her body. How did this nymphomania burn through my hypnosis?

I whipped Jenny ahead of me and sent her tripping over a stack of wooden pallets. My fangs sprouted. After a glance to see that we were alone, I knelt to hold her by the shoulders. I pulled her head back and curved her delicious throat toward me.

Afterwards, I walked her back to the sidewalk tables and left her slumped in a chair, her sweater buttoned tight to her neck to hide my bite marks. Within a few minutes she'd wake up, confused and oblivious to our meeting.

On the way home I couldn't keep my thoughts from careening into one another like bumper cars. So much had happened that didn't make sense. Once back in my apartment, I sat in the armchair with an old-fashioned glass in my hand, scotch and boar's blood served neat. Midway through the second glass, my thinking had calmed enough for me to analyze with some degree of coherence what I did and didn't know.

My first break had been the revelation from Tamara that Dr. Wong possessed the Tiger Team report about Building 707, but that in turn raised more questions. Why would the head of Radiation Safety keep the report from his boss, Gilbert Odin? Who was the report intended for, and what did it describe? Tiger Teams were special national-level committees convened to investigate serious concerns about nuclear-weapons safety. They never issued a finding that didn't cause someone's head to roll in the dust. I hadn't heard of any heads rolling at Rocky Flats . . . yet. Maybe my friend Gilbert Odin was afraid that ax would fall across his own neck.

The second revelation was this mysterious yellow aura emitted by the nymphomaniacs and their ability to resist vampire hypnosis.

Third, someone had come after me with a rifle. Why? I doubted they were soliciting memberships for the NRA.

Last, and equally troubling, was Jenny's mentioning that someone had been asking about vampires. This someone knew about the nymphomania, and yet what he queried Jenny about was vampires. A human asking about vampires? Impossible. Or maybe he wasn't human. And why would he make the connection between the outbreak of nymphomania and us vampires?

I set my empty glass on the end table. Tomorrow I would keep digging into the nymphomania until I found out who was asking questions about me.

CHAPTER
8

AFTER A RESTLESS NIGHT, I commuted to
Rocky Flats the next morning. During the drive, I ate
my usual morning pick-me-up, an apple and a low-fat cin-
namon scone washed down with a blend of dark Sumatran
java and goat's blood.

I "worked" in the same building as Dr. Wong and knew
him in passing. I was one of many health physicists at Rocky
Flats, most of whom were contractors or on loan from another DOE facility, so my presence was no novelty. As a
government contractor, it didn't take much for me to look
gainfully employed. I walked around with a notebook full
of whatever papers I had found in my desk. I signed up for
meetings I would never attend. In general, I kept a lower
profile than a bedbug in a mattress.

Dr. Wong was the key to the next step in my investigation. To bait him into revealing the Tiger Team report, I
created a bogus excerpt from an incident summary about

Building 707. Using details Tamara had given me, I entered the names of the three RCTs, their contamination levels, and a description of their survey.

I printed out the document and knocked on Dr. Wong's office door. He invited me in.

The room smelled of talc and miconazole nitrate, the active ingredient of antifungal foot spray. Stacks of binders, spiral-bound reports, and thick folders covered every horizontal surface of his office except the floor, flotsam created in the wake of any bureaucracy.

Dr. Wong sat hunched at his desk, reading a book and finishing a chocolate snack cake. His comb-over flopped away from his brown, bald head. A computer monitor and in- and out-boxes formed a barricade across the front of his desk.

Arranged left to right on the wall behind him were his framed diplomas: a bachelor of science in chemical engineering from Rensselaer Polytechnic Institute; a masters in health physics from Georgetown; and a doctorate in health science from MIT. On an end table in the right corner of the room rested a gray safe the size of a single-drawer cabinet. A magnetic placard on the safe's door read: CLOSED.

Narrow-shouldered and with a sloppy gut, Dr. Wong's pear-shaped body settled into the chair. As a senior health physicist, DOE paid him well, yet he wore clunky government-issue black-framed glasses, a cheap short-sleeved shirt, and a clip-on tie. Dr. Wong dressed like he was moonlighting at Radio Shack.

He crinkled the empty cellophone wrapper of the snack cake and looked up from his book: *Pathological Effects of Thermonuclear Weapons, Volume IV—Maximizing Civilian Mortality.* He tapped the cover. "Oh for the good old days, when working here had a purpose."

"Sorry to disturb your nostalgia, Doctor, but I found something that might concern you."

Dr. Wong looked at his monitor and jiggled the computer mouse. "I don't see that we have an appointment."

"We don't." I held up the summary. "This will only take a minute."

He squinted at my badge. "Mr. Gomez, first make an appointment. That's the protocol, and this is why DOE has an undeserved reputation for sloppiness. People keep circumventing protocol. The nuclear industry is governed by rules, at every level."

"It's an excerpt from an incident summary," I insisted. "I think you should review it."

He gestured to the in-box. "Drop it there."

I couldn't just leave the form, I needed to see his reaction. "This looks serious. Something about three RCTs getting seventeen rems in Building 707."

Dr. Wong's bland, round face turned dark with shock. He scurried around the desk and snatched the summary from my hand. He studied the form with a quiet, smoldering intensity, turning it over and over as if he couldn't believe what his eyes told him.

He stood barefoot, his trouser cuffs rolled up to mid-shin, his crooked toes dusted with white powder, the source of the miconazole nitrate smell. He was a short man, so I couldn't see why Tamara had called him Big Wong. If it involved the doctor dropping his pants, I didn't want to find out.

"Where'd you get this?" he snapped, oblivious to the comb-over hanging from his head like an open pot lid.

"In my desk, out there." I pointed to the cubicles beyond his door.

"Well, Mr. Gomez—I mean, Felix," he camouflaged his distress with a smile, "I wouldn't be too concerned about this."

"It looks serious to me. I've been in this business a while," I lied. "British Nuclear Fuels. DOD. The EPA. Lawrence Livermore."

Dr. Wong strained to keep his toothy grin while his eyes seemed ready to burst like the bulbs of overheated thermometers. "This summary is nothing to worry about, believe me."

I offered my hand. "Then where should I file it?"

"I'll take care of this." He stepped back to the safe, peeled off the magnetic placard, and flipped it over. The reverse side read: SECRET OPEN.

Dr. Wong grasped the combination dial. He looked over his shoulder at me. "That's all. I'll take care of this."

At last I was on a hot trail. In that safe sat the Tiger Team report. Gilbert Odin could pull his head off the chopping block; and I could wrap this case up, pocket my fee, and go back to California.

I left Rocky Flats, ate dinner—red enchiladas smothered with bull blood—and returned to the office late that evening. The building was empty and dark. Putting on a pair of latex gloves, I entered and removed my contact lenses. In the shadowy interior, everything looked remarkably clear to my vampire vision.

Like any resourceful private detective I carried a locksmith's kit and readily picked the lock of Dr. Wong's office door. The room still smelled like foot spray. I walked directly to the safe and inspected it. A chain looped from the safe's lifting shackle and ran through an eyebolt along the baseboard. I didn't see any wires for an alarm.

This was going to be easy. Closing my eyes to focus my attention, I placed my hands on the safe and delicately turned the combination dial, first to the right and then to the left. I heard and felt the faint clicks when the notches of each tumbler rotated under the bolt-release mechanism. Discerning the subtle differences between the three tumblers, I lined up the first tumbler, then the middle, then the third. Pressing the release button, I twisted the handle.

The safe clicked, and the door swung open.

I was as heady with pride as if I'd hit a home run.

But wait. Inside I found a box of Little Debbie chocolate snack cakes, a can of foot spray, and a dog-eared *Sports Illustrated* swimsuit issue, dated 1986. Stacked to the right in folders marked SECRET were documents detailing rad-contaminated biological waste. These papers were dated from last year and described mice, pigeons, and a cat found dead inside the Building 776 glove boxes, an incident of no relevance to me. Next to these I found my bogus incident summary but nothing else about the nymphomania or the Tiger Team report.

Damn. My home run had just turned into a pop fly.

After closing the safe, I shed the gloves, replaced my contacts, and drove home, sour with disappointment. I could think of nothing better than to snuggle into the comfort of a warm coffin and forget the day. I unlocked my apartment and leaned wearily against the front door to push it open.

A stream of cayenne pepper spray splashed my face. My eyes burned. In the instant before I clamped them shut, I glimpsed the brilliant-red aura of my attacker. I bent over, gagging, and rubbed my face to wipe away the searing liquid. Something hard slammed into the back of my head. My thoughts exploded into a thousand colored sparks that quickly dissolved into blackness.

CHAPTER
9

A BARKING DOG WOKE ME. I opened my eyes—
they burned. I reeked of pepper spray. Pushing off the
carpet, I sat up and noticed the morning sun trickle around
the edges of my window blinds. Outside, the dog finally
shut up.

A bent tire iron lay on the carpet. Somebody had whacked
me with a blow that would've killed a human, and I'm sure
that's what they had intended for me.

With a headache that felt like an electric bell ringing in
my frontal lobes, I staggered to the front door and locked
the deadbolt.

I retreated into the bathroom to treat my wounds and wash
up. I'd been hit so hard that my contacts had been knocked
out. If I could've seen my reflection, I'm sure my swollen eyes
would've looked like stewed prunes. Dried blood flaked from
my scalp. On my head, I felt a crease atop a lump the size of
my thumb. When I laid the tire iron against my head—only

barely touching the tender flesh—the crease fit into the bent part of the tire iron. The angle of the blow coming from behind meant my attacker was probably right-handed.

Right-handed like the man who had come after me with the M16. Pranging me across the skull with this tire iron would've seemed a practical tactic to a man of his large, muscular size.

I sniffed the handle of the iron, smelling talcum powder and latex residue, then tossed it aside. The attacker had worn disposable gloves, so unless I discovered his name or Social Security number engraved on the metal, I couldn't expect to find much of a clue on it as to his identity or motive.

He knew plenty about me, though. My home address. What kind of car I drove. For now, I was sure he thought I was dead, or close to it. Once he figured out that I was on my feet, he would attack again.

I put on a fresh pair of contacts and folded a compress over the wound. My head throbbed with an ache that four tablets of aspirin weren't able to quell.

In the second bedroom, my desk had been smashed apart. Shattered drawers and torn folders lay scattered on the floor. The computer power cords and modem cable dangled over the desk, where my hard drive and backup had been. What he didn't know was that he had taken a decoy.

Though that wasn't exactly reason to gloat. There had been two attempts on my life—as close to a life as a vampire had—and my apartment had been pillaged.

I checked the kitchen and found my laptop safe behind the false panel in the pantry. I still had my files and I was still alive. The lump on my head started to throb.

What hurt worse than the lump or the nauseating headache was the humiliation of getting KO'd by the human goon who had ransacked my place. Being a vampire, I was heir to the legacy of the most feared ghouls in history,

Dracula and Nosferatu. I was supposed to be the terrorizer, not the terrorized.

The attack left me obsessing. Bob Carcano had cautioned me about my refusal to drink human blood, accusing me of ignoring my vampire nature. Was he right? What consequences did that bring? My wounds hadn't healed overnight, which worried me. Last year, I'd been shot in the back and by the following morning, I was fit enough for my Pilates class.

Had the lack of human blood in my diet affected my recuperative powers? Or was it my guilt? Maybe, too, my vampire senses had dulled, and that's why my attacker had gotten the better of me. Or not. I wasn't sure.

Dizzy and spent, I went into my bedroom and pulled the Murphy bed from the wall, exposing my coffin. I climbed in and spent the rest of the day listening to the built-in stereo while I medicated myself into a dreamy haze with ibuprofen and vodka tonics.

When the buzz wore off I remembered Bob's invitation to *The Hollow Fang* party for tonight. A vampire party. They're either as sedate as an art reception—I've been to one where the guests critiqued watercolors and noshed on scabs they picked off the corpse centerpiece—or they're as raucous as an orgy choreographed by Attila the Hun. I wasn't in the mood for highbrow conversation and scabs—or orgies, for that matter—but if I stayed here, I'd be looking at the same damn ceiling I'd been staring at since morning. Plus I should meet members of the local *nidus*. Can't have too many undead friends.

When it came time to go, I showered and then jolted my nerves with a tall cup of Costa Rican dark roast spiced with goat's blood. The lump was almost gone and if I fluffed my hair over it, no one could tell that my head had been used for batting practice. And if someone asked, I'd tell him that I'd accidentally let the lid of a coffin slam on me. Clumsy me.

The party was in an east Denver home, a gabled Tudor. Techno music boomed from inside. A chubby woman answered the doorbell, wearing an obscenely tight latex cat suit that pinched a wedge of fat cleavage out the front. Her thick legs teetered on stiletto heels. No mistress of the dark, she looked more like a matron of the refrigerator. Her eyes had a vampire's gleam from costume contacts. "Welcome to our crypt, fellow vampire," she lisped through plastic, glow-in-the-dark fangs.

What a sad poser. No self-respecting vampire would dress like her, not unless there was serious money involved. I excused myself and squeezed past.

Most of the guests wore black, some gaudy latex, others trashy Goth getups with chains and leather, and a few were dressed in dark clothing that looked ordered from Lands' End. Everyone's eyes shone bright, the same as the greeter's from the front door.

I surreptitiously removed my contacts. Instantly, the color of the auras let me know who was vampire and who was human. Makes for an interesting switch when we vampires have to remove our contacts to fit in.

As soon as I got something to eat, I'd start to mingle. I forgot about this being a mixed crowd—vampires and humans—so there weren't many real blood treats on the buffet table in the den, mostly human food. A chocolate cake in the shape of a casket lay in the center of the table. Tamales wrapped in black cornhusks were piled in a chafing dish. Black candles dripped wax on bone-shaped candelabras. A steaming fondue pot held what looked like blood, but it was only marinara sauce—sans garlic, of course. A pyramid of blood-pudding canapés sat on a silver platter. No scabby corpse, thankfully. The cake looked especially rich, so I grabbed a serving knife.

Someone tapped my shoulder. "Cut me a piece of that."

I turned around.

A woman grinned at me. A bright-green aura radiated from her body as if she were plugged into a xenon lamp. With an aura that color, she was not human, and she definitely was no vampire.

"Felix Gomez," she said, "welcome to Denver."

CHAPTER 10

MY *KUNDALINI NOIR* jumped so hard I thought it would leap through my belly button.

After last night's attack, my defenses went to maximum alert. This woman made no threatening gestures, so I strained to keep my fangs and talons from springing out and revealing myself to the human guests.

She stood about five feet tall and was narrow-shouldered with broad hips. Wavy brunette hair fell alongside a pixieish face. Her green eyes looked a size too big for her face, her mouth a size too small. She seemed to have been put together from God's spare parts bin, though somehow it worked. She was cute.

So far, this investigation into the nymphomania at Rocky Flats had introduced me to the paranoia and intrigue within DOE. Soon after that a nympho put a gun to my head, later somebody knocked me unconscious and ransacked my apartment, and now I meet this woman with her mysterious green aura. Perhaps she was a super-nympho.

I fixed a vampire glare on her, strong enough to make the toughest biker whimper in fear. "How did you know my name?"

"Bob Carcano told me," she answered, oblivious of my attempt at zapping her.

What was *with* this woman? She was no vampire and deflected my powers like no human could. Her green aura became like the pleasant glow from a string of Christmas lights.

She set her hands on her hips and gave me the once-over. "Felix, if you get this excited when I have my clothes on, what would you have done if I'd been naked?"

"What do you mean?"

"Your aura," she replied. "If your erection throbs like that, I'm one lucky girl."

She read my aura? How? Her eyes didn't have *tapetum lucidum.*

I said, "You're no vampire."

"I"—she mugged nonchalantly as if it were obvious to all but the densest of morons—"am a dryad. Forest sprite to you nontechnical types."

"A forest sprite? That some kind of fairy? Like Tinkerbell?"

"I never cared for *her* sense of fashion." She wore a wooly red sweater and loose jeans with the cuffs bunched over suede clogs. "Too frou frou for me. I don't have the hips for it."

"What's a dryad doing here among vampires?"

"You got something against me? None of the other vampires do." Her smile eased, then disappeared. "Let me simplify it for you. I could leave and pretend we never met. Would that work?"

The idea that we'd never met disturbed me. I wanted to see her smile again. I barely knew this woman—forest sprite, fairy, whatever the hell she was—and frankly, I didn't want her to go. Her spunkiness excited me. And since my aura was flashing my emotions like a billboard, she had to know that, too. But I couldn't make it too easy for her.

"I notice you're still here."

"Maybe I like dumb challenges." She pointed a finger at me. "You know what I mean?"

"Much too well." I offered my hand. "Miss Dryad, you have a name?"

"A rather nice one, I think." Her pearly grin returned. "Wendy Teagarden."

We shook hands. Her touch was firm and warm.

"Wendy? So you *are* like Tinkerbell. Who's your old boyfriend? Peter Pan?"

That pearly grin flattened a tight line. "Keep that up and you'll go home the same way you got here . . . alone."

I raised my hands to signal surrender. "My bad. Forgive me."

Wendy shook her head and gave a self-deprecating laugh. "Considering what I have to work with, okay, you're forgiven."

"How do you know Bob?"

"Friends of friends."

Wasn't much of an answer. "What do you want from me?" I asked.

"Since my offer for sexual favors went right over your head," she waved a hand over her hair and made a *whoosh* sound, "I'll have to settle for chocolate cake."

"What offer?"

"Jeeze, talk about your dumb challenges." She rolled her eyes. "The cake. Please, while I'm still in the mood for *that*."

I plunged the serving knife into the cake and flipped a piece onto a paper plate.

Wendy looked at the plate and twitched her nose in disapproval. "Kinda small."

"I thought size didn't matter.".

"We're talking about chocolate cake."

I cut a thicker portion. "Is this okay? What else would you like me to do?"

Wendy lifted the plate and started away from the buffet table. "Cork that opened bottle of merlot and bring it. And a couple of glasses."

"Where're we going?"

She motioned to the other guests. "To get some privacy."

How much privacy would we need?

We went out a side door, into a night barely lit by the dim street lamps. We walked around the corner of the house into a shadow between two elm trees.

Wendy approached the wall. She planted one foot on the siding and began walking up, vampire fashion, while keeping the paper plate level with the ground so that the chocolate cake wouldn't slide off. Stepping over the eaves, she disappeared onto the roof.

I lifted my leg and set my shoe against the siding, then stepped upward with my other foot. The climb was a simple, sixteen-foot vertical walk. But my movements became sluggish, and the higher I climbed, the harder I breathed. The wine bottle and glasses clinked together and almost slipped from my hands.

I hoisted one leg over the eaves and then the other. My feet planted themselves on the steep, shale-shingle roof. I felt like a fat man who had sprinted up three flights of stairs. Thoughts about my weakening vampire prowess led me to brood about my refusal to drink human blood, and that, in turn, resurrected my guilt over shooting the Iraqi civilians.

Wendy's aura brightened with concern. "You okay? What's with that bump on your head?"

"Coffin lid fell on me. Occupational hazard." I rested my

hands on my knees until I gained enough breath to ask, "Now that we're up here enjoying the penthouse view, explain your green aura."

Wendy set her plate on the swamp cooler and stabbed the cake with her fork. "You got a weird set of priorities. We're alone. We've got wine. And you ask about my aura. Why?"

"Humor me."

"It's green for the reason yours is orange."

"Mine is orange because I'm a vampire." I set the wine and glasses on top of the swamp cooler.

"Sort of. Your aura is orange because, being a vampire, your psychic energy level is centered on the second chakra, which is here." Wendy touched her lower abdomen. "It's all explained by Tantric mysticism."

My stay in Denver had taken a tight turn into the even-more-weird. Radiation and nymphomania weren't enough, now there was this New Age wackiness to consider. It was a good thing she was easy on the eyes. I worked the cork out of the bottle and poured the wine.

"You know anything about chakras?" She palmed one glass and sipped.

"I've tried not to." The question reminded me of a hippie-dippy granola chick I dated in college. I put up with her Birkenstocks and patchouli stink for the sake of tapping her hairy nookie.

"Haven't you wondered," Wendy asked, "why humans have red auras and vampires orange ones?"

"Figured it was the same reason humans have blunt teeth and I have fangs. Part of the prey-predator arrangement."

"Chakras are your body's psychic energy centers," Wendy said. She set her glass on the swamp cooler. "There are seven major chakras and each corresponds to a distinct psychic energy level. Each level is analogous to the color reflected by your aura. Red auras mean that the being is concerned with manifestation. Orange, connection."

"Connection to what?"

"Of the material world to the spiritual," she said. "That's why vampires can see auras. You were surprised by my green aura, weren't you?"

"Of course. But once you explained that you were a dryad—a forest sprite—then I figured it's because you ate leaves and bean sprouts." And granola.

"My energy is centered on compassion. The fourth chakra. Here." She stroked her sternum. "Its color is green."

During my interrogation of Tamara, Sofia, and Jenny, their auras had gone from red to yellow when the nymphomania took over.

"What are the chakra colors?" I asked.

"Red, orange, yellow, green, light blue, dark blue, and white."

"You're green. I'm orange," I said. "If we're supernaturals, why aren't our energy levels next to each other?"

"I don't mean to insult you," Wendy replied, "but despite your powers, you vampires are closer to humans. That's what you came from. We dryads were born this way."

"Then explain yellow."

"Who has a yellow aura?"

"Somebody I've met."

Wendy raised an eyebrow. "Was this somebody a supernatural? Like us?"

"I'm not sure," I replied. "They were human when I first met them. Under vampire hypnosis their auras turned from red to yellow."

Wendy kept quiet for a moment. "Maybe that has something to do with it. Yellow is transformation."

"Transformation from what?"

"One psychic level to another," she explained. "I don't

know of any supernaturals with yellow auras. Doesn't mean they don't exist." The intensity of her green aura notched up. "Why did you hypnotize these humans? Was it part of an investigation?"

"How do you know about that?"

"Bob Carcano told me you're a private detective."

My anger with Bob kept the words from forming. I had to force them out. "Yes, I'm an investigator."

"He said something about an outbreak of nymphomania at Rocky Flats." Wendy crossed her arms. A mischievous smile traced across her mouth. "Sounds kinky. Could be fun."

"Bob talks too much. And why do you ask about me?"

"A request."

"By whom?"

"Someone far away."

Who did I know from far away? "The Araneum?"

"If it was, I couldn't say so, could I?"

"What else do you do?" I asked.

"In other words, what pays the bills? I work at Denver Health, the local public hospital. It's a good place to keep tabs on things."

"What if I want to keep tabs on you?"

Wendy reached for me. "I'll make it easy for you." Her fingers clasped my wrist.

My *kundalini noir* rustled at the expectation of pleasure. Since becoming a vampire, I've never given thought to being close to another being, not this way. And certainly not to a supernatural creature I knew little about, however cute.

Wendy abruptly pulled away and lifted the hem of her sweater. She flashed a narrow band of white skin above her belt. Lusty excitement heated me. She didn't waste time. The steep slope of the roof could demand some interesting positions.

A pager clipped to her belt buzzed and its red light flashed. She pressed the pager button to illuminate the display. "It's the trauma center, a.k.a. the knife and gun club. Must be short-staffed again." She smoothed her sweater over her waist. "Sorry. Gotta run. Give me your number."

I handed her a business card.

She kissed my cheek. "I'll call." She stepped off the roof and floated down between the elm trees like a leaf. She scurried over the lawn toward a silver Mazda coupe parked along the sidewalk. The coupe's alarm beeped twice. Wendy got in. The car shot away from the curb, honking goodbye.

The air cooled my skin where she had kissed me. Wendy was a good distraction from the mess of my investigation. The mystery about her intrigued me. Was she from the Araneum? If I wanted to learn more about Wendy on my terms, I should've gotten her number.

Now to get down. The drop from the roof looked forbidding now that I suspected my vampire powers were weakened.

Come on Felix, trust yourself. Walking off the edge, I hovered for a second. Then the air collapsed under me, and my legs slammed into the ground. I tumbled backwards over the grass and thumped my head on the siding.

Clutching my scalp, I cursed, pushed myself up, and brushed dead grass from my clothes.

I needed another belt of wine to nurse the pain, but then I remembered that I'd left the merlot on the roof. I wasn't climbing back up there, so I limped inside and guarded a spot at the buffet table next to the liquor. Humans in capes took out their fake vampire teeth. They dipped breadsticks into the marinara sauce and acted as if they had been impaled. Their voices melted into the blur of conversation and music.

I downed one glass of a red wine I poured from a box, a

wine whose two major attributes were that it was wet and had alcohol.

The humans dared one another to try the blood-pudding canapés, all of them behaving as if they were trying to out-dork the others. One of them, a man of about thirty and clearly the leader in this informal dork contest, threw his cape back and unfolded a cell phone. He stared at the tiny screen and started text-messaging. Even here at a party, humans were obsessed with documenting their lives.

Documenting. The thought echoed in my head.

The rush of ethanol and the fall from the roof must have jogged a loose connection in my brain, and I had a "Eu-reka" moment. The Tiger Team report couldn't exist in the bureaucracy of DOE without generating a tide of paper-work. Documentation such as access logs, visitors' files, and expense reports.

If I looked hard enough, I could find a trail within that documentation. A trail that would lead me to the truth.

CHAPTER
11

BOB CARCANO ENTERED the den. His round head swiveled to pick through the crowd as he scanned the room. His aura simmered with the disarming cheeriness of a smiley face. He looked about the room and, finding me, waved.

I waved back and resumed drinking my second glass of wine.

Bob remained in a pleasant mood upon seeing me, which was a surprise, considering the nagging lecture he had given me as a going-away present at our last meeting. I didn't want to spend another evening sparring with him over my vampire dining habits. I didn't drink human blood because . . . guilt bubbled into my thoughts. Blood from the Iraqi girl I had murdered came flinging at me across time and space. What I wanted more than anything else was to have the girl forgive me and expunge this guilt. But her little rotting corpse was buried in a forgotten dirt patch on the other side of the world, so my absolution was impossible.

The wine soured and I put the unfinished glass down.

Bob stood on a chair, clapped his hands, and announced, "Everybody, we're playing zombie twister in the basement."

The humans around the buffet table cackled like happy chickens at the news. They reinserted their fangs and joined the others filing down the stairs.

Bob and I remained alone in the den. His eyes went moody and his expression tightened.

"Felix, it's good that you're here." He grasped my arm and pulled closer to me. His voice lowered to a whisper as if to emphasize the importance of what he was about to tell me. "There's trouble. We've got serious business."

"We? You mean you and I?"

Bob's gaze lifted abruptly to the top of my head. "What the hell happened to you?"

Here came the lecture. The tone in my reply had no humor. "I got a little clumsy."

Bob raised a hand to stop me. "Forget it. Right now I've got bigger concerns than worrying about your brown ass."

I'd gotten so worked up about arguing with him that his answer muzzled my resentment. What concerns? I was about to ask when a tall, older man approached from the kitchen.

He had a white, wispy beard and matching droopy eyebrows. Orange aura. Vampire. His lanky arms draped over the shoulders of a younger woman and man flanking him. Red auras, humans.

The woman had a kerchief tied around her neck. The man wore a thick, black leather collar. Covering their necks like this meant they were hiding puncture marks, the sign they were chalices. For all but these humans, the fascination with vampires was just a playful diversion. Even the most die-hard posers thought that having someone suck blood from their necks was a perverse game played only by sickos too taken by the vampire fantasy.

Bob extended his hand and introduced me to the tall vampire. "Felix, this is one of the snaggletoothed plasma guzzlers I told you about, Ziggy Drek. He's been around longer than the calendar."

"It's Siegfried von Drek," Ziggy corrected. Resplendent in his starched white shirt and black waistcoat, Ziggy's visage should've been on a painting hanging inside a castle. "At one time, I was a Prussian baron." The words came from his mouth in a bothered drawl, delivered with the creaky, Teutonic accent of a B-movie vampire.

"And now you manage a Kinko's."

Ziggy hugged his chalices, then allowed them each to kiss him on the neck, the gesture saying, Screw you, Bob, I don't need your goddamn approval. "Is that why you asked for me? To remind me of where I work?"

"We have private business." Bob selected a blood-pudding canapé from the table and gestured to Ziggy that his companions should leave.

Bob munched on the canapé while he waited until the chalices were out of earshot. "I'm going to call a special council of the *nidus*. As you are one of our senior vampires, I'll need your help."

A ring of light descended Ziggy's aura, the psychic equivalent of an irritated sigh. "What now?"

"Jody Pasquales and Erwin Flakes are dead." Bob turned to me. "Jody and Erwin were vampires from New York."

"You've spoiled the party to tell me this?" Ziggy tugged at his shirt cuffs. "Vampires die all the time."

"Not like this. Seven of us have been offed in the last month," Bob said. "If you trace the deaths on a map—New York, Philadelphia, Kansas City, Lincoln—it's a path that leads here, to Denver. This could be another church-sponsored extermination."

"In America?" I asked. "Now?"

"Did the Araneum say that?" Ziggy added.

"No," Bob replied. "That's my guess."

"Your guess? Then say so," Ziggy said. With every word, Ziggy's accent became less Mannheim and more Milwaukee.

"I've been around," Bob said. "I've seen this before."

"And so have I. A couple of vampires get smushed and suddenly everyone's Chicken Little." Ziggy flapped his arms and squawked. "The sky is falling. The humans have their stakes and pitchforks out. All vampires stick their heads up their collective ass and hide."

Ziggy clasped my shoulder and gave a jovial shake. "Felix, the way Bob's acting, you'd think he's about to start menstruating."

Bob's aura flared like the burner on a furnace. His quick glance to me said, Better not betray me.

Bob turned his anger back to Ziggy. "Don't mock me. According to the Araneum, the vampires were quickly found out and killed. Such tactics point to *vânätori de vampir.*"

Every undead bloodsucker knew those words. Vampire hunters.

Maybe my attacker wasn't concerned about the Rocky Flats investigation. Maybe he was one of these vampire hunters, perhaps the one who had questioned Jenny, the RCT.

Ziggy chuckled with skepticism. "Ridiculous. And where are these *vânätori* from?"

"Romania. Specifically, Transylvania."

"According to whom?" Ziggy asked.

"Rumor."

"Rumor?" Ziggy laughed and raised his voice. "*Vânätori de vampir* from Transylvania? Who's helping them? The bogey man?"

"Make jokes, you old fool," Bob said. "How do you explain the deaths?"

"The usual. Stupidity. Carelessness. Driving while intoxicated. That lush Erwin couldn't walk two city blocks without stumbling into a tavern."

"These killings followed a ritual pattern. Decapitation."

"Stake through the heart—all that, I'm sure," Ziggy interrupted. "Yes, we are familiar with the lore of vampire killings. I've been around for three centuries and not once have I seen any *vânätori de vampir.* I even owned a brothel in Bucharest, so it wasn't hard to find me."

"Maybe *you've* stumbled through the world with your eyes locked on every available crotch, but I've seen *vânätori.*"

"Good for you," Ziggy replied. "Someday when I'm bored to tears, I'd love to hear every detail. I don't suppose the murders could've been caused by another vampire? Or an envious chalice? Hasn't that happened before? Right here in Denver, as I remembered it."

Bob thrust a finger at Ziggy. "I've survived the exterminations. I've seen the worst of it."

"Which was when?" Ziggy cupped a hand behind an ear.

"The Mausoleum Purge of 1810."

"Which was where?"

"Aquitaine, France."

"I thought so. France, not Colorado. Two hundred years ago, not yesterday." Ziggy waved for his two chalices to return. "Bob, as the *nidus* leader you know better than to stir up the nest with your paranoia. When your Transylvanian *vânätori* show up, silver crucifixes in hand and wreathes of garlic around their necks, then call me. Better yet, tie a note to the leg of a bat and send it."

The woman and man returned and wrapped their arms around Ziggy's waist. He rested his arms first on their shoulders, then let his hands drop down their backs to caress their round bottoms. The three of them walked out of the den.

"Didn't that lecherous old bastard say it was stupid vampires who die?" Bob leaned against the table. "I hate to say it, but if the *vânätori* do attack, I hope they go after Ziggy first."

"What if these *vânätori* are already here?"

Bob's gaze cut to me. "What do you mean?"

I shared what Jenny had told me. The more I talked, the more Bob's aura acquired a prickly surface indicating alarm.

"Why didn't you say something before?"

"Because it had to do with my investigation. You've already blabbed to Wendy Teagarden and I don't want to make what I'm doing any of Ziggy's business."

"Don't you worry, unless it involves engorged genitalia, it won't ever be Ziggy's business," Bob said. "I'll pass along what you told me to the Araneum. In the meantime, I'll need proof about the *vânätori*."

"What Jenny told me is proof."

"What Jenny told you was the talk of a medicated crazy woman. That's what Ziggy would say. Felix, bring me proof. Something I can show to the *nidus*."

"Proof? Bob, I've got my own investigation to run."

"This takes priority."

"To you maybe, not me," I said. "If I run into the *vânätori*, I'll see what I can get as a souvenir."

"I'm surrounded by comedians. Go, then. Do what you have to." Bob turned to the table and sorted through the wine. "The hell with this. I can't solve these problems with grape juice. Where's the scotch?"

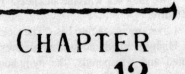

CHAPTER 12

MRS. ANGELA FINAMORE, civil servant level GS-13, managed the Rocky Flats Personnel Records Department. She was the custodian of Dr. Wong's file. Documents that could lead me to the secret Tiger Team report and the truth behind the outbreak. I'd corner Finamore in her office, put her under vampire hypnosis, and make her show me Dr. Wong's file.

Surprisingly, when I arrived, the Records Department was unoccupied except for a fellow at the front desk. Boxes bulging with files surrounded him. Behind his desk stood rows of steel filing cabinets and empty desks. In his late twenties and wearing a light-blue oxford shirt hanging limply on his trim body, he exuded the clean-cut and overworked demeanor one expected from a trustee of federal records. His badge read Gary Higby.

I asked, "Where's Angela Finamore?"

"Ms. Finamore is not here"—Gary Higby's eyes focused on my badge—"Mr. Gomez."

"Do you know when she'll be back?"

"No, she's out with the sickness." He studied me a bit too intently.

I fixed my gaze into his. "The sickness?"

Higby blushed and averted his eyes. "You know," he hesitated and whispered, "the nymphomania. It affected the women in the office, and I'm here alone to cope with all this." He waved to the mounds of documents awaiting his attention. Dots of perspiration shined along his brow. What the hell was heating him up?

So what if he wasn't Angela Finamore; I'd give him a good dose of vampire hypnosis and have him hand over Dr. Wong's file.

Higby abruptly swiveled in his chair toward the cabinet behind him, as if he were hiding something and I had made him uncomfortable. No problem, I'd uncover his secrets soon enough.

With his back turned to me, I quietly closed the door and removed my contacts to expose my *tapetum lucidum*.

I cleared my throat to get his attention.

His aura flashed, yet he remained still, ignoring me.

I rushed around the desk, seized his arm, and jerked his face toward mine.

His eyes closed, Higby sprang from his chair and embraced me. He kissed my lips.

Turning my face to avoid his mouth, I pushed him away. "What the hell?"

He clung to me. "You made me so hot the second I saw you. I was praying you felt the same way."

Was the nymphomania turning into homosexual satyriasis?

Higby clasped the back of my neck. "Why should the women here have all the fun?"

Higby unbuckled his trousers and let them drop past his knees. His erection formed a tent inside his royal blue briefs. He swept the files off his desk and scooted his butt onto the desk. I needed to put him under before he tried to bone me.

But Higby wouldn't open his eyes for me to hypnotize him. I tugged at the collar button of his shirt, hoping to subdue him with a bite of my vampire saliva.

Caressing my back, Higby tilted his head to one side as if expecting me to nuzzle him. I sank my fangs into the jugular of his warm neck. Gasping with desire, he squeezed me hard. His blood spurted into my mouth. I spit into a wad of tissue—no telling what contaminated him.

Holding him still, I sucked at his neck again and worked my saliva into the wound. His grip loosened. The tent inside his briefs began to deflate. With my mouth still attached to his neck, I lay his relaxed body across the desk. His hairy, naked legs dangled over the edge, his trousers bunched at his ankles.

The door opened, and a security guard entered. He hollered in surprise and reached for his pistol.

I released Higby. His head thumped on the desk.

I froze the guard with my vampire glare. Leading him into the office, I locked the door. At the rate things were going with these interruptions, I'd have to hypnotize all of Rocky Flats. In order to erase his memory of me with Higby, I'd have to bite the guard as well.

I sat the guard in a chair and bit him. I tried not to gag on his Aqua Velva aftershave.

With Higby and the guard sedated, I searched for Wong's file in the cabinets. Meanwhile the phones rang and rang. Someone jiggled the doorknob. Whoever it was beat on the door for several minutes and then left, cussing, "Goddamn lazy-ass records people are never here."

When I couldn't find the file, I revived Higby just enough

for him to give me his computer password. His spreadsheet listed an entry for Wong dated two weeks ago and noted that his file was stored in Building 371, inside the Protected Area.

I had found the trail. Dr. Wong's otherwise innocuous personnel file contained something worth keeping secret.

Before I left the Records Department, I put my contacts back in. I dropped the guard's trousers and sat Higby on his lap. When the two men came around, I'd let them sort the situation out for themselves. Maybe they'd start dating.

I was hoping that Higby had attacked me because he mistakenly got the gay hots for my body; otherwise the outbreak had made the jump to those of us with XY chromosomes.

Getting into the Protected Area was routine, considering that I had the appropriate clearance. I entered the concrete tunnel building straddling the perimeter wire. In the locker room I stripped to my skivvies and socks. I grabbed a set of baggy, white overalls from the laundry cart and put them on. Blots of grease on the legs and yellow circles under the armpits stained the fabric. I sorted through a pile of work boots until I found the only pair my size. The stink from the boots was so bad it made my toes curl. Whoever wore them before hadn't been familiar with the concept of hygiene. Hell, a strong dose of radiation would probably have done this pair some good.

I took off my watch and set it on the shelf in the locker. The rule was don't take anything into the Protected Area that you can't afford to lose, in case it gets contaminated.

Properly attired as an anonymous worker ant, I presented my badge to the guard. He slid it over the scanner and when the indicator flashed green, he motioned me to proceed through the metal detector.

The tunnel connected to Building 371. A sign in the

foyer gave directions to the materials containment facilities and the archives office.

The dilapidated appearance inside Building 371 startled me. In the movies, nuclear facilities are always futuristic beehives made of stainless steel and glass tubes filled with glowing liquids. Everything runs with the precision of a European racing car.

The reality was that Rocky Flats, including within the Protected Area, where plutonium manufacture had taken place, had the feel of an old factory mill that had seen better days. The rough edges from layers of paint applied to the walls and floors revealed the constant battle against decay. Capped, discolored pipes hung from the ceiling.

All the workers, exclusively men, had shaggy mustaches and proud bellies that strained the waistbands of their overalls. Several of them had their sleeves rolled up, showing arms covered with tattoos. Again, in the movies, nuclear workers look and act like buff robots. These guys at Rocky Flats had this ambling beer-guzzling, blue-collar manner about themselves. It was as if America's nuclear arsenal had been entrusted to bikers.

A worker turned into the hall too sharply with his supply cart and bashed into a protruding corner, adding another gouge to the already scarred surface. He backed away from the corner and continued, crunching over chips of plaster that he had knocked loose.

Down the hall I found the archives office, entered, and locked the door. The two male clerks on duty heard the click and turned toward me. One was as skinny as the other was fat. Standing next to each other they looked like the number 10.

I removed my contacts and hypnotized them both. I left them standing like a couple of zombies who had forgotten what to do next. Spit drooled from their open mouths. I unhooked the key rings from their belts.

Banks of file cabinets shared floor space with stacks of safes. I asked the skinny clerk for Dr. Wong's file.

He twitched and gagged in the effort to answer me. "Redlight."

I asked him what "Redlight" meant but he was too stupefied to reply. The fat clerk wasn't any more coherent.

I could bite them and let my saliva do its work, but for the moment I wanted to keep my lips off another man's body.

Scanning the cabinets, I bypassed those labeled PERSONNEL. Too obvious. At the far end, against the wall, stood a gray cabinet with a TOP SECRET placard. It took two different keys to unlock the cabinet, a safeguard to prevent any one individual from getting access. Fortunately, between the clerks I had both keys, and within a minute I was rustling through the drawers, looking for anything marked "Redlight."

I thumbed through the folders and felt my anxiety rise as the minutes ticked by. Nothing mentioned Redlight.

At the back end of the bottom cabinet I discovered Dr. Wong's file. After feeding his papers through a copy machine, I returned the originals to their place and tucked my copies, which I had neatly folded, into the waistband of my underwear. I'd study the documents later.

Confident that this case was starting to break open, I walked back to the tunnel. I joined a group of five workers waiting to exit through the metal detector and radiation monitors.

An alarm shrieked, sending a grating, pulsating blare through the building. Lights along the walls flashed.

The worker in front of me spun around. His braided ponytail smacked me in the face. "Holy shit, that's the criticality alarm."

That meant there was plutonium nearby that was ready to explode. The deafening scream of the alarms gripped my ears with their shrill cry of doom.

One guard stepped in front of the metal detector to block our passage through the tunnel. He pointed to the nearest door inside Building 371 and shouted, "Everybody outside."

The six of us rushed outside. We slipped on the dirt and gravel surrounding the building. We remained trapped inside the wire of the Protected Area. The wail of the alarms echoed around us, screaming of danger.

The man behind me went, "Uff," and he sagged against the wall. A red blot appeared on his chest.

Bullets tore at the wall. I grabbed the collars of the two closest men and yanked them to the ground. We flattened our bodies against the dirt. One slug ricocheted in front of me.

What the hell was going on? First the criticality alarms. Now a crossfire. Were we under attack by terrorists?

Another volley of bullets stitched the wall above me.

The guy with the ponytail began to sob. "We're going to die, man. If we don't get crapped up from the plutonium, we're going to eat lead."

"No one's going to die," I shouted to him. "Stay calm."

The wounded man lay on his back. I crawled over to him and unbuttoned the torso of his overalls. Warm blood bubbled from a hole in the left side of his chest. I slid my hand through the blood and crammed my index finger into the hole. The smell of the fresh human blood excited my vampire hunger. My fangs grew. I wanted to attack, to feed.

Then I remembered the other time I had done this, had washed my hands in human blood. The wail of the Iraqi girl tore into my skull. My arms tensed and I fought the urge to spring up and run away. My left hand trembled and started to slip away from the wound. I grasped my left wrist and kept my hands steady.

The wounded man clasped my shoulder and gave a weak squeeze.

I patted his head and left clumps of blood in his hair. "Stay with me. We'll get out of this."

We lay still and waited for another volley of bullets. The scream of the alarms overwhelmed my vampire hearing. I might as well have been deaf.

My breath puffed into the dirt. Blood ran down my sleeve. The folded copies of Dr. Wong's file dug into my belly. Was this a terrorist attack or simply the work of a lousy shot gunning for me?

The alarms abruptly became silent. From inside the building, someone shouted, "All clear!"

"You see?" I told the group. "We're okay." I patted the wounded man on the forehead.

"Don't move, any of you," growled a voice. "Stay on the ground. Put your hands behind your head."

Two pairs of black combat boots tramped around my head. The blast deflector of an M16 rifle knocked against my temple. "You—I said to put your hands behind your head."

I arched my neck and stared up the barrel of the rifle. Both guards looked like demons in their black helmets, hoods, and tinted goggles.

"But this man has a serious wound."

The guard rapped the rifle muzzle against my forehead again. "I didn't tell you to look up. Do like you're told. Let us worry about that bastard."

Dropping my head, I withdrew my bloodied hand.

The guard nudged my cheek with his boot. "All right, Florence Nightingale, give me your badge."

I scraped my hand under me and pulled my badge free.

The guard took my badge. "So you're Felix Gomez? Get up." He grabbed my collar. "You're coming with us."

CHAPTER
13

TWO SECURITY GUARDS LED me to the plant manager's office. The taller of the guards hurried ahead and opened the door. Cradling his HK submachine gun in his left arm, he beckoned us to proceed.

I entered the office and walked across a plush maroon carpet to a chair in front of a massive wooden desk.

The plant manager, Herbert Hoover Merriweather, sat in a high-backed leather chair behind the desk. This was the first time I'd seen him in person, though I recognized his face from the official DOE photos that hung about the plant. Merriweather was a retired U.S. Navy captain, a former nuclear submariner—what DOE wags called a "sewer-pipe driver."

Merriweather's black complexion was as dark and bumpy as the creosote on a wharf piling. He had a squat face, a low crinkled brow, and a nappy flattop haircut that made you think that at least once in his naval career someone had slammed a deck hatch on his head and squashed his skull.

His flat nose and wide nostrils accentuated the horizontal impression of his features.

He wore a navy-blue polo shirt that fit snug around his broad chest. The silhouette of a submarine and the designation "SSN 42" in gold thread decorated the left breast of his shirt. Like most newly retired officers, the beginnings of a paunch swelled his belly.

On the wall over his left shoulder hung a gold submariner's badge, two dolphins flanking the cylindrical conning tower of a submarine. To the untutored eye it looked like a couple of carp fighting over a garbage can.

A tall glass case stood against the wall, next to a large picture window covered with slat blinds. Inside the case hung a white naval officer's uniform with four gold stripes on the sleeve cuffs indicating the rank of captain. Badges and rows of military ribbons decorated the left breast of the coat.

Merriweather's dark pupils tracked me as I approached the pea-green leather chair centered before his desk. He nodded to the guard, who turned sharply on his heels and left the office, closing the door.

I sat in the chair, careful so as to not cause the papers tucked inside my overalls to bend and crackle.

"Do you know why you're here, Mr. Gomez?" Merriweather asked in a voice that sounded like gravel rattling down a pipe.

He was playing with me. This theater of bringing me into his office, with a couple of heavily armed goons outside the door was an intense mind-squeeze. He knew why I was here. They had caught me stealing the file and rather than confront me outright, they tightened the psychological screws.

I could remove my contacts and use vampire hypnosis to control him, but I was certain that I was under video surveillance. One suspicious move and those two guards would rush in like Dobermans and blast me to pieces with their submachine guns.

The papers hidden inside my overalls felt as hot as plutonium. I rubbed my sweaty palms across the dirty knees of my overalls. "I'm not sure."

"Can you tell me what happened?"

His question came at me with the intensity of a magnesium flare. So certain was I that he was referring to Dr. Wong's file that I thought the papers in my shorts would burst into flames.

"I brought you here to broaden your perspective of what happened today. I don't want you to report the wrong information to Lawrence Livermore." Merriweather drew a deep breath and exhaled. His nostrils fluttered. "We experienced the unfortunate confluence of two separate situations. A criticality alarm and a live-fire terrorist drill."

"You're talking about the shooting?"

"There was the discharge of weapons. Yes."

"What about the guy in front of me who got hit?"

"There were three . . . injuries," he elaborated.

"Injuries? The man had a sucking chest wound."

Merriweather knit his fingers together and leaned on his desk. "Are you a medical doctor?"

"No. I'm a health physicist."

"Then you would appreciate the need to let a medical expert render the proper judgment."

"The man didn't have a sucking chest wound?" I held up my right index finger that was smeared with dried blood. "I used this finger to plug the hole."

"Your point?"

Confused, I muttered, "My point . . . my point is that I don't understand what you're getting at."

Merriweather pushed away from his desk. "Then I'm glad that I brought you here. A layman could look at what happened today and come away with the wrong conclusion. I'm not going to let anything happen on my watch that could tarnish either my own reputation or that of the Department of Energy."

"What happened today was a little more than tarnish."

"How so? My guards reacted appropriately. Nothing was compromised within the Protected Area."

"What about the three casualties?"

"Injuries," Merriweather corrected promptly. "The last time this happened—"

"This happened before?"

Merriweather frowned at my interruption. "The first time, the results were disappointing. Even I will admit to that. Six hundred and thirty-eight rounds fired. One injury. The second time, one hundred eleven rounds fired, two injuries. This time, ninety-six rounds expended, three injuries. By anybody's measure, that's a big improvement, in marksmanship alone."

"That's not much consolation for those who got shot."

"I hate the word 'spin,' but I don't want people to draw erroneous conclusions about what happened today."

I remained silent, stunned by his logic.

Merriweather stood and walked over to a thick steel pipe behind him. He pressed a button on the wall. There was a hum as the pipe rose until handles and a viewfinder along its side appeared from a hole in the floor.

"What's that?" I asked.

"A Mark 4 attack periscope. A memento from my days at sea."

"How did it get here?"

"Not that it's any concern of yours, but since you asked, it was paid for with discretionary funds." Merriweather folded the handles down from the periscope. He grasped the handles, closed his left eye, and pressed his open right eye to the rubber gasket surrounding the viewfinder.

"In my navy career, it was my privilege to serve four tours aboard a submarine, the last as captain." Merriweather paced in a circle and rotated the periscope. "I learned that, above all, loyalty was the most important attribute of a good sailor. A loyalty that manifested itself in selfless devotion, discipline, and dedication. Are you following what I'm saying?"

"That I should be loyal."

"The ultimate test of loyalty, of the trust that our government and commander-in-chief set upon me, was to execute our nuclear attack plans when that the time came . . ." Merriweather stopped his pacing. "Regrettably, that opportunity never materialized."

I didn't regard nuclear holocaust as a missed opportunity.

"You would've been impressed by the thoroughness of our planning. After we expended our load of twenty-four Trident missiles, do you know what our orders would've been?"

"I'd say cruise to the Caribbean, break out the sunscreen, and water-ski after the fallout settled."

Merriweather shook his head, oblivious to my attempt at humor. "No. Our orders would've been to rendezvous with a supply ship, reload, and continue the attack."

Attack what? By that time most of the world would've been radioactive rubble.

"Can you understand the depth of my loyalty?" he asked.

"I can. But the next question is—loyal to whom?"

"If you ask that, then you're thinking too much. In this post-9/11 world, none of us has the luxury of thinking too much. Leave the thinking to the government. Otherwise you run the risk of not being serious about your oath of federal service, specifically about defending our country against all enemies, both foreign"—Merriweather pulled his face from the periscope and looked at me—"and domestic."

"I fought as a soldier in the United States Army. There's no question about my loyalties."

Merriweather slapped the handles flush against the side of the periscope. He touched a button on the wall and the periscope retracted into the floor. "Excellent answer. Then you're dismissed."

I know that we had been eavesdropped upon because at this point the door opened. Both guards waited for me to leave.

I rose from the chair, dizzy with confusion and a growing dread that our nuclear weapons had ever been entrusted to this lunatic Merriweather.

I returned to the locker room, where I stripped out of the overalls, showered, and put on my street clothes. I tucked the copied file into the interior pocket of my jacket and went home.

I tried to relax and drank wine while I lingered over a quick dinner of *posole* and bull's blood. I spread Dr. Wong's file on the table and picked at the food as I studied the report. The blood congealed and formed a red scab over the stew.

The file was the collection of Dr. Wong's travel and expense vouchers. Why these had been stored with classified documents mystified me. I was confident that a bureaucrat's love of documentation would lead to a slip and allow light into the crevasses of DOE security.

The forms listed flights from Denver International to McCarran Airport in Las Vegas, Nevada, and then back to Denver. Had to be for visits to the Nevada Nuclear Test Site. Once in Las Vegas the doctor didn't claim any travel, meal, or hotel expenses, so I figured he stayed on a secure compound.

Two weeks after the outbreak, Dr. Wong took a commercial flight from Denver International to McCarran Airport in Las Vegas, Nevada. From there he took a Janet flight to an unknown destination.

A Janet flight? What was *that*? And three days later, why did this Janet flight return him to the Jefferson County Airport when his usual home destination was Denver International? Could the reason be that the county airport was only a few miles from Rocky Flats?

I sat at my laptop and searched the Internet for Janet flights. The first hit took me to a Web page for UFO conspiracies. I scrolled down to a photo of a Boeing 737 sitting on the ramp of McCarran Airport. According to the text, "Janet flights" took federal employees and contractors of DOE and the U.S. Air Force on a short hop to an airfield north of Nellis Air Force Base, a site known as Area 51.

I gulped the rest of my wine. Area 51? The notorious, not-so-secret base at the center of every modern American conspiracy. Either I was on a snipe hunt, or suddenly I had caught the tail of something huge.

CHAPTER 14

WENDY TEAGARDEN AND I climbed the steps to the wooden door under a tattered green-and-white-striped awning. Above the awning, a neon sign, *El Pingüino*, in white script, cast a cold, inert light into the dark street. An outline of a penguin, complete with top hat, spats, and holding a martini, glowed beside the letters. Taped to the door was a hand-lettered sign scrawled with a broad tip marker: CLOSED TONITE AT 8.

I held the door open for Wendy and we entered a short, dingy hallway. A petite yet well-toned Latina wearing mirrored wrap-around sunglasses, a black leather halter-top dress, and matching open-toed pumps stood before the next door. Her brunette hair, pulled into a bun, contributed to her sleek appearance. She peeked over the tops of her sunglasses and revealed briefly her *tapetum lucidum*. She smiled and nodded, indicating that we could proceed.

Wendy pushed open a battered metal door, heavily

scratched and mangy with hand-sized blotches where the latest coat of paint had flaked loose.

We walked into the lounge. A karaoke singer was mangling "I Got a Line on You." A row of dim amber lights above the bar illuminated the room. Most of the frayed vinyl stools around the heavy wooden bar were empty. Cigarette smoke curled from ashtrays and mingled with the luminescent ribbon of silvery haze that snaked above the patrons' heads. A conglomeration of smells—hair spray, drugstore cologne, perspiration, spilled drinks, and cigarette ash—told me that I'd probably have to soak in bleach to get the funk out of my skin.

Wendy waved to the bushy-haired man behind the bar. "Hi, Mel."

He lifted his head and nodded. The mass of his gray hair wove into bushy sideburns that sprouted from his jaw. Thick muscles and a substantial belly filled out his shirt. Mel's eyes, like most of those that flashed toward us from the clientele, glowed from the reflection of his *tapetum lucidum*.

A small microwave on the bar counter pinged.

Mel grabbed a potholder and pulled a 450-milliliter bag of blood from the microwave. He snipped a corner of the bag and poured steaming red liquid over a bowl of nachos already drenched in melted cheese.

A waitress in a pink tube top and black stretch pants squashed her cigarette into an ashtray on the bar and placed the nachos and two bottles of Fat Tire ale on her tray. She took the tray and circled past us. The incandescence of her vampire eyes matched the luster of the fake rhinestone in her belly ring.

Wendy led me to a booth between the bar and the stage. I sat next to her, careful not to peel the duct tape from the vinyl seat.

I was glad that Wendy had asked me out for an evening of entertainment. My investigation was at an impasse. I'd learned that such interludes can allow my subconscious to work on the next step, or at least keep me pleasantly distracted until the next break happens. For now, my worries hovered in the distance.

I took out my contacts. Around me, everybody shimmered from their auras, the vampires in orange, the few humans in red, and Wendy in green.

Against the wall to our right, two men with orange auras stood on a stage, or rather on a slightly raised platform covered with worn and stained carpet. The large mirror behind them was chipped and cracked along the edges. The mirror showed a room with a few humans, though vampires were also present.

One of the vampires operated the karaoke machine, which occupied the top of one table, while the other vampire, bald, with a white turtleneck and black suit, held a cordless microphone and sang. He glanced at the words scrolling across the television screen hanging above him. Long fangs protruded past his upper lip and into the gape of his smiling mouth.

Mercifully the song ended. The vampire hummed the last bars of the tune, became silent, and bowed. A group at the far end of the room clapped and hooted. The vampire acted as if he had treated us to a musical masterpiece, though the best part of his performance was when he shut up at the end.

"The acoustics back there must be better," I whispered to Wendy. "Because from up here, I've heard better notes from a wood chipper."

The waitress stopped by our booth. "The drinks include rabbit blood. For an extra three bucks, we can make it human. Type O-positive is the special."

"I'll take a Dos Equis," Wendy said. "Hold the blood."

"Carta Blanca for me," I added. "With a rabbit blood chaser."

The waitress nodded and left.

The karaoke crew dismantled their machine before anyone else could wreck our Western musical heritage. Faces in the lounge turned toward a commotion in the back. Six vampires in black mariachi outfits appeared from the rear of the lounge. They carried guitars, cornets, and violins at the ready as if the instruments were rifles. Lights glittered off the spangles sewn to their jackets and trouser seams and the sequins stitched along the brim of their sombreros.

The mariachis got onstage and did a sound check. The leader of the group adjusted the microphone stand and introduced himself and his colleagues as Nahualli. The name of sadistic Aztec clerics who had presided over human sacrifice was now the moniker of this cantina festivity.

The group started with the song "Mariachi Loco," which got the crowd moving with laughter and shouts of *ahu-a*.

The song ended and the lights went dark. A single spotlight beamed toward the back of the lounge and illuminated a lone voluptuous figure surrounded by an orange aura. This vampire was so covered with emerald sequins that she looked wrapped in green foil. The spotlight followed her progress through the lounge. The shank of a leg flashed in and out of the slit in her tight dress. Her bosom jiggled like firm pudding. An aromatic banner of perfume trailed her.

The lead mariachi introduced her as "our own *chupacabra*"—the demon who drank goat's blood. Smiling seductively, as if her lacquered lips alone could make us all swoon into orgasm, she grasped the microphone. The group started to play Selena's "Bidi Bidi Bom Bom." The *chupacabra* singer bounced her hips in tempo to the music and began to wail.

Couples—combinations of human and undead—took to the floor and danced. The rest of us had to crowd close to converse over the musical din. All the auras modulated into a fuzz of glowing static, a measure of our collective good mood.

The waitress brought our drinks, the beer in tall glasses and the blood in a tall porcelain cup. Wendy and I clinked our glasses and sipped.

We sat contentedly and absorbed the homey ambiance. Vampires shared cigarettes, joked, and slapped each other on the shoulder. At the tables before us, chalices rolled their sleeves and cut their forearms with razors or penknives. They let blood drip into the martini and highball glasses of their vampire masters. The chalices' eyes fluttered and their red auras spread out from them as they swam in the pleasure of their sacrifice.

"Wendy Teagarden," I said.

She turned to look at me, her expression warm and full of anticipation.

"Don't suppose that's your original name?" I asked.

"Oh, I've had lots of names through the years."

"Figured you'd been around a while."

"You don't date older women?" Wendy looked about twenty-eight, though I'm sure she was several hundred. Supernatural immortals age well.

She wove her arm into mine and pulled it under the table. Her hand slipped past my wrist until our fingers clasped. With her face fixed on the singer, Wendy nudged against me, crossed her legs and let her ankle drag across my shin.

Since I've been a vampire, I never needed a woman to express affection for me. When I had the urge, a flash of *tapetum lucidum* was enough to get into a vagina. Lust and eroticism, these were tools to manipulate humans. What need did the damned undead have for romance?

Wendy's interest kindled a forgotten desire within me. A wave of excitement coursed through my body. My aura sizzled. I tried to calm my aura before Wendy noticed the effect she had on me.

Wendy brought her right hand across and stroked my upper arm. My aura sizzled more intently, fueled by anticipation.

She snuggled closer.

My aura radiated as if I were plugged into an electric socket.

A human woman bumped against our table. "Have you seen Ziggy?"

I turned to her and a male companion beside our booth. Because of their red auras I recognized them as the chalices serving Siegfried von Drek, the old vampire I'd met at *The Hollow Fang* party.

They wore similar white shirts, wrinkled, and the sleeve cuffs unbuttoned. Their glassy eyes cast worried looks at me. Chalices can become slavishly devoted to their vampires and often pine after them like junkies for their dealer.

The man's eyes teared. "He was supposed to meet us here." His voice cracked. "We haven't seen him since Sunday."

This distraction caused my aura to fade to a safe, even glow.

Wendy relaxed her grasp of my arm and fingers. "Have you tried calling him?"

The woman reached into the hip pocket of her pants and pulled out a cell phone. "Constantly. There's no answer."

I resented the intrusion from these addle-brained chalices. "How about going by his house?"

The woman closed her eyes and raked trembling fingers through her hair. She opened her mouth and it took a moment for her reply to croak through her lips. "Ziggy won't let us visit without an invitation."

Probably so that these two airheads wouldn't disturb his interviewing other chalices.

"Do this for me," I said. "Go by Ziggy's place. If he doesn't like it, tell him to take it up with me."

The woman hugged her companion and kissed his cheek. She panned her head toward the mariachis, as if suddenly aware of the music—it would be like ignoring a freight train—and said slowly, "We'll do that."

"Now would be a good time," Wendy replied.

The woman took the man by the hand and led him out the door.

"They're as stupid as they are cute," Wendy said. "Maybe they've given up so much blood that it's affected their IQ."

"I doubt their SAT scores were very high to begin with," I replied. "Ziggy didn't keep them around for stimulating conversation. Then again, for an old pervert, he is being a bit too indifferent toward his pets."

"Maybe he needs time to recuperate."

"Ziggy recuperate? Gossip is he buys Viagra by the carton."

Wendy clasped my arm again and squeezed. "And how much Viagra do you need?"

"I've never had cause to use it."

"Why? Lack of opportunity?"

"You're talking to a young vampire, a fountain of concupiscence."

"Is that what you call it?"

"Call what?" I asked.

"When your aura went to full burner a few minutes ago. Didn't think I'd notice?"

I didn't want her to know the effect she had on me so I said, "It wasn't you. It was the singer. The lady *chupacabra*."

Wendy released my arm. "Oh." Her aura cooled to a pale yellow-green. Even a supernatural divinity felt the sting of rejection.

My cup of blood was still warm enough to release a wisp of vapor. I chugged it and washed my mouth with a hearty swallow of beer.

If this was about sex, I'd pull Wendy close and nibble on her neck before working my way to her mouth as I fingered her. But Wendy was more than a mortal woman, she was a dryad with supernatural powers at least equal to my own. And I was certain she was smarter than me. But the real complication was that I liked her and felt energized by her attention the way I'd been before my life as a vampire.

With every passing minute, the moat of silence between Wendy and myself grew wider and deeper. The mariachis churned through their repertoire of ballads. Every song about romantic betrayal and loss raked bitter words over me.

What happened to the simple days when vampires merely prowled the night and sucked on necks? Or did the tales leave out all the messy details in the retelling? Messy details like this one before me.

I felt pressed into an emotional corner, queasy with the rush of uncomfortable feelings.

My cell phone started to vibrate. Caller ID gave me Bob Carcano's number.

I pressed the receiver to my ear and answered.

Bob replied, "I'm right outside. Come see me." His clipped tone relayed his distress.

I grasped Wendy's hand. "Let's go. The change in venue might refresh our conversation."

Bob waited under the awning. His aura burned bright orange and flashed in rhythm to the agitated beat of his pulse. As soon as he saw us, he started down the stairs and across the sidewalk. "Felix, let's take your car. I'm too upset to drive."

"Where are we going?"

Bob held up his cell phone. "Ziggy's chalices called. He's been murdered."

CHAPTER
15

I SPED NORTH ON Colorado Boulevard in my
Dodge Polara. The wind drummed across the convertible top. Wendy sat beside me while Bob gave directions
from the backseat. Considering it was a Tuesday night, I
didn't have much problem running red lights and weaving
through traffic.

Bob and I wore sunglasses, with just enough tint to hide
our eyes while still allowing the use of vampire night vision. Around us, human auras glowed in their cars and on
the sidewalks.

"What did the chalices tell you?" I asked.

"Those idiots didn't say much. Mainly blubbered about
how scared they were going into Ziggy's house, and then
they found him dead." Bob craned his neck to read the
street signs. "We're getting close."

"Could it be *vânätori de vampir*?" Wendy asked.

Bob rubbed a meaty hand across his face. "Don't know

yet. I'd hate to be right about that. Ziggy liked skimming the margins of human society, so he could've been murdered by a hoodlum or a speed freak."

Wendy looked back at Bob. "Or another vampire?"

"Yes, that's a possibility," Bob replied. "Ziggy had lots of enemies, both human and undead."

Wendy shifted her head to check out the passenger's-side mirror. "We've got company."

Headlights closed rapidly on my rear bumper. I tensed my grip on the steering wheel and readied my foot to stomp on the accelerator. Who followed? Humans? Vampires? Auras being psychic energy, they didn't reflect through mirrors. A glance over my shoulder revealed three orange auras inside the car. With the recent mention of Ziggy's many enemies, the unannounced arrival of vampires alarmed me.

Bob twisted around to look out the back window when his cell phone chirped. Ironically enough, the chime was a funeral dirge. He answered the call, speaking quickly, then snapped his cell phone closed. "It's my friend Andre and his pals. They'll be going the back way to Ziggy's house."

I turned east into an older, fashionable neighborhood. Ranch-style houses of brick and stone stood behind manicured lawns and neatly arranged shrubs. The car behind us careened up the next street.

Wendy rolled her window down. The night chill blasted into the car. She wrinkled her nose. "Phew. All I smell is arsenic trioxide and sodium nitrate. Americans don't garden, they wage chemical warfare on their plants."

Zipping up her jacket, she tipped her head out the window and made a faint hooting sound.

Bob pulled off his sunglasses. I took his cue and removed mine. The fuzzy auras of cats and small rodents slinking beneath the hedges sharpened. I spied two bright-red auras clumped together behind a thick bush along the wall of a house. A pair of very excited humans. Ziggy's killers waiting in ambush?

"On the left," I said. "Two humans."

Bob scrambled to his left window. He chuckled. "Relax. It's a couple of kids fooling around. One of them's getting a blow job."

"Homework for a sex ed class?" I asked.

"Hope she gets an A," Wendy added.

"They're both boys," Bob replied. "I doubt they'll ask for extra credit."

Something darted in front of the windshield. I tapped the brakes. The flying streak vanished as rapidly as it had appeared. "What the hell was that?"

"What was what?" Bob gripped the top of my seat and searched past my shoulder.

"I don't know." I rubbed my eyes. Maybe I was hallucinating.

Wendy rolled her window back up. "It's safe. No one's waiting for us."

"How do you know?"

"A little bird just told me."

Bob pointed to a house at the right where a cottonwood tree grew in the center of the lawn. The curtains were drawn across an illuminated picture window. A small, battered sedan sat beside the curb. "That's the chalices' car. Pull up behind it."

I parked my Dodge close to the rear bumper of the little Toyota. Stickers of rock bands and slogans were plastered across the trunk lid and rear window: Guano Apes. Devotchka. Depression Is Anger Without Enthusiasm. A Clear Conscience Is Usually the Sign of a Bad Memory. And my favorite: Oral Sex Won't Cause Brain Freeze.

Wendy jerked her door open and started for the house. We followed her across the lawn and past the cottonwood tree. Bob and I surveyed the area as we approached the front door.

"How come you're so sure it's clear?" I asked.

A horned owl fluttered to a tree branch above us. The owl hooted and flew off.

Wendy hooted back and remarked, "Like I said, a little bird told me."

"Got any more tricks, Dr. Dolittle?"

"Lots, but the night's young yet."

Bob strode ahead and his silhouette crossed before the picture window. He placed his hands on the wooden front door. Bob stood quiet for a moment, then declared, "I'm not detecting anything dangerous."

Nudging Bob aside, Wendy grasped the brass door handle and clicked the thumb latch. "How many times do I have to say that the coast is clear? Whoever did this is long gone."

"How would the owl know?" I asked.

"That's what the cat told the owl." Wendy pointed to the small red aura hiding underneath a car across the street. She pushed the door open, leading us into a foyer. Most of the interior lights were on. Plush carpets in beige accented the restrained furnishings of pale oak and earth-toned leather.

"I figured Ziggy to be heavy into industrial fetish," I said. "This place looks like a Marriott hotel."

"For a Kinko's manager he lived well," Wendy noted. "Where'd he get the money?"

"Besides satisfying his carnal appetites," Bob replied, "Ziggy polished his skills as a scam artist, hence his many enemies. Don't act surprised. Vampires aren't known for their moral scruples."

We followed a soft sobbing drifting from the back of the house.

The closer we approached the sobbing, the more my vampire senses tingled. My fangs grew. I pulled Wendy's petite frame behind me. She elbowed me in the ribs and took a place next to me.

We stepped into a sunken den. The male chalice lay

curled in the fetal position. Shivering, he sobbed quietly and stared up at the woman chalice, who knelt beside a prostrate figure. Tears dripped from both chalices' reddened eyes. Wrinkled white shirts clung to their sweaty bodies.

Despite Wendy's assurances that we were safe, the hairs on my skin stood in fear. I walked forward a step to examine the body.

Ziggy's decapitated corpse lay supine, surrounded by the flakes of his dried vampire blood. What had been his sternum was a black pit marked by a ragged hole in his shirt. The gruesome stump of his neck looked like a rolled slice of bacon. His head rested against the leg of an end table, a lock of long white hair flopped over his eyes, which stared emptily up at the ceiling. His mouth gaped open, as if he'd been killed in mid-howl. Our collective gaze lifted to a darkly spattered pattern of holes punched into the wall.

I said, "Looks like someone pressed a shotgun to our friend Ziggy and gave him both barrels."

Wendy opened a pocketknife and knelt beside the body. She poked into the wound and dug out a pellet of buckshot the size of a pinkie fingernail. Polishing the pellet on her sleeve, she revealed a shiny ball. "Sterling silver. Someone's taking their vampire killing seriously."

"You've noticed? I thought the decapitation was a good clue."

Orange auras shone through the blinds covering the French doors along the back wall.

"It's Andre," Bob said.

The doorknob clicked. One door swung open. A vampire wearing a green velvet sport coat and denim jeans entered, crawling upside down like a spider across the header above the door. Bracelets on his wrists reflected the den lights. His ponytail dangled to the floor. He crept across the ceiling and scowled suspiciously at us and Ziggy's corpse.

Two more vampires came through the door, walking onto the carpet in normal fashion. The woman was the petite brunette we'd seen earlier at the El Pingüino lounge. A padded-shoulder leather motorcycle jacket covered her torso, giving her a muscular, intimidating appearance. The man was older and thin. His close-cropped gray hair started from a well-defined widow's peak.

Bob welcomed him. "Andre. Sorry I couldn't tell you more over the phone. We just got here ourselves."

They made introductions among us all. Andre spoke in a heavy accent. Carmen, the vampire woman, unzipped her jacket and displayed the cleavage within her leather halter-top. Dan Sky-Pony, the vampire on the ceiling, let his cowboy boots swing down and he hung for an instant by his fingertips before dropping to the floor. He paced around the female chalice and caressed her head as he licked his lips.

Bob picked up Ziggy's head and pushed the upper lip back to reveal holes in the jaw where the incisors had been pried out. "*Vânätori de vampir.* This was a ritual killing, and they've taken his fangs as proof."

Andre stroked his face in a gesture I'd describe as nervous. His eyes flitted from side to side as if looking for something the rest of us hadn't seen.

"You okay, Andre?" Bob asked. "You look . . ."

Scared, I thought.

"I'm fine," Andre blurted. He coughed to mask a glint of embarrassment. Vampires aren't supposed to show fear.

Dan stood over the body. "I can't figure how this happened. Ziggy hasn't lived this long by being careless."

"I'm not so sure," I interrupted. "Remember how he scoffed when you first brought up the question of the vampire hunters. I think maybe he did get careless."

"Or maybe it was someone trying to make it look like vampire hunters," Wendy said.

"What do we know about these *vânätori*?" Carmen asked.

"Very little, unfortunately," Bob answered.

"So what *do* we do?" Sky-Pony asked.

Bob took Ziggy's head and cradled it under his arm like a basketball. "Learn more. Stay alert."

Carmen pointed to the corpse as if it were a heap of misplaced trash. "What about that?"

"The usual means of disposal. Solar immolation." Bob studied the layout of the den. A large bay window faced east across an open yard. "This place is perfect."

He told the chalices, "Find a tarp or a shower curtain." Bob dragged his shoe through the flaked vampire blood on the carpet. "And a vacuum cleaner."

The female chalice returned with a shower curtain, a plastic one of yellow and blue stripes. The male chalice found a Hoover upright in the closet.

We pulled Ziggy's corpse to the middle of the curtain, which we then dragged against the wall. Bob had the female chalice strip the body. He ordered the male chalice to vacuum the dried blood and clean the wall.

"We'll spackle and paint the holes later."

Carmen took Ziggy's Tag Heuer watch and wallet. Wendy bundled the clothes and shoved them into a plastic garbage bag.

Using the shower curtain, we dragged the corpse to the middle of the room and arranged the body so the feet pointed toward the bay window. Bob set the head upright by the neck.

As a final touch, Wendy bent over and adjusted the scrotum and penis. "Wouldn't want Ziggy to be uncomfortable."

Carmen and Sky-Pony shared a pack of cigarettes and lit up. She tapped her toe and exhaled a jet of smoke. "So we have to wait here till morning?"

"Patience. When morning comes, we'll divide the spoils." Bob tipped his head toward the chalices. "You'll enjoy it."

Bob and Andre rummaged in the kitchen, collecting food

for an impromptu wake. Bob cooked steaks, hash browns, and corn on the cob. Like every modern vampire, Ziggy kept jars of animal blood in his refrigerator. Sky-Pony and Carmen went to the bar on the opposite side of the den. One of them found the stereo and played jazz. Carmen made drinks. Andre took a paring knife and sliced the arm of the female chalice and ordered her go to every one of us and offer blood as if she were dispensing gravy. I declined the offer.

We lounged in the den, ate dinner, and sipped drinks. Andre chuckled as he recited vampire anecdotes in his bad English, much of which Bob had to translate.

Wendy and I shared Manhattans. With the rye whiskey seeping into our bloodstreams, she and I set our plates aside on the coffee table. She kicked off her shoes and, before I could protest, climbed into my lap and rested her head on my shoulder. Wendy's body settled against mine. She didn't weigh much, a hundred pounds maybe. Her green aura softened and pulsated in tempo to the low purr coming from her throat.

Where our auras overlapped, my orange and her green took on an iridescent shine, something I'd never witnessed. Then again, I'd never had a dryad sit on my lap.

Wendy didn't ask to impose on me. She simply assumed that I wanted her close. Which I did. Problem was, I didn't want to admit my desire to her . . . or myself.

Wendy wove her fingers into mine and snuggled against my neck. My aura grew brighter and other things stirred. Sky-Pony tapped Carmen on the knee and then pointed to me.

Was I the first vampire ever to feel embarrassment? We were fearsome killers, rapacious as wolves, and yet at this moment, I, Felix the vampire, felt as awkward as a schoolboy at a dance.

Wendy whispered into my ear. "I can slide off you. Just say the word."

I didn't.

After a moment, she brushed her lips against my cheek. "I knew you wouldn't."

Bob turned on the TV by the bar and switched to the Weather Channel. Sunrise was to be 6:27.

The other vampires searched Ziggy's room and brought out a tray of Dermablend and sunblock, which we gooped on. At 6:00 A.M. we put on our sunglasses.

Carmen opened the blinds on the bay window. We vampires tucked ourselves into the shadows of the den. The dawn sky lightened, turning from black to purple, and now to blue. The rays of the sun peeked over the roof of the house on the other side of the yard. The sunbeam splashed against the wall. Minute by minute, the beam widened and scrolled down toward Ziggy.

When the sunbeam touched Ziggy's head, his skin wrinkled and smoldered. The stench of burning, rancid meat smacked us like a wave. The sun's rays lapped down Ziggy's body like a ravenous tongue of fire. His flesh turned black. Smoke curled against the ceiling.

The smoke detector went off. Centuries of death held at bay reclaimed Ziggy's corpse. His charred body collapsed into a pile of ash. Carmen closed the blinds. We took off our sunglasses. Sky-Pony crawled up the wall and yanked out the smoke detector's battery to silence the wail. The chalices started to cry again.

"How do we explain Ziggy's disappearance?" I asked.

Bob replied, "The Araneum will arrange it that he died of 'natural causes' while vacationing in Panama. We'll appoint someone to take care of his estate. Now to clean this mess."

We lifted the shower curtain by the corners and carefully poured the ash into a garbage bag.

"What would happen if we added water?" Carmen joked. "Would we get instant vampire?"

"Yuck," Sky-Pony said. "I don't even like instant coffee."

A garbage bag filled with ash and another bag stuffed with his clothes, this was all that was left of Ziggy.

"You vampires aren't very sentimental," Wendy said.

"I doubt Hallmark makes a card for this," Bob replied.

Carmen stepped behind the female chalice. "Now that we've finished our janitorial duties, time for the vampire initiation. As reward for your loyalty, welcome to the ranks of the damned."

Carmen's eyes glowed in bloodlust. She grasped the female chalice's shirt collar with both hands and yanked. The chalice staggered to remain on her feet. Carmen wrestled with the chalice until the shirt and bra tore free. The chalice stood before us, bare-breasted. Sweat trickled down her pale face. Her eyes stared out into nothingness.

Sky-Pony grabbed the male chalice by the hair, ripped off his shirt, and forced him to kneel beside the female.

"We've lost one vampire and gained two." Sky-Pony slapped the male chalice. "This is what each of you wants? Immortality as one of us?"

Both chalices whispered a frightened duet. "Yes." Their auras turned an incandescent red like heated metal.

All the vampires bared their fangs and circled the chalices. The vampires stripped naked and tossed their clothes behind them. Their orange auras merged and lit the darkened room with the fearsome intensity of a bonfire burning out of control. They would attack without hypnosis so that the screams of the chalices would fuel their undead ardor.

Carmen and Bob each took an arm of the female chalice and sank their fangs into opposite sides of her neck. The chalice squirmed—now a pale form of jiggly flesh—and shrieked in agony, for they bit without secreting anesthetic enzymes. Blood streamed down between her breasts.

Sky-Pony and Andre wrestled the male chalice to ground.

Giving in to panic, he fought them. They fended off his blows and laughed as they relished this opportunity to prolong the kill. Their bare feet tracked blood across the carpet. So much for our tidiness.

So long as I never drank human blood, I would be immune to this descent into the lurid recesses of our feral nature. I've spilled enough human blood as a soldier.

Wendy looked me over. "Why are you still dressed?"

"I have my reasons."

Bob's loud snarl surged above the screams of the tormented chalices. He called me. "Felix, join us." Blood smeared the stubble of his beard and dotted the hairs on his chest.

"You know I can't, Bob," I said. "And after tonight? What do we do about the vampire hunters?"

Bob's blazing eyes narrowed. "The *vânători de vampir* will get what's coming to them."

CHAPTER 16

I HADN'T MUCH CARED for Ziggy, to be honest. What disturbed me was that a vampire was murdered. It just happened to be him.

My personal dangers had escalated. The conspiracy behind the outbreak of nymphomania remained guarded by trigger-happy federal maniacs. Someone had tried to steal my computer and conked me on the head, and I'm sure that same guy had used me for target practice. Was he one of the vampire hunters prowling the streets of Denver?

My fingertips tingled. My vampire senses grasped a hunch and alerted me that perhaps—no, certainly—these events were connected.

If so, then time to reenergize my investigation and draw out those stalking me. My leads pointed to one man, the person at the center of the conspiracy behind the outbreak. Dr. Bigelow Wong.

I'd kept my distance, fearing that I would compromise

my investigation if I pressed him too eagerly. My adversaries, whoever they were, weren't worried by such concerns.

From my Internet source I learned that Dr. Wong had managed his dollars well during his career with the Department of Energy. He had recently bought a home in Tucson, Arizona, and moved his family there. While he waited for retirement, he lived alone in a high-rise condominium in the Park Hill neighborhood of Denver.

The condo building was new, accented with rounded corners and oval windows that repeated the architectural rhythm of the gently arched roof. Each story had recessed balconies and stuccoed walls, the floors alternating in pastel green and beige, and separated by narrow ledges that looked like icing squeezed between the layers of a cake.

Entrance to the building was through a small, unadorned lobby. Banks of mailboxes and an intercom occupied the wall to the left. An elevator stood on the other side of a partition of green-tinted glass. Access to the elevator was through a glass door, which was locked. I couldn't very well ring Dr. Wong on the intercom and ask to be let in to discuss the outbreak.

Sifting through a trashcan under the mailboxes, I pulled out a piece of discarded junk mail. Standing against the glass partition, I pretended to read the mail and waited for someone to unlock the door.

The elevator chimed. Out stepped a young, stylish couple. They chatted about dinner plans with friends and exited, ignoring my presence.

I caught the door before it closed and went to the elevator, which I took to the third floor. Once there, I found Dr. Wong's unit, number 313. I removed my contacts, slipped on leather gloves, and knocked on the door.

Someone called out in a bothered voice. "What is it?"

"Mr. Wong, this is maintenance."

"It's Dr. Wong. It's late, why are you bothering me?"

"Excuse me, Dr. Wong, someone reported a gas leak and we're trying to track it down."

"There's no gas leak here."

"I wish I could take your word, but we need to play it safe."

The lock snapped, and the door opened.

"Very well," he groused. Dr. Wong turned away before we made eye contact. "You can be sure that the manager will hear about this tomorrow. I'm not paying those outrageous association fees to be bothered like this."

His red aura bristled with spikes and signaled his annoyance. Spindly brown arms and legs jutted from his yellow T-shirt and baggy shorts. "Come in. Make it quick."

I entered and shut the door. The living room opened to a kitchen. A cool breeze from the balcony swept through a sliding door and rustled the newspaper on the kitchen counter.

I put my hand on Wong's shoulder. He spun around to parry my arm. My grip held him firm.

His eyes drew wide and his scowl went flat when I locked my vampire gaze upon him. I pushed him backwards onto a sofa seat.

I let go of his shoulder. Holding his hands, I kneaded the webs of flesh between his thumbs and index fingers.

Dr. Wong's breathing eased. His muscles relaxed. His aura softened. I kept my gaze locked on his until his aura swirled around his body like warm syrup.

"Dr. Wong, tell me about Project Redlight."

Though his face remained expressionless, he replied with a chuckle. "Redlight? That's been my ticket to financial independence."

Under hypnosis, victims' answers were shaded by their subconscious biases. I had to guide the interrogation to get the facts I needed.

"Your success? In what?"

His chuckle resumed. "In DOE. What I know makes me very important . . . and dangerous."

"Dangerous to whom?"

He pointed his nose to the ceiling. "The bigwigs. The men who run this country. The guardians of the truth."

"What truth?"

"The world did go crazy." He giggled. "I, Dr. Bigelow Wong, the nerdy, anal-retentive scientist, suddenly had to fight off the pussy. All those beautiful women who ignored me for so many years couldn't drop their panties fast enough. Who would've expected? It was better than any retention bonus. For a few beautiful days, I *was* the Big Wong."

"Yes, I know about the nymphomania. But what was the cause?"

His aura spiked again. *Warning.*

His hands suddenly pulled loose from mine, and he seized my wrists. I immediately yanked free and grabbed his shoulders. To subdue him, I had to use my fangs. I aimed for his throat.

Perhaps screwing the nymphos had contaminated him and this was how he resisted my hypnosis. But his aura remained steady and hadn't changed to yellow, as had the infected radiological control technicians.

He acted cooperative. My fangs retracted. I caressed his eyes shut and cradled his face in my hands. As my aura melded with his, siphoning his psychic resistance and strengthening my hypnotic hold, his muscles relaxed. His pulse slowed. I asked again, "What was the cause?"

"Red. Redlight," he whispered. "Hg-209."

"What?"

"Hg-209. Red mercury."

"What about red mercury?"

Wong started to raise an arm. I let him, and he motioned to a shelf of books on the opposite wall. "The cause was red mercury. And the EBEs."

"EBEs?"

"My diary explains everything."

DOE forbade any mention of classified information except in authorized documents. "You keep a diary?"

He wet his lips. "Yes."

"Why?"

He tilted his head back toward the ceiling and replied in a quiet, smug tone. "Consider it blackmail against the gods."

Carefully withdrawing my hands, I turned and followed the direction of his upraised arm. I didn't expect to find a book labeled Dr. Wong's secret diary. "Where is it?"

"Inside the copy of Audubon's *Birds of America*."

I found the volume. Tucked into a cutout within the color plates, was a slim composition book. I opened the composition book and found it filled with neat columns of handwritten notes. It was a diary. Could unraveling the conspiracy be this easy?

I maneuvered an ottoman in front of the doctor and sat. I would peruse the notes and ask Wong to explain everything. At last I'd find out about the Tiger Team report, Project Redlight, his trips to Area 51, the red mercury, and, now, the EBEs. By this time tomorrow I'd be at Rocky Flats, giving Gilbert Odin my report and collecting the remainder of my fee. Case closed.

I heard a thwack.

"Dr. Wong?"

He remained silent. His red aura faded, collapsing into his slumped form.

I shook him. "Dr. Wong. Dr. Wong."

He tipped forward. Blood seeped across the back of his T-shirt. Wong's aura faded to nothing. He was dead.

A tuft of stuffing curled from a hole in the upholstery. Something had punched through the back of the seat. A bullet?

I snapped a look over his shoulder, past the kitchen, and

to another tall building beyond his balcony. My ears and fingertips tingled from my vampire senses going to maximum alert. I ducked. A bullet whizzed past. The lamp on the end table shattered.

With the diary tucked to my side, I scrambled for the front door and out into the hall. The elevator chimed. Much too coincidental an arrival. I spied an exit sign in the other direction and sprinted.

The elevator doors whooshed open. I turned my head for an instant to see who came out.

Two men, bearded and middle-aged, burst into the hall. They wore hats and long, open coats. Red auras flared around them. Large silver crucifixes hung from their necks. One brandished a sawed-off shotgun and the other a double-bladed ax—the type of weapons used to murder Ziggy. The men yelled at each other in a harsh foreign dialect.

Vânători de vampir.

I kicked open the metal fire door leading to the stairwell. Just as I cleared the threshold, a blast of pellets ricocheted off the door.

I used my vampire powers to glide above the steps to the next landing. The man with the shotgun leaned over the railing and took aim. I huddled against the wall, outside his line of sight. A volley of pellets splattered along the stairs.

Pain stabbed my left leg. One pellet tore into my shin. I limped down the stairs, suddenly too weak to float over more than a few steps at a time. I continued to the bottom of the stairwell and went out the door, into the crisp, night air of the alley. A row of sodium lamps threw their yellow glare into the gloom.

I ran to the left, the shortest path to my car.

In front of me, where the alley emptied to the street, appeared a man with a coat similar to my pursuers. His aura burned with hatred. He cradled a hunting rifle with a scope. I was sure he was the one who had shot Dr. Wong.

He jerked the rifle to his shoulder and fired a wild shot that missed.

The stairwell door behind me opened with a bang and the two men rushed into the alley.

I was trapped. I halted. The silver pellet burned against my left shinbone. Blood oozed into my shoe.

My throat tightened in panic. My ears and fingers tingled so hard that they buzzed. The only escape was to crawl up the wall. I hobbled over and planted my toes and fingertips against the stucco. Managing only two feeble steps against gravity, I knew that I couldn't reach the balcony above in time to avoid getting shot and decapitated. I slid back to the ground.

The man with the rifle tracked me through the scope. The other two men called to him and he held his fire.

Shadows falling from the wide brims of their hats shrouded their faces. In this meager light, I couldn't easily hypnotize them. Not all at once. And not until they got closer. They approached warily. Their auras crackled with hostility and determination. The older one with the ax held his crucifix before him and chanted in Latin.

An approaching police siren echoed through the alley.

The man glanced over his shoulder toward the siren and let the crucifix dangle. He gripped his ax with both hands, his fingers flexing. He hissed at his companions and their steps quickened.

With this wounded leg I couldn't escape, not in human form.

A Dumpster stood against the wall to my left, midway between the man with the rifle and myself. I ran toward it as best I could. Bolts of agony shot up my left leg.

Ten feet from the Dumpster I leapt and dove for the inside. I didn't figure that the cover might be secured. Instead of landing within, I bounced off the metal top. I landed hard on the asphalt, between the Dumpster and the wall, knocking the wind out of me and scraping my knuckles.

Gasping and dizzy, I struggled to my feet, tilted open the Dumpster's cover, and crawled inside . . . to land on top of piles of stinking garbage. I burrowed into the trash, into the slime and yuck at the very bottom, and tucked myself into a ball.

I commanded the transformation and channeled pain and fear into the energy needed to change my shape. My heartbeat quickened. My bones and joints stretched and popped, each crack a torture that I endured in silence. My skull distended. Saliva washed from my mouth, dripping from many sharp teeth. Skin prickled as my hair thickened and spread across my body. Smells flooded my growing snout. My ears picked sounds too faint even for vampires.

I shook off the man garments choking me. I waited hunched inside the Dumpster, naked and hairy, no longer vampire but wolf.

The man creatures approached the enclosure, their breathing guarded and anxious. They exuded smells—of digested cow meat, perspiration, and the greasy odor of their deadly fire weapons.

The hairs on my spine bristled. My lips curled back to bare vicious canines. I felt the urge to rip their flesh and taste blood. But escape was my priority. Revenge could come later.

The long end of a human weapon pushed over the top of the enclosure. Just as the man's head appeared, I lunged for him and knocked aside the weapon.

He screamed. The weapon released its explosive bark. The loud noise stung my ears.

I landed between him and his companion. My left hind leg collapsed and I yelped, reminded painfully of my wound.

Springing to my paws, I raced down the canyon between the human nesting structures and hid in the shadows.

Another weapon barked and its bite pinged well away to my side. I turned the corner and continued down the wide path. The wail of the siren became louder.

Several humans emerged from one of their carriers. The two males smelled of a recent dinner and the female of estrus. I snarled at them. They shouted in fright and jumped away.

I was surrounded by mountains of human dwellings. Sniffing river water, I turned toward the source, knowing that I could hide in the reeds and wait until later to transform back into a vampire.

A human carrier roared in front of me. Lights flashed along its top. I stumbled and turned. My wounded leg buckled under me. I lunged off my good hind leg and started again. The smell of river water grew stronger. I lifted my head to look for any signs of bushes or a shoreline.

I headed west and slinked through the bushes and shadows surrounding the dwellings. Human carriers rolled past. Some slowed and made honking noises. One of the human carriers with the flashing colored lights shined a powerful light in my direction. I hid within a lilac bush along a fence and waited for them to leave. The moon crested the tallest dwelling.

I welcomed the opportunity to rest. My wounded hind leg burned with pain.

The light went dark and the carrier left. I trotted from under the bush and continued west. I moved carefully from cover to cover and did my best to avoid humans. There were few of their carriers on the roads. By the time the moon had risen high above, the smell of the river was strong and inviting.

I loped from the shadows toward an open dirt lot. Colored

lights flashed on. A bright white light caught me. I dashed to the left.

A sudden sting, like from a bee, popped me beside my tail. Desperate to escape, I ran faster.

My legs grew clumsy. My paws knocked against each other. I slowed and dragged my numbed hind legs. A feathered human weapon clung to my haunches. I tried to gnaw it off but my head felt too heavy to hold upright. Drowsiness smothered my panic. I lay on the cool ground and watched through dimming eyes a human approach, a rope in her hands.

CHAPTER 17

T HE YAPPING OF EXCITED dogs awakened me.
"Felix."

I lifted my groggy head in the direction my name had
come from. Recognizing the scent, then the voice, and finally the orange aura, I struggled upright to my paws. A
cone of white material encircled my head.

A familiar man stepped close. His hand reached into my
cage. I whimpered in anticipation of regaining my freedom and clumsily turned my head with this cone around it.
His fingers stroked my muzzle and I licked them in appreciation.

The man fumbled with the front of the cage and opened
the door. He spread a blanket on the floor and beckoned me
with a soothing whisper.

I limped out of the cage and lay in the center of the blanket. Shutting my eyes, I summoned the transformation.

Pain enveloped me. I clenched my teeth to keep from

yelping. Saliva bubbled through my lips. My legs trembled and my tail twitched from the agony.

The dogs in the cages around us whined and barked nervously.

Fur retracted into flesh. My skin felt on fire. This cone around my head dug into my neck. My bones twisted and realigned from the shape of a wolf into that of a vampire. The toes on my forelimbs stretched into fingers. My hearing grew dim. The smells in my nose became simple. Abstract thought returned, and my awareness swelled with the names of things inside the dark kennel, especially this plastic doggie cone I found wrapped around my head.

I ripped the thing off.

The man laughed. "You're lucky I didn't bring a camera."

I wiped the drool and sweat from my face. "Screw you." I pulled the blanket over my nakedness.

"How the hell did you end up here?" Bob Carcano lifted the blanket away from my left leg. "What happened?"

"Shotgun. Vampire hunters. Then a dog catcher nailed me in the ass with a tranquilizer dart."

He felt my swollen wound. "They could've done a better job treating you. Mind if I help?"

I flinched. "Be my guest."

Bob dragged the razor edge of his fingernail over the lump and cut my skin. He squeezed tainted blood through the incision. I clenched my fists to withstand the anguish. Sweat trickled from my brow, pooled in my eye sockets, and stung my eyes. Blood spurted from the slit. The pellet popped out and rattled across the linoleum.

"Silver," Bob said. "Must have been agony."

"It hurt like hell, if that's what you're getting at."

Bob spit on his fingers and massaged my wound.

The pain ebbed as his vampire enzymes deadened the nerves and began healing the injured tissues. I lay on the floor and breathed deeply, relieved that I had survived and was back in the form of a vampire.

Bob offered his hand. "Let's go." He helped me up.

Walking stiffly, I dragged the blanket along and followed Bob to the exit. "How'd you know I was here?"

"A wolf gets trapped in Denver—news like that has a way of making it to my ears." He reset the alarm by the door and pocketed the key. "You aren't the first vampire I've rescued from the Denver Municipal Animal Shelter."

We went outside and proceeded toward his Buick Regal. The chill caused me to wrap the blanket tight against my naked body. The muffled barking inside the shelter carried into the darkness. Cold gravel in the parking lot poked the tender soles of my bare feet. I leaned on Bob's shoulder to offset my still-weakened left leg.

"What time is it?"

Bob pulled back the cuff of his jacket to read his watch. "A little past three."

"Thursday morning?"

"Yeah." Bob aimed his remote at the Buick. Its lights flashed and the honk chirped twice. He opened the rear door for me. The interior dome light blinked on. "Don't take this wrong, Felix, but you stink like a sewer."

"That's a relief. I thought you were going to say I smelled like I had spent the night in a kennel."

"There's a grocery bag with some clothes," he said.

I found old trousers and a frayed sweatshirt. I shrugged off the blanket and put the clothes on.

Bob's gaze lingered on me. "You're in good shape, Felix, even if there is shrinkage of the important parts. Blame that on the cold. It's been a while since I've had a nice-looking naked man in my car."

"I thought you were celibate."

"I'd make an exception for you." He squeezed behind the

steering wheel. "Vampire to vampire. What you don't know, I'll teach."

"Think I'll pass." I pulled the door closed. The dome light went off. "Thanks, though."

Bob handed a large plastic 7-Eleven cup over his shoulder. "It's half cappuccino-yogurt shake and half goat's blood. Should perk you right up."

We left the parking lot. I sipped the shake, its rich coolness refreshing me. Coffee and goat's blood go so well together.

"Make sure you stay on that blanket," he cautioned. "I don't want your funk stinking up the upholstery."

"Where we going?"

"Isn't it obvious? Take a whiff of yourself. The closest shower or bath. I ought to dip you for fleas."

"Take me to Wong's place first." I related what had happened at the condo.

"*Vânâtori*?" Bob's aura throbbed in concern. "Could you recognize them?"

"By their auras but not by their faces. It's kind of hard to loiter when someone's drawing a bead on you with a shotgun."

"And you ran *down* the stairs?" he asked. "Why not up to the roof and then crawl down the outside wall? They'd never be able to follow you."

I paused, too embarrassed to answer right away. "I've been having problems clinging."

Bob slapped the steering wheel. "Goddamn it, Felix, I told you that not drinking human blood would weaken your vampire powers."

"And Ziggy? He was never more than five minutes away from a human neck and the vampire hunters still got him."

"Ziggy's arrogance did him in." Bob's voice sharpened.

"As for you. Clinging against gravity is the first power to go. Then your sixth sense falters. After that—"

"Take the next right at Broadway," I interrupted.

"Aren't you listening?"

"Stow it, Bob. I'll deal with this on my own terms."

"On your own terms all right. Until your head is cut off and your fangs carried away as a trophy by those fanatics."

"No one knows the risks better than I."

The silence in the car became thick with antagonism. I liked Bob, respected him, but he knew better than to broach the subject of my not consuming human blood. We said nothing until I gave him directions to the condo. We turned off Broadway and continued on side streets. A police van, a cruiser, and two government sedans were parked in front of Wong's building. A police officer stood guard at the lobby door.

"I'm not surprised to see the cops here," Bob said. "Didn't think that someone blasting a shotgun in the halls would go unnoticed. Sure you want to stop?"

"I need to get my things from the Dumpster."

We turned the corner toward the alley. A police cruiser was parked between the Dumpster and the rear door of the building. The car's hazard lights flashed.

"Shit," I said. "Keep going past the alley and park down the block."

Bob slowed and halted alongside the curb. "What's so damn important that you can't replace?"

"For one thing, cops find my ID and they'll know I was here." I cracked the door open and got out. "Plus, I hid Dr. Wong's diary in the bottom of the Dumpster."

"This diary has sensitive information?"

"According to Wong it explains everything."

We rounded the corner and headed up the alley. A perimeter of yellow tape surrounded the Dumpster. I walked lightly, the rough asphalt and litter pricking the bottoms of my feet. In these thrift-store castoffs, I felt like the lowliest of bums.

A cop sat in the cruiser. The dim blue glow of a cell phone splashed alongside his face. He whispered romantic palaver. "Yeah, babe, she doesn't mean anything to me. Not like you . . ."

"Let me do the talking," Bob said. "I'll bet he doesn't understand Romanian, and that will buy us time."

The cop glanced up and snapped his cell phone closed. He jerked open his door, climbing out.

"You're going to have to leave," he commanded gruffly.

The gloom hid our eyes, allowing us to get closer.

The cop came around the rear of his cruiser. "You two deaf? I said leave. Now."

Bob started talking Romanian and gesticulated over his shoulder. We kept approaching the cop.

He put his right hand over the grip of his pistol. "I don't understand a word you're saying. But stop right there." He looked at my bare feet, my rumpled clothes, and then back at Bob. With his left hand, the cop clasped the radio microphone clipped to his shoulder.

I sprang forward and gripped the cop's head. His left arm twisted out to parry me, but . . . too late. My gaze locked onto his eyes. He froze.

Bob pulled the cop away from me and sank his fangs into the cop's neck. The cop gurgled and went limp. Bob knelt beside him, sucking on his neck.

Bob stood, wiping his mouth. "Pure beef cake, this one. Definitely filet mignon."

The cop lay sprawled on the asphalt, twitching.

"Can't leave him like that," I said. "Someone finds him, they'll go ape-shit."

"You're right. Better put him back in the car."

We carried the cop to the cruiser.

The back door of the building opened. A uniformed female cop and a man in a suit with a badge hanging from his neck stepped out. "What the hell?" he muttered.

Bob and I dropped the cop and he plopped to the asphalt.

The female cop sprang into the alley, her pistol leveled at us. "Don't move."

CHAPTER 18

I STANK LIKE COMPOST and an unconscious po-
lice officer lay at my bare, dirty feet. What could I say?

The plainclothes cop drew a snub-nosed revolver from
inside his sport coat.

Bob raised his arms. "We found him knocked out. Just
like this."

The cop's forehead wrinkled. The spikes of his aura
blunted as his mood changed from anger to confusion. Why
would two men—meaning us—be carrying a uniformed
cop? Maybe we were telling the truth.

Bob pointed to the ground. "He was right there. We were
gonna put him in the squad car and then get help."

The female cop's aura remained as prickly as a thistle.
She kept her big semiautomatic trained on us. "On your
knees. Put your hands on your heads."

I turned my back to the lamp on the opposite alley wall
and let the early-morning darkness conceal my *tapetum*

lucidum, and Bob did the same. We knelt and carefully set our hands on our scalps. Our one chance to escape was to get the cops close enough to subdue them with vampire hypnosis.

The cop in the suit circled past us for the cruiser. "Keep 'em covered. Call for backup."

Damn. Backup. The situation was complicated enough without more cops on the scene.

The cop stopped in mid-stride. "What the . . . ?" He squinted at me. "What the hell is with his eyes? I've never seen eyes *shine* like that."

Bob motioned to me with his elbow. "Yes, he's got a medical condition. He blacks out and wanders the streets. That's why he looks like this."

The cop stepped close, then grimaced. "Oh yeah—and that explains the smell."

"You should get a whiff of him after he's been out a couple of days. He smells like a rose now in comparison."

I knocked Bob's elbow with my own to let him know that I didn't appreciate being the butt of his snarky jokes.

The female cop set her flashlight parallel to her pistol. "Let me see."

I closed my eyes and turned my head.

"Open your eyes," she said. "Come on, it's for your own good. You might need medical attention."

The flashlight beam shone through my eyelids as a red haze.

Bob nudged my arm. "Go ahead. Open your eyes now."

I did. Both cops stood close and leaned into one another. Their heads almost touched. Their two pistols remained pointed at my face.

Their eyes popped wide open, as at such close range, my *tapetum lucidum* bore into them like lasers. The female cop's jaw slackened. The male cop lowered his arm. His revolver clattered to the ground.

Bob yanked the male cop's necktie and jerked him down. Bob clasped the cop's head and tilted it back to expose the neck.

I kept my gaze on the female cop and unbuttoned her shirt midway, then spread her collar to examine her neck. I traced my fangs across the inviting contours of her throat. Her warm blood beckoned me. I sank my fangs into her fat, welcoming jugular.

Her blood filled my mouth. I dammed the flow with my tongue and proceeded to work my saliva into her wounds.

She relaxed. Her aura became muted. I took the pistol and flashlight from her hands and returned them to her belt.

Bob smacked his lips. "Mmmm. My cop had a note of Johnnie Walker in his blood. Black Label. Somebody's got problems with the bottle."

"This isn't a tasting party." I motioned to the Dumpster. "Let's get that diary and beat feet before more cops come along."

Bob dragged his cop to the cruiser. "You go Dumpster-diving while I take care of these three."

I rested the female cop against the front tire of the cruiser. I pushed aside the yellow police tape, climbed into the Dumpster, and searched through leaking bags of garbage. Damp coffee grounds clung to my hands. Slimy, rotting vegetables lapped my wrists.

I found my trousers and jacket, and examined the pockets. My wallet, keys, cell phone, and scout knife were still there. I kept digging to the bottom of the Dumpster until I discovered Dr. Wong's diary. Garbage water dripped from the soaked pages as I climbed out of the Dumpster.

Bob had arranged the three cops in the rear seat of the cruiser, the female in the middle. They slumped, shoulder-to-shoulder, their heads resting on the back of the seat.

Bob stroked his chin as he studied them. "They look bored."

He got back in the car and unzipped the male cops' pants, then shoved the female's hands into each of her companions' crotches. As a finishing touch he opened her shirt to the navel and pulled her bra down.

Bob shut the door, locking them in. "What do you think?"

"Nice rack on her."

"I'd love to hear them try to explain this. 'Vampires hypnotized us,'" Bob whined satirically, "'made us play with each other and locked us inside.'"

We walked out of the alley and back toward his Buick.

"Don't take this wrong," Bob said, "but you stink even worse than before."

"I don't care what I smell like, as long as I have this." I showed him the diary.

Bob examined it. Sections of wet pages disintegrated at his touch.

"Hey, careful." I took the diary back and smoothed the pages to see if the writing remained legible.

We reached his car and climbed in.

"What's that diary prove?" Bob asked. He started the Buick and drove away from the curb.

"That Wong knew what had caused the nymphomania, and that he helped cover it up."

"What caused it?"

"He said red mercury and EBEs."

"Which are?"

"Red mercury, I assume, is a material used at Rocky Flats for making nuclear weapons. I've never heard of it before."

"And EBEs?"

"I'm going to let Gilbert Odin explain that."

Bob's aura flashed. He tapped the brakes. The car lurched. "What's to explain? The investigation's over. Give your friend the diary, collect your fee, and disappear. Case closed."

"I've got to tell him about the people who killed Dr. Wong."

Bob resumed normal speed. "Are you crazy? You're going to tell your friend, a federal employee, that vampire hunters are on your trail?"

"Of course not. But they did murder Wong, so why not let the police catch them? And if they capture the *vânätori*, think the police will believe their story that they killed Dr. Wong by mistake when they were aiming for a vampire?"

"So what the hell were we doing back there, ditching those cops? I thought you wanted to stay clear of that."

"I needed to get the diary first. Let me tell Gilbert about the murder when I see him." I caressed the damp cover of the diary. Instead of drawing assurances that my investigation into the nymphomania was definitely closed, I felt a twinge of doubt. My fingertips tingled to alert me of danger. But of what? And from whom?

"I'm not so sure this investigation is over," I added. "There's more to the conspiracy than what's in this diary."

Bob pulled the Buick to the curb and jammed the transmission into park. He turned to me. His *tapetum lucidum* glowed hot in the reflection of the street lamps. "And so what? That book explains the outbreak, and that's all that you were hired to do. Our priority now is the *vânätori*. I'll inform the Araneum and call for a council of the *nidus*. You'll testify about what you know."

"Not yet, Bob."

"Your investigation is *over*."

"Sorry. This investigation is far from over." I held quivering fingertips before him. "I can feel it. You and I, all the vampires in Denver, are in greater danger than ever because of this. Something's been set in motion, and the more we try to ignore it, the worse it will get for everyone."

CHAPTER 19

L IKE THE LAST TIME when I'd seen him in his office, Gilbert Odin put his telephone inside the credenza behind him, along with a boom box playing heavy metal turned up full volume. He closed the credenza door, muffling the screaming of guitars and the hammering of drums.

Gilbert folded his hands on his desk and gave me a genial smile. "It's safe to talk now."

"Couldn't there be any more bugs? In that, for example?" I pointed to the lamp on his desk.

"Oh no. I know exactly what listening devices Security has. I'm on their budget-approval committee. A Seven-Sigma telephone eavesdropping microphone is all they're authorized to use on me."

I suppose the logic made sense to a professional bureaucrat, but it gave me a headache. I pinched the bridge of my nose to ease the pressure.

"How's the investigation going, Felix?"

The investigation. That word alone worsened the headache. When I handed Wong's diary over to Gilbert, I wanted him to kiss me in gratitude, then write a check and send me on my way.

"Well, Gilbert, for starters, Dr. Wong is dead."

"We all know that." Gilbert tapped the newspaper on his desk. Page one of the Metro Section showed a picture of the doctor under the headline ROCKY FLATS NUCLEAR SCIENTIST MURDERED. Gilbert added, "The police say it was a botched robbery."

The cabbage smell swirled from him, not as strong as before but enough to make me think he needed to vary his diet.

"It was no robbery," I said. "I know who killed him."

"Who? Terrorists?"

"No. Enemies of mine."

Gilbert held a hand up. "Whoa. Back up. What enemies?"

I couldn't tell him the truth, that they were vampire hunters. "Enemies with a vendetta from a previous assignment. Wong got shot by mistake."

"A vendetta?" Gilbert asked. "The Mafia's after you?"

"No," I answered. "I have enough enemies, thank you."

Enemies savvy enough to ambush me. I had the mysterious gunman and the *vânători* after me, a lethal double threat. Suddenly I realized that Wong had been shot only moments after I arrived at his condo. How did the vampire-hunter marksman set up his rifle so soon? Unless he had the place staked out. Which meant he, and his companions, knew I was going to see Dr. Wong. But only I knew about the visit. A chill ran up my spine and out to my hands. My fingertips tingled as my vampire senses went on alert.

"Hey. Hey," Gilbert snapped his fingers. "You okay?"

I rubbed my hands together to calm the tingling. I wished

I didn't have to hide my eyes behind contacts—I needed the reassuring ability to read auras, even my friend Gilbert's.

"I'm all right," I answered.

"I thought you were having a seizure." He gestured to my face. "Something related to that Gulf War Syndrome of yours."

"I appreciate the concern. The question now is, what should I tell the investigators?"

"About what?"

"What I know about Wong's murder."

"Let the police worry about it. You said it wasn't terrorists, so there's no threat to Rocky Flats."

"Only a threat to me," I replied.

"And you can't handle it?" His question was a dare. "You said that it was enemies from a previous case. Should I be concerned?"

"No. It's my problem." I didn't want the cops to find the *vânätori* until after the *nidus* had torn the vampire hunters to pieces. "You don't want anyone to know that I've been talking to Dr. Wong, correct?"

Gilbert nodded. "That's right. Keep this between you and me."

"You're saying this investigation into the nymphomania is more important than Wong's murder?"

Gilbert focused his gaze into my eyes. "Yes. Even more important than Wong's murder."

Or mine for that matter. What kind of a conspiracy was this? "Why?"

Gilbert shook his head. "Because if you go blabbing that you were with Dr. Wong when he got killed, then you're likely to be locked up as a person of interest and forgotten. The wall of security around the conspiracy will only grow more formidable and I'll be SOL forever."

People with guns had already tried to stop me, so I appreciated Gilbert's well-grounded concerns.

I pulled out a Ziploc bag containing Wong's diary. "The doctor didn't have the chance to tell me much. He did mention"—I paused to gauge Gilbert's reaction—"red mercury."

Gilbert narrowed his eyes. "Red mercury?"

I laid the Ziploc bag on his desk. "It's all right here. Dr. Wong kept a diary."

Gilbert's face reddened. "A diary? With classified information?"

"According to him."

Gilbert sighed. "What the hell did he do that for?"

"Wong was convinced that safeguarding the secrets behind the outbreak would serve as insurance."

"For what?"

"His safety."

"Bullshit. This was about Dr. Wong and his inflated opinion of his own work." Gilbert used a mechanical pencil to slide the diary out of the bag and flip it open. The damp, filthy pages clumped together and exuded a disgusting smell. Gilbert stifled a gag reflex. "Where did this come from? A toilet?"

"I hid in a Dumpster to escape."

"I suppose that is better than a toilet." Gilbert adjusted his spectacles as he studied Wong's notes. "Red mercury, huh? Anything else?"

"EBEs."

Gilbert shrugged. "Got me there. I've never heard of that."

I homed in on Gilbert's expression as I asked, "Project Redlight?"

Gilbert rocked back into his seat. "Sorry, Felix, I'm drawing a blank on that one." His expression matched the flat tone of his statement.

"Area 51?" I asked.

"Nevada?" Gilbert set his hands on the armrests of his

chair and sat up straight. "That I can answer. Here at the Flats we generated waste streams of classified material. Dr. Wong was our liaison with the U.S. Air Force in Area 51 to make sure that we didn't inadvertently release sensitive information about these materials during our clean up. Secret? Yes. Mysterious? No."

I tapped the inside cover of the diary. "Look. It gives the dates. From two years ago to last week. Wong started making entries long before the outbreak." Carefully, I turned to the middle of the diary. The damp pages tore. "The writing's smudged but you can make out his comment about twenty-three kilograms of Hg-209, red mercury, moved from Building 707. That's the curious thing. There's no mention of red mercury in the historical discharge reports."

"Of course not. The only mercury we've used was quicksilver in instruments. And perhaps some mercuric-oxide, in minuscule amounts, for laboratory analysis. That's all."

"That's what I'm getting at. Existence of the red mercury was so secret that it was even kept out of the Classified Safety Analysis Files."

Gilbert shook his head the way a professor might at a confused student. "Red mercury is a sham. Supposedly the Russians used it as a catalyst for fusion weapons. It is mildly radioactive and very toxic. And useless. Quantities pop up on the European black market every now and then. Some sucker pays a few thousand bucks for crap he thinks is weapons-grade material."

"So why did Wong mention red mercury?"

"Maybe our good doctor wasn't so good. Maybe he had something cooking on the side."

"But twenty-three kilograms? That's more than a minuscule amount."

"True. It's quite a lot. And if he had any, it wasn't produced here."

"But he mentioned it specifically when I asked him about the outbreak. That and the EBEs."

"Let me tell you something about Dr. Wong. He was a fossil, a relic of the Cold War. When DOE consolidated its weapons operations in Los Alamos, Wong was left here. Out to pasture. I'm sure he was upset because of his treatment by DOE. Maybe that's why he concocted this chimera about red mercury and EBEs . . . whatever those are."

I pushed the diary toward Gilbert. The damp pages left a slimy trail on his desk blotter. "You asked me to find the cause of the nymphomania. Here it is."

Gilbert got up from behind his desk and opened the blinds of his window. A hundred meters away, on the barren ground inside the concertina wire of the Protected Area, waited a long white semi-trailer. A tent covered the rear of the trailer. Security guards in camouflage and carrying submachine guns patrolled the vicinity.

"Dr. Wong's death spooked a lot of important people," Gilbert said. "I spent my breakfast hour on a conference call with Germantown and D.C. Because of what happened to Wong, the shipment of the material I'm concerned about has been accelerated." Gilbert rapped the window for emphasis. "The material will be loaded into that trailer, which will leave for the WIPP facility in New Mexico within days, not weeks."

"You have Wong's diary. It's enough for you to demand to personally inspect the trailer."

Gilbert pulled a folder from his in-box. "That ain't how it works." Gilbert opened the folder and produced a sheaf of forms. "As the Assistant Manager for Environmental Restoration, my signature verifies the accuracy of these shipping documents for the trailer. If I don't sign them, I'd better have an excellent reason. It's called playing the DOE game."

"And if you refuse?"

Gilbert closed the folder. "Then I get reassigned. Some political hack will take my place behind this desk and whatever's in the trailer will get buried deep in Carlsbad Caverns. After which, the cause of the outbreak will remain a mystery forever . . . until the next wave of nymphomania, or worse. Meanwhile, I take water samples in Idaho for the rest of my career."

"You hired me to find the cause and I told you."

"Felix, give me something I can work with and I'll get a warrant. I'll have a team of federal marshals knocking down that fence and cutting that trailer open."

Gilbert slid the folder back into his in-box. "But red mercury? Why not magic dust or dilithium crystals while we're at it? Wong yanked your chain real good."

The book shriveled under the glare of Gilbert's desk lamp. The pages wrinkled and tore. My ego felt the same way. I was at another dead end.

Frustration turned into suspicion. Maybe Gilbert wasn't so clean himself. I tipped my head and reached to remove my contacts so that I could hypnotize him. I stopped. Gilbert had asked me as a friend to help him, so why would he keep secrets from me? I felt guilty for suspecting him and lowered my hand.

"Felix, the key word in this investigation is 'deception.' The only way I can get at the truth is to call their bluff."

"Whose bluff?"

"The ones who know what caused the nymphomania. What are they hiding? And why?" Gilbert leaned against the window frame and rubbed his temples. "I need proof to show that the inventory reports about those shipments are a lie. I know it seems like an impossible task, but that's why I asked for your help. If that trailer leaves Rocky Flats without answering that question, I'll have failed. You'll have failed. Don't let that happen."

The anguish of defeat pressed upon me. I loosened my

collar. Sweat tickled my brow but I couldn't wipe it or I'd smear my makeup.

This was my job. Sure, I could quit and can the hassle. Then what? Go somewhere else and quit that, too? Maybe this failure was the result of the gradual loss of my vampire powers because I wouldn't drink human blood.

No, that couldn't be it. I'd prove Bob Carcano wrong. A pulse of determination surged through me. My fangs extended. Gilbert had his back to me so he didn't notice. I held my lips closed until the sharp incisors retracted and then I touched the tips to make sure they didn't protrude.

Gilbert turned from the window. He glanced at me. "You got dental problems?"

"Something like that. If I find out what's in the trailer, that will solve the conspiracy?"

"Yes."

"That simple?"

"If you call breaking into the Protected Area and getting shot simple."

"Consider it done."

Gilbert's forehead wrinkled in doubt. "How?"

"I don't know yet. Let me surprise you."

CHAPTER
20

AFTER THE MEETING WITH Gilbert Odin, I spent a few hours trolling the Internet for red mercury, EBEs, and Project Redlight. Every hit on red mercury confirmed what Gilbert had told me, that it was hokey material. EBEs, I discovered, stood for "Extraterrestrial Biological Entities," a long-winded way to say "aliens." The proverbial little green men from Mars.

This led me back to websites devoted to Project Redlight, supposedly a secret air force program either studying UFOs and their EBE occupants or debunking the whole extraterrestrial story. I wasn't sure which, but as every paranoid conspiracy nut would confirm, all interplanetary flights to Earth lead to Area 51. In this mishmash of crackpot theories I didn't find anything that mentioned nymphomania or Rocky Flats. All this work and so far I had nothing to show for my investigation but wasted time stumbling through a labyrinth of hoaxes concerning flying saucers.

Bob called and asked that I join him for dinner. I needed a break from the frustration of my case and agreed to go. I drove us that evening to a taco stand on South Federal Boulevard where we met Andre. We sat around a wooden picnic table, in the warm envelope of air radiating from the space heater slung under the metal awning. Loud motorcycles, tall pickups, and garish low-riders cruised by. Not even the most reckless of *vânätori* would dare attack us here, out in the open.

I reached for the plastic basket containing my tacos.

Bob lifted a pouch of human blood from a paper bag on the bench. He snipped the pouch open and squeezed blood over his *chile relleno* combination plate. "Smothered. The only way to eat Mexican food. Of course, come tomorrow, this chile and beans are going to turn my ass into a weapon of mass destruction."

Andre, sipping on his beer, choked and shot suds out his nose.

Bob offered a plastic bottle to me.

I took the bottle and uncapped it. The aroma smelled of pig's blood. "Thanks." I poured the blood into my tacos.

Andre wiped his face with a paper towel. His gaze shifted from the plastic bottle to the pouch resting beside Bob's plate. "What's this, Felix? You're choosing animal blood over human?"

Bob was about to shovel *chile relleno* into his mouth. "Felix doesn't drink human blood."

Andre's face took on the astonished, injured expression of a priest hearing that a friend is an atheist. "This is . . . obscene." He turned to Bob. "Why?"

Bob pointed his fork at me. "Ask him."

I had been looking forward to a relaxed meal. "It's because of the war."

"Which war?" Andre raised his hands in supplication. "Humans have caused so many."

"The recent Gulf War. With Iraq."

"It's not healthy," Andre blurted. "We need human blood. It's the most nourishing."

"That's what I've been telling the jackass," Bob mumbled over a mouthful.

Andre's hands curled into claws. He held them before me as if they were weapons. "Human blood replenishes our vampire powers. It makes us strong. It makes us *monsters*."

"I don't want to be a monster," I replied. At this moment I hated being a vampire. I wanted to quit hiding behind these contact lenses and layers of Dermablend and be a normal human.

"But you are undead. You are vampire. You have no choice." Andre pushed the pouch toward me. "Drink and revel in this pleasure God has given us."

"What pleasure? God has damned us with this existence."

"Quit wasting your time, Andre," Bob said. He tapped his fork against Andre's plate of burritos and rice. "Eat before it gets cold."

Andre emptied the pouch of human blood over his food. "Felix, we are your friends, your brothers in fangs."

"Is this why you invited me to dinner?" I replied. "To pester me like this?"

"No," Bob answered. "I asked you here to discuss what you're going to tell the council. And to see how we could help in your investigation."

"My investigation?" I glared at Bob. "What did you do? Post it on your Internet newsletter?"

Bob quit chewing and wiped his mouth. "Before you wet your panties, listen. You're tangling with DOE, and vampire hunters have got us on their hit list. Considering that you've got to be looking over both shoulders at the same time, I'm surprised that you're not grateful for our help."

"You're right. I'm not. I don't need you two stumbling behind me."

"As if you've been so surefooted. Didn't you get conked on the head? And do I have to go over the how and why of my rescuing you from the animal shelter?"

I didn't want to answer. This was my business. My appetite waned and, regretfully, I watched the pig's blood congeal on my tacos.

Andre whispered in an accusing tone. "And now we have this revelation that you won't drink human blood. Deny your nature and you stand naked before the danger with your eyes closed."

I gulped my beer and let it settle in my stomach. Okay, I was a vampire. Maybe I was blinding myself to the risks. And I shouldn't be so headstrong, especially if it put me in the position of being lectured by this geezer. "All right. I am grateful for your help. Where would we start? . . ." My fingers tingled.

I looked around. "Somebody's watching us."

"I feel it, too." Bob hunched his shoulders and looked about.

All three of us removed our contacts and examined the area.

We were alone under the awning. Cars whooshed by on the boulevard. The red auras of humans shimmered in the black dome of night that surrounded us beyond the glow of the parking lot lamps. None of the auras bristled with threatening emotion.

The tingling stopped.

"Whatever it was, it's gone now," Bob said.

"Not it," I corrected, "but who."

"*Vânätori de vampir*?" Andre asked.

"Who else could spook us like this?" Bob answered.

"In my centuries as a vampire I've never seen the *vânätori de vampir*," Andre said.

"Never?" I asked.

"Not one. I spent most of my time fanging humans in the Orient. The eastern provinces. Siam. Java. Moved to South America for the fifteen through seventeen hundreds." Andre sat, his expression tense. "How many *vânätori* are there?"

"Four," I replied. "At least, that's how many I've seen."

Andre wrung his hands. In this light, withdrawn and circumspect, he appeared frail and weary. He was, after all, close to a thousand years old.

"Up until these attacks," Andre said, "I regarded the *vânätori* as Ziggy had, more exaggeration than truth. No human could be capable of stalking and killing us so easily."

Bob collected the plastic ware and napkins on his tray. "And look what happened to Ziggy. Standing out here like this, I feel like I'm the center target in a shooting gallery. Let's go."

We tossed the remnants of our food into the trash. I jingled my keys and hurried to my car.

Bob and I climbed into my Dodge. Andre got into his Pontiac.

The comforting rumble of the Dodge's engine alleviated my fears. The needle on the tachometer quivered as if daring the *vânätori* to come after us. I squealed the tires and fishtailed out of the parking lot.

Slowing down, I waited for Andre to follow. In the rearview mirror I saw that Andre's headlights were on but he hadn't left his parking spot. A set of high beams from another car crowded behind him. My fingers tingled, then vibrated in alarm.

Bob turned around and looked out the rear window. His aura burned with rage. He shouted, "Andre's in trouble."

"Yeah, I know." I whipped the Dodge into a U-turn. We looped in front of oncoming traffic and smacked the opposite curb. Cars swerved around us, horns blaring.

Bob snarled at them, his fangs extended.

I gunned the V-8 and shot into the southbound lane. My *kundalini noir* reared up and readied my body to strike. Talons grew from my fingers. Fangs extended to my lower lip.

Bob squinted. "Those damn high beams are blinding me."

In the parking lot, the high beams went dim and a darkened car with three glowing red auras zoomed backwards. The car spun around and retreated into the mass of auras and vehicles at the far intersection.

I raced the engine to catch them.

Bob beat his hand on the dashboard. "Stop. Stop. What's happened to Andre?"

I veered into the parking lot and skidded to a halt beside the Pontiac.

Bob jumped out. The Pontiac's motor still rumbled. Inside, a faint orange glow grew dimmer. Bob switched off the motor. He hung his head and leaned against the door pillar.

I got out of my Dodge. "Is he . . . ? Did the *vânätori* get to him?"

Bob nodded.

My *kundalini noir* remained still, disappointed at having lost the chance to tear flesh. I looked inside the Pontiac.

Andre's body lay across the center console, decapitated and with a hole in his chest. Vampire blood flakes were strewn like confetti across the instrument panel and the inside of the windshield.

The door of the *taquería* opened and a woman, round as a bell pepper, stood silhouetted in the threshold. "Hey," she called out in a *barrio* accent, "you guys making trouble?"

Bob's fangs retracted. Shielding his eyes, he shook his head. "We're okay. My friend's having trouble with his car."

"Well, it sounded like someone was starting shit," she said. "Don't make me call the cops."

Bob waved at her. "No trouble. Everything's fine."

"Then why are you and your friends driving through the lot like it's a goddamn racetrack? I expect *cholos* to act that way, not a bunch of *viejos* like you *cabrones*. If you're done eating here, go somewhere else and do your *chingaderas*." The woman closed the door and peered at us through the take-out window.

Bob opened the car door. Andre's head rested between his knees, upside down. The raw stump of his neck stared at us.

"What about his fangs?" I asked.

"Gone."

CHAPTER
21

THE BRAZENNESS AND THE stunning deftness of Andre's murder shook both Bob and me. These *vânätori de vampir* were expert assassins.

Still, I had my investigation to complete, and that clock was ticking away. The next day Bob and several of the other vampires arranged for the solar immolation of Andre's remains. I attended the ceremony, or, rather, the perfunctory arranging of his remains to be burned to dust by the dawn sun. All the vampires kept unusually quiet. The *vânätori* had us worried, something that as vampires we were ashamed to admit. Even though we were undead, none of us was eager to trade our animated forms for mounds of ash.

Wendy had left a message on my voice mail saying that she had something important to tell me. I hoped it was about my investigation. She lived in the Washington Park neighborhood. Her home was a modest brick bungalow, known locally as a "Denver square." I circled the block with my contacts out, reconnoitering the area to make sure that no *vânători* waited in ambush. The area clear, I put my contacts back in and parked.

Wendy answered after the second ring of her doorbell. Her elfish face peeked through the small window in the door and greeted me with a smile. She opened the door and looked past my shoulder. Her gaze surveyed the street. A rainbow-colored scrunchy gathered her hair into a ponytail.

"We're okay," I said to reassure her.

Inviting me in, she stepped aside to let me enter a compact living room where a humid plant smell overwhelmed me. Spider plants and ferns hung from baskets along the edges of the ceiling. Flowers and herbs crowded the buffets and built-in shelves lining the walls. Instrumental music—a sub-Saharan beat—drifted from unseen speakers.

Wendy locked the door. A loose blouse hung to her plump hips.

"Your message on my voice mail was vague," I said. "I hope you have news about my investigation."

"I've found something. Maybe it's useful. You decide." Wendy reached up to the closest shelf. The contours of her muscles showed where the blouse clung to her torso. She opened her day planner and unfolded a sheet of paper.

Printed on the paper was a disjointed series of paragraphs that looked lifted from other documents. Certain words practically jumped at me, as if they had been highlighted with electricity. "Where'd you get this?"

"People owe me favors. Your story about the nymphomania at Rocky Flats fascinated me. I wanted to see if it had happened before."

I read her notes aloud. "The first outbreak was reported in 1947. According to the Chaves County Health Department, five women in Roswell, New Mexico, succumbed to what they called heightened female sexual nervosa."

"Nymphomania," Wendy interrupted.

"I figured that. The second outbreak was recorded by Greene County, Ohio, health officials in 1952. Three women treated for heightened sexual nervosa."

"Nymphomania," she interrupted again. "Just in case you forgot."

"Fine. Thanks." The next dates startled me. "Two women treated for nymphomania in 1969. Here in Denver?"

She motioned for me to sit on the cushions grouped around a coffee table. There weren't any chairs in the room. "Actually, it was in Jefferson County. There's not much more than that. The Department of Energy confiscated the records."

DOE? How far back did this conspiracy go? "When did they confiscate the records?"

"Shortly afterwards. In 1969."

I settled into a cushion and rested my elbows on the coffee table as I reread the list. "What's the connection between all this?"

She sat next to me. "You're the detective. You tell me."

My eyes sifted through the words and searched for clues that would hook into my investigation. But at the moment, nothing. "It's interesting. Let me study it more." I folded the paper and slipped it into my pocket. "Thanks. Good work."

Wendy got up and padded on bare feet toward the kitchen. "You're not too busy for drinks, are you?"

In the time I've been a vampire, this was the first occasion a woman, even if she was a dryad, had asked me into her home for a visit. The sensual coziness surprised me. "Make it something special," I said.

I settled into a big cushion, removed and put away my contacts. A dim pinkish aura washed over the plants. There was a ceramic water pitcher, a wash towel, and a flower vase on the table.

Wendy returned holding a plastic cafeteria tray with a

bottle of shiraz, a creamer, and two goblets, which didn't match. Her aura looked like transparent green glass. She set the tray on the table and sat cross-legged next to me. Wendy's naked feet had an inviting sexual allure. Her manicured toes added the notion of erotic preparation. My aura pulsed in anticipation.

Wendy looked away. This made my aura brighten in annoyance. We supernaturals used our ability to read auras to outwit humans. Now this power betrayed me. I took a calming breath and let my aura smooth out.

Wendy pushed the creamer toward me. "I got ewe's blood for you."

I mixed it with my wine. The opaque blood turned the shiraz cloudy. "The myth is that ewe's blood and certain red wines enhance sexual potency."

Wendy's green eyes sparkled. "Really?"

Her teasing made my aura burn. Being the vampire, I was supposed to manipulate the woman.

She pulled the scrunchy off and shook her head. The ponytail separated into luxurious curls.

My aura burned brighter. I sipped the blood-wine cocktail. A coppery aftertaste slid down my throat.

Smiling, she twisted a lock of hair between her fingers. "How many of the nymphomaniacs have you talked to?"

"Three."

Wendy tapped her foot against my ankle. "Did they try to seduce you?"

"Actually, they did."

"At the same time? Lucky you."

"No, it wasn't like that."

Wendy placed her hand on my knee. "Were any successful?"

"No. There were difficulties."

"Man problems?" Wendy held a finger out, then curled it. "There were *no* problems of that sort," I replied and masked my irritation at the suggestion. "What's this interest in nymphomania, anyway?"

"What's not to find interesting?" Wendy sipped and then chuckled. "The idea of women shucking their panties and humping men—what a great image. It's hysterical."

"Wasn't funny to the nymphos."

"The ones you interviewed, they didn't enjoy themselves?"

"I didn't say that."

Wendy's cheeks dimpled. "So they did have fun?"

"At a price, yes."

Wendy brought her face to mine. "And what would the price be for me?"

The price would be a good screwing. My desire percolated into lust. We kissed. I grasped her shoulders and pushed so that she rolled onto her back.

Wendy resisted. "Wait."

She unbuttoned my shirt and exposed my translucent vampire skin. "Felix"—she ran her mouth across my neck and collarbone—"can vampires get hickeys?"

I didn't answer because I didn't know. We'd find out. Closing my eyes for a moment, I focused on the touch of her lips.

Wendy sat back and reached for the pitcher on the coffee table. She moistened the towel and dabbed my nose to remove the makeup and sunblock.

"It doesn't look right for your face and hands to not match the rest of your body."

The damp towel caressed me like a cool tongue. She held up my right hand and admired the veins pulsating within the sheath of my pale skin. My aura rippled where her fingers traced along my flesh.

Wendy released my hand. She pulled the flower stems from the glass vase on the table. When she turned the vase around, I saw that it wasn't a vase but a bong. She retrieved a butane lighter and a small plastic bag from a drawer in the coffee table. When she opened the bag, the pungent odor of marijuana leaked out. Wendy crammed a wad of the pot into the small metal bowl of the bong.

I tugged the tails of my shirt from my trousers. "Is this a way of connecting to your forest nature?"

"Not really. It's about getting high and horny. You've been downing that ewe's blood cocktail and I wanted to catch up. Haven't you heard about the aphrodisiacal powers of ganja?"

"I have. Aren't you afraid of a drug test at the hospital?"

"I'm a dryad. I could drink vinegar and pee chardonnay if I wanted to."

I glanced at my wine.

"Don't worry. That came from the liquor store." Wendy aimed the blue flame of the lighter into the bowl. She sucked on the barrel of the bong and gurgled the water. The burning weed glowed orange. She held her breath and passed the bong to me.

I took a big hit and immediately coughed.

She exhaled a puff of smoke and giggled. "What the hell was that? Weren't you in the army?"

"I haven't gotten toasted since I've been a vampire." I tried again, taking shallow breaths.

Wendy took the bong and inhaled several more hits. Her aura took on a creamy haze. It changed from green to yellow, then orange and finally red, like a human's.

I blinked to make sure I wasn't hallucinating. "What was that?"

"Marijuana, like a lot of other drugs, causes your spiritual center to shift from chakra to chakra."

My own aura darkened from orange to red. My center of gravity sank from my chest to my groin, as if it were an elevator, going down. My head became light and a warm sensation swelled into my crotch.

Wendy watched and nodded. "I like what's happening to you."

And so did I. "But the yellow aura. The only time I've seen that before was when I questioned the nymphos under hypnosis."

Wendy closed her eyes. Tendrils of smoke drifted from the corners of her smile. "Perhaps the nymphomania is rooted in spiritual displacement."

My center of gravity floated upward into my torso. I set my hand on the floor to steady myself. My aura turned orange again. "Maybe there's a level of psychic awareness between the planes that vampires and dryads occupy. A different type of supernatural. Not with an orange or a green aura, but yellow."

Wendy grinned, her eyes remaining closed. "Hmmm. What could that be?"

She blew smoke rings and relaxed against a big cushion. Her aura changed again, like a liquid jewel turning different hues. Tiny rosebuds in all colors sprouted among the curls of her hair.

Was there no limit to her surprises? A euphoric numbness muted my senses. My heart matched the tempo of the music seeping through me. The sexual tension grew into a thirst I had to quench with her body.

Her hooded eyes pulled with a magnetic power. I set my arms alongside her head and lowered my face to kiss her. My orange aura curled through the air, like a flame.

The scent of a thousand blossoms swirled around us. Her warm lips found mine. I pushed away to reposition my hands so I could unbutton her blouse. The roses in her hair had grown into a crown. Wendy plucked a red blossom and fed it to me.

The petals disintegrated between my teeth, leaving a taste I could only describe as a mood. Passion. "If this is what grew from your head, I'm wondering what's waiting between your legs."

She nipped my chin. "You'll have to pluck that one yourself."

Wendy peeled off her blouse and revealed small, enticing breasts. She wrapped her arms around me and whispered. "Did you bring protection?"

The question broke the mood as it always does. "You're supernatural, why would you need protection?"

Wendy relaxed against the cushion and propped up on an elbow. "Because there's lots of nasty bugs that even I can't defend myself against. No offense to you. The only souvenirs I want from this afternoon are good memories." She pointed to an end table. "There's protection in there."

Awkwardly, trying to act both nonchalant and romantic about looking for condoms, I opened the drawer, looked inside, and hesitated. "Don't take this wrong, but there might be a problem."

Wendy shimmied out of her jeans and red bikini panties. "Aren't there any?"

I lifted a packet. "Oh, there's plenty. Problem is, they're all supermagnum triple-extra-large."

Wendy raised an eyebrow. "And the problem?"

"There's no problem for me but I don't mean to disappoint . . ."

"Oh," Wendy gasped, "I get what you mean. Those were from an old boyfriend. He was big down there, really big. Whew." She held her hands apart as if she were describing a trophy catch. "The guy belonged in a zoo."

"Thanks for sharing." Nothing like the mention of an old flame and his humongous wanger to cool my ardor, even if I *am* a vampire. "Was he a supernatural, too?"

Wendy took the condom and dropped it back into the drawer. "No, human. He was an intern from the hospital. It was purely physical."

Physical. Like that was supposed to make me feel better.

I was a vampire, a notorious king of seduction. How the hell was I being upstaged by a mortal?

Wendy rummaged in the drawer and found a regular-sized condom. "After a while the novelty wore off, and we called it quits. No big deal. Except for that, I mean. A penis that size was quite a find. Made for some great visuals in the mirror."

Oh, trample my ego some more. My orange aura sizzled with jealousy at the image of Wendy gleefully impaling herself on that meat missile.

Wendy sprawled her naked body across the cushions and hugged me. "Why don't you direct some of that emotion in my direction and give me a good banging? Where's this Latin machismo I've heard so much about? And you're a vampire. My first. You should have me pinned to the floor already."

She rubbed her neck against my face. The sensation of her blood surging through juicy veins only millimeters beneath her skin inflamed my desire. My fangs grew. I'd show her a vampire.

We rolled on the cushions to smooch and fumble until I was naked too.

"Fang me," she groaned and arched her neck back.

I dragged the tips of my elongated incisors against the tender skin of her throat. I'd pierce her skin but not drink the blood.

Wendy's aura flashed bright, like an alarm. Finally I had her libido on full burner. She would forget all about Moby Dick.

She pushed me off and sat up. The roses scattered from her hair. "Someone's at the back door."

Wooden steps creaked faintly. So it wasn't my prowess that had set off her aura. Could it be *vânätori de vampir*?

Adrenaline pumped into my muscles and prepared me for a fight. I yanked my trousers on, stood, and went through the kitchen to the back door. Suddenly modest, Wendy pulled on her blouse and crept behind me.

The silhouette of a man darkened the curtain on the door. He raised an arm.

I pushed Wendy back. Our feet tangled, and we toppled over.

The window glass exploded. A clay jar on a kitchen shelf shattered and sprayed us with flour.

A gloved hand reached through the broken window and fumbled with the doorknob.

I rolled away from Wendy. She placed her hands and feet against the wall and climbed up. I sprang to the ceiling, attempting to cling and haul my body upward where I could surprise the attacker from above.

But my fingertips couldn't hold and I dropped to the floor. This vampire power failed me again. Instead I crouched, my legs flexed and readied to propel me forward. My fangs jutted out. I'd strike at his face, blind him, and then rip open his throat. Gun or no gun, our attacker was about to die.

The door lock released. The door swung open.

CHAPTER
22

THE INSTANT I SAW the intruder block the open doorway, I zapped him with my vampire glare.

Dark wraparound sunglasses shielded his eyes.

Damn, I couldn't hypnotize him.

I took a mental snapshot.

A red aura blazing like the fire from a rocket nozzle surrounded his hefty bulk. Tall, easily six-four. A big man who knew how to use his muscles. Black leather jacket. A head like a rectangular hunk of stone topped with short, wiry blond hair.

Was he the same gunman who had chased me into the ditch with an M16? And the guy who broke into my apartment and whacked me on the head? How did he know I was here? Was he stalking me? Who did he work for?

Wendy tucked herself next to the overhead cabinets above me, like a moth trying to hide.

He shifted his weight to one side. The afternoon sunlight

burst around him and flooded the kitchen to scald my naked torso.

I stumbled backwards toward the counter and clutched the air in pain. Through tearing eyes, I glimpsed the long barrel of a silencer jerk toward me. A plastic bag covered the pistol, a professional killer's trick to catch ejected casings.

I knocked over a row of bottles on the counter. Instinctively, I snatched one bottle and blindly hurled it at the gunman. He ducked when the glass bottle shattered against the doorframe by his head and splashed olive oil. His pistol fired. A bullet tore into the ceiling. Wendy flinched. Flakes of plaster rained down.

Fumbling with the next bottle, I threw it wildly and smashed it on the floor between his feet to make him dance as vinegar doused his legs.

I clutched the next bottle and knocked loose the glass stopper. The liquid splashed on my skin and burned like acid. The pungent odor of garlic oil stung my nose. I yelped and jumped back.

A bullet gouged the countertop inches from my hand.

Desperately, I grabbed another small round bottle and cocked my arm.

"Not that one," Wendy shouted.

Too late. My arm whipped around and the bottle shot from my hand. The bottle struck above the door and sprayed the gunman with liquid that immediately turned into a white cloud of vapor.

The spikes of the gunman's aura blunted and writhed, signaling his confusion. His pistol trembled. He teetered against the doorjamb, fired again and missed.

A fine mist from the vapor settled on my skin and soothed the burning pain. An intense sweet flowery smell overcame me. Dizzy, I leaned against the counter to keep from falling over.

Wendy groaned in disbelief and floated to the floor.

The sunglasses couldn't hide the alarm in the gunman's expression. The spikes of his aura became short and dense like fuzz. His posture relaxed. He smiled, a wide slash of big teeth.

The gunman walked toward me, holding his left hand up to reach for my face.

I wanted to shrink away from him but didn't. From the depths of my confusion, I felt the swoon of anticipation.

His thick fingers clasped the back of my neck. He pulled me forward tenderly. Wrinkles and tiny pockmarks marred his complexion, yet I found him irresistible. His smile condensed as his lips pressed together. Our lips barely touched.

Droplets rained on my skin. Immediately my desire turned into mortification. The face which seconds ago seemed handsome now repulsed me. Both the gunman and I shoved each other away.

He squeezed his tongue between his teeth as if to scrape away any taste of me.

Likewise, I wiped my mouth in disgust. More droplets drizzled onto my skin. Wendy worked the trigger of a small brass spritzer to mist the gunman and me. As my skin absorbed the droplets, my revulsion intensified.

The gunman retched and staggered out of the kitchen doorway and onto the back porch. "Next time, Felix," he yelled. "Next time."

He lurched toward a wooden gate at the far end of the small yard. I lost my would-be assassin in the dazzle of the afternoon sun. A car door slammed in the alley. The sudden squeal of tires meant someone had been waiting for him.

Wendy set the spritzer on the counter and didn't move until the sound of the car faded. She tiptoed over the broken glass on the floor, seemingly unaffected by the lingering vapor. She pushed the kitchen door closed and pulled the curtain tight over the window. The darkened room calmed and soothed me.

I slid against the counter cabinet until I rested on the floor. Spots danced across my vision. "What the hell happened?"

"You threw a bottle of love potion. That's what saved you." She raked her fingers through her tresses, now stringy and oily. "You can see what it does to my hair."

"I'll buy you shampoo."

Wendy pointed to the spritzer. "I had to counteract the potion with a repulsion tonic. Not that I wasn't tempted to watch you and our visitor go at it. But I have dibs on you. He can wait for his turn."

"It'll be a long wait."

"I hope so. He wasn't a vampire hunter, was he?" she asked.

"No. He wasn't from the group who attacked me before. But I'm positive he was the guy who whacked me on the head. He's come after me at least twice already."

"Then who is he? And who sent him?"

"I'm guessing the same people behind the cover-up at Rocky Flats. I was warned my investigation into the nymphomania was more important than murder. I didn't figure that might have meant my murder."

I picked up a fragment of the bottle that had contained the love potion. "Maybe this was the cause of the outbreak."

Wendy shook her head. "I doubt it. It's love potion, not Spanish fly. Did any of the women mention falling for their . . . uh . . . conquests?"

"No. The outbreak was all about grinding genitals. Plus, their auras changed colors from red to yellow. The gunman's didn't."

"So why come after you?" She pulled a candle and matches from a counter drawer. "What makes you such a threat?"

"That's the frustrating part. I wish they'd tell me. So far I haven't discovered anything worth killing someone over.

At least from what I understand." I squinted at the candle. "More magic?"

"Depends on your definition of magic. I prefer to think of it as chemistry humans haven't yet discovered." Setting the candle into a glass holder, she lit the wick. Smoke from the candle flame carried the smell of sage through the kitchen.

The spots in my eyes faded. The fog of dizziness eased.

Wendy's aura crackled again. Glancing to the door, her eyebrows narrowed and creased her forehead. "Think he'll come back?"

"Not if he figures he might end up kissing me again. But if the question is, are we still in danger? That answer is yes." I pushed to get off the floor but was too weak.

Wendy opened the refrigerator and pulled out a steel bottle. She squatted beside me and uncapped it. "Here. It's bull blood. The taurine should rejuvenate you. I was hoping to use it to prolong our play time but that can wait."

I sipped the cool blood and rested. Wendy brewed herbal tea and sat opposite me on the floor. She folded her legs and the hem of her blouse covered her hips. The steam from her mug carried the aroma of chamomile and lemon.

"That was pretty ballsy of you," she said.

"What do you mean?"

"You could've clung to the ceiling and attacked from above. At first I thought that's what you were going to do. Instead you faced him head-on."

I didn't want to admit that my *ballsy* head-on attack was the fault of my weakening powers. Wendy's love potion is what saved us, not my heroics.

As dusk fell, the curtains on the windows became dark rectangles. Strength returned to my limbs. I went to the living room to retrieve the rest of my clothes. I decided to contact Bob Carcano and have him watch my back while I hunted for the gunman.

Wendy followed. "You leaving?"

I buttoned my shirt. "Some asshole just tried to kill me—us—so I need to do more than watch you drink tea. Let's get going."

"What's this 'Let's get going?'" Wendy rattled her mug of tea against a saucer. Her green aura surged up a notch in intensity. "I can take care of myself. I've got plenty of potions. If he comes back again, I'll turn him into a frog and feed him to a duck."

I found my cell phone and keyed Bob's number. "I'd like to see that. Until then, I need to find the gunman. He's got answers to my questions."

"And he's got a pistol, too. Don't forget that."

"I won't." Bob didn't answer, so I left a message for him to meet me at my apartment.

Wendy escorted me to the front door. She rested her head against my shoulder and hugged me. "Be careful, Felix. We have unfinished business here." She gave my crotch a light squeeze.

My fangs popped out. I touched them to her neck, then pecked her forehead and left.

Outside, I detected nothing unusual. With the onset of night, I didn't need to worry about the sun burning me. Once inside my car, I slid my makeup kit from under the driver's seat and covered my pale vampire complexion. I drove home. Bob's Buick waited alongside the curb in front of my apartment complex. His engine was running.

Seeing Bob in his car, I parked my Dodge and walked over to him.

"I got your message," he said. "You need to come with me."

"Why?" I pointed to my apartment. "We can talk inside."

"No time." The lock on his front passenger door snapped open.

I got into the Buick and buckled up. "Where're we going?"

Bob headed down the street. "The *nidus* council is meeting tonight to discuss the *vânätori de vampir.* We've already lost Ziggy and Andre. If we lose a third vampire, all hell will break loose. You know, fang first and ask questions later. The mood is ugly."

"It'll get uglier if they hear about this." I described the attack at Wendy's.

Bob's aura lit up like napalm. "Damn it, Felix. Trouble follows you like a shadow. And we aren't supposed to cast shadows. How do you know this gunman wasn't a vampire hunter?"

"Because he came after me with an automatic and a silencer, not with a crucifix and a wooden stake. And he knew my name."

"No shit! this *does* make things uglier. That settles it."

"Settles what?"

"Tonight you tell the *nidus* what you know about the vampire hunters and this hit man. After that, you leave Colorado. Disappear."

"Bullshit. I'm staying to finish my investigation."

"Because you gave your word to a friend at Rocky Flats?"

"It's a matter of principle."

"What about your principles regarding the rest of us? And Wendy? Have you bothered to think about what that gunman intended to do to her after he plugged you? I doubt he was going to give her a sympathy card and flowers."

"You let me worry about Wendy."

Bob stared at his outside mirror. His aura shrank around him.

"Did you hear me, Bob?"

"Yeah, I heard you." He divided his attention between the road and the rearview mirrors. "We're being followed."

Immediately my fingers and ears buzzed. I tipped my

head to check the mirror outside my window. A Ford Crown Vic pulled close. A black one. "They're right on us."

"*Vânätori?*" Bob accelerated until we about tapped the bumper of a delivery truck in front of us.

I turned my head around to see.

The Ford surged into the oncoming lane of traffic and gained on us. A familiar aura filled the passenger side of the windshield.

"Not vampire hunters. It's him," I said. "The gunman from Wendy's place."

The gunman's aura flared.

"Get down," I yelled to Bob.

A swarm of bullets punched out our rear window.

CHAPTER
23

THE GUNMAN PAUSED, as if reloading. His big hands manipulated the pistol. He kept his gaze fixed on me. His eye sockets seemed chiseled out of a head massive enough to use as a battering ram. He leaned from the window of the Ford and waved the driver to speed up.

My fangs sprang out. I reached across Bob and grabbed the steering wheel.

He tried to push me away. "What the hell you doing?"

"Taking the offensive." I spun the steering wheel to the left.

Our Buick bashed against the Crown Vic. Sheet metal crumpled. Trapped within the door window, the gunman flailed his arms and yelled in panic as I slammed our car inches from his body.

After enduring these last days of having been chased and shot at, my *kundalini noir* coiled in vengeance within me. "I've had enough. This son of a bitch is going to pay."

I let go of the steering wheel. "Take it, Bob. Keep our rear window even with the gunman."

I dove into the backseat. I smacked the window and shattered it. I reached for the gunman and seized his thick arm. We locked gazes. I didn't hypnotize him, as I wanted him to feel the pain of every cut and bruise I was about to inflict.

I bared my fangs and growled.

He blanched with terror and tried to yank free. "What are you?"

I laughed at him. "Your executioner."

The cold night air whistled past as we hurtled down Speer Boulevard, he and I bridging the gap between our cars. I couldn't reach to bite him so I punched him in the face. Blood spurted from his nose and over my fist. His pistol fell and bounced onto the street.

"I don't care what kind of a freak you are, Felix," he shrieked. The wind pushed blood across his cheek. "We'll stop you."

"We *who*?" I paused from punching him again. "Stop me from *what*?"

"Stop you from living." The gunman drew his free arm and brandished a switchblade.

"Too late for that." I parried the knife and grabbed this arm as well. Bracing myself against the inside of the Buick's door, I yelled, "Now, Bob! Stop!"

He slammed on the brakes. Our car skidded and swerved. The gunman's arms tugged against mine. He screamed. His bones cracked. I held fast until his body jerked from the Ford's window, then I let go. His shoes flew off. He helicoptered in the air and flopped face down on the street. A car behind us had nowhere to turn and skidded over him, *thump, thump*.

Bob revved the engine. We whipped around to the opposite direction. Centrifugal force flung me across the backseat. Cars honked and dodged around us.

The Ford locked its tires and stopped. The driver hustled out and fired a pistol. Two slugs whapped into our trunk lid.

We raced away and took the on-ramp to Interstate 25, heading north. No one followed. I climbed back into the front seat.

Bob merged into traffic. "You like to make enemies, don't you, Felix?"

"Doesn't have to be about me. Maybe they don't like Buicks."

Bob smiled. "Too bad we couldn't have finished them off properly. Shame to think of all that fresh blood getting dumped on the street." The reflection of passing headlights twinkled along his fangs.

I massaged my knuckles. "Yeah, it would've been great to have fanged him but my fist breaking his nose felt good enough."

Bob leaned toward me. "Is that his blood on your hand?"

"Yeah." I opened the center console and found a small box of tissue.

Bob sniffed. "Smells good."

I wiped the blood from my knuckles and handed Bob the tissue. "Here, have a taste."

Bob put the tissue in his mouth. He rolled his window down and spit out the tissue. "Mmmm, not bad. It's the adrenaline. Drinking donated blood gets bland after a while."

A police car with flashing lights approached on the opposite side of the highway and continued past us.

"You just killed a man," Bob said.

"I know."

"And you feel no guilt about it?"

"Only that I didn't kill him earlier."

"So you're okay now to drink human blood?" The question sounded hopeful, as if the correct answer would eliminate any lingering tension between us.

"The death of that goon changes nothing," I said.

"What would, Felix?"

"Forgiveness." I was surprised I let myself admit it.

"That simple?" Bob looked at me, his fangs peeking from under a dismissive grin. "Sounds like you need religion."

"Sounds like you need to shut up."

Bob's grin went flat. He stared straight ahead and floored the accelerator. The highway curved to the right. Bob cut across the lanes to the next exit and zoomed between two cars. The exit took us into the Five Points area north of downtown. He turned on Brighton Boulevard, a long strip of industrial businesses and warehouses deserted at this time of the evening, then slowed for a red traffic light.

My fingers tingled. "We're not safe."

Bob's aura simmered. He adjusted his rearview mirrors. "I sense it, too. Where are they?"

The light turned green. Bob tapped the gas pedal. We rolled through the intersection.

An older-model Dodge cargo van zoomed at us from the left. The intense glow of red human auras filled the windshield. Familiar auras. Vampire hunters.

"*Vânätori*," I warned. "Look out!"

Bob accelerated and veered to the right. The van turned sharply, came parallel to us, and rammed our front fender.

Our Buick hit the curb and ricocheted back against the Dodge. We careened up the street, fender bashing against fender. The side cargo door on the van sprung open. A bearded man in a long coat and a wide-brimmed hat pointed the muzzle of a double-barreled shotgun at Bob's window.

The window exploded into a shower of glass. Blood sprayed inside the Buick. Bob clutched his neck and gagged.

The vampire hunter lifted the shotgun and aimed for me. I snatched the top of the steering wheel and pushed. The Buick surged to the left. The door pillar knocked against the shotgun just as it went off. The muzzle blast deafened me. A swarm of pellets gashed through the ceiling upholstery.

The Buick bounced over the curb. We flattened a stop sign and smashed into a telephone pole. The airbag deployed and slapped my face.

The Buick perched at an angle, the front end balanced on the stump of the telephone pole. I sat silent, stunned by the collision. My ears rang. The Buick groaned and hissed like a dying animal. Pushing the deflated airbag from my face, I groped for Bob.

He rested against the steering wheel, swaddled by the fabric of his airbag. His aura pulsed and grew dim. Overcome with desperation, I cradled his head and lifted gently. Blood gushed from a wound in his shoulder at the base of his neck. Moaning, he stroked my arm with a bloody hand.

The Dodge van screeched to a halt and backed up, its transmission grinding. Three vampire hunters jostled in the open cargo door, two hulking bearded goons flanked the older man, all of them pointing guns. They opened fire. Their shots cracked against the Buick's windshield and peppered me with glass.

Energized with panic, I opened my door and dragged Bob by the arm.

The van jumped the curb, scraped alongside the Buick, and stopped with the cargo door aligned with Bob's window. At this distance they couldn't miss me.

If I held on to Bob, there would be two dead vampires. I hesitated for a microsecond and weighed self-preservation versus loyalty. Dead, I'd be of no help to him. So I let go and tumbled out through my door. Bullets tore the upholstery inches from my head. I landed on the sidewalk and put the Buick between the vampire hunters and myself.

The closest refuge was behind a stack of rusted metal drums at the corner of the sidewalk and an alley. I scrambled over the concrete like a bug and dove over the drums just as another volley of bullets came searching for me.

I couldn't abandon Bob. Turning around, I peeked between the drums.

The older vampire hunter aimed a crucifix at Bob and shouted in Latin. His burly companions reached through the Buick's window and clutched Bob by the collar. They dragged his limp body through the window and into the van.

The vampire hunter with the crucifix waved his shotgun in my direction and fired. I ducked. Pellets rapped against the drums. The van tore back into the street and picked up speed.

Why did they take Bob? Why didn't they blast him to pieces with their guns?

I dashed from around the barrels and into the street. The van's taillights receded up Brighton Boulevard. I ran after the van, faster and faster, spurred by rage and the need for revenge. The van kept pulling away. My lungs sucked the cold air. Running at vampire speed, I should've been able to catch the van. But I wasn't able to keep up. My legs tired. In one final effort, I lunged forward and then slowed to a trot. From the pit of my belly came that burning craving for human blood. A craving that turned into guilt. If I had overcome my aversion for human blood, then perhaps I would have been able to rejuvenate my failing vampire powers and rescue Bob. Perhaps.

The rear doors of the van opened. Out dropped a body. A round object followed and bounced lazily like a lopsided ball.

My guts tightened when I realized what I was seeing. Massaging a runner's stitch between my ribs, I jogged forward and approached the body lying on the street. The round object rolled to a stop over a sewer grate at the curb.

I stepped close to Bob's decapitated corpse. A wooden

stake jutted from a bloody stain in his breast. His head faced me, lying sideways atop the sewer grate, his mouth frozen open in an silent scream. His upper lip was torn apart and revealed two gashes where they had pried out his fangs.

A great sadness crushed me. My knees buckled. I sat on my heels, my arms drooping to my sides. Breath wheezed through my dry throat. Far ahead, the taillights of the van merged into one and then disappeared.

At this moment, I wished that vampires could cry.

CHAPTER
24

I STOOD WITH TWENTY other vampires under the night sky, on the shoulder of an asphalt road beside a dusty field near Last Chance, eighty miles east of Denver. Against the dark contours of the terrain, our orange auras looked like gems floating on black velvet.

A cold, dusty breeze stirred the morning air. As dawn approached, the twilight sky faded from inky black to purple and then to blue.

Bob's naked corpse hung from a sheet of salvaged plywood propped to face the sun. His head rested on a crude shelf above his shoulders. A ragged hole the size of a fist showed where the vampire hunters had pounded a stake through his sternum. Frayed polypropylene boating rope looped under his armpits and across his chest, holding him flat against the plywood.

To us vampires, the first rays of the morning were the most savage to our flesh. For protection, five of the vampires used the satin robes they usually donned for choir with the Temple Baptist Church. Carmen, as usual, was ensconced in tight black leather, looking like a petite dominatrix making a rural house call. My jacket and trousers rustled in the wind. Everybody wore balaclavas, gloves, and welders goggles.

A corona of yellow light spread over the eastern horizon. A tremor of awe surged through me. Since prehistoric times when the first vampires stalked human prey, this moment of dawn has meant the dreaded finish to us, the undead. Now we watched, standing with impunity in the open, protected by thick tinted glass and layers of polyester, leather, and wrinkle-free cotton.

The sun rose over the edge of the earth. A terrible, incandescent wave bore upon us like the flash of an atom bomb.

Bob's head and corpse sizzled. His skin turned black and wrinkled. Flesh peeled away from bones and turned into smoke. The tangled mass of his organs spilled from underneath his rib cage. His bones broke apart like brittle twigs. Everything that had been Bob Carcano disintegrated into flakes of ash as centuries of arrested death came back to reclaim their due. The ash swirled and scattered in the eddy of wind twisting before the plywood. After a few minutes, nothing remained of Bob except for a discoloration in the dirt and a last smudge of smoke dissolving into the air.

As a vampire, Bob was lucky to get this modest little ceremony. Solar immolation was our way of destroying the evidence of our presence to humans, nothing more. Bob would be missed, certainly, but as undead creatures who walked in step beside the Grim Reaper, we accepted the inevitability of our final destruction.

The vampires in robes gathered around the plywood sheet and kicked free the two-by-fours holding it upright. The sheet slapped the ground with a whap. The vampires dragged the plywood and lumber down the slope and tossed it into the trash littering the gully.

Carmen and I walked back to her Audi TT roadster, a sleek, flattened lump of metal with narrow windows. We got in, she in the driver's seat, I next to her. Protected by the Audi's tinted glass, we pulled off our goggles, hoods, and gloves. Behind us, the other vampires dispersed into three groups and climbed into a copper-colored station wagon, an SUV, and a long-bed pickup with dually wheels.

Carmen unsnapped the collar of her leather jacket and pulled the zipper midway down her cleavage. Neither of us had said much on the way out here last night, consumed as we were with dismay and outrage at Bob's death.

She plucked a plastic bottle from between her seat and the center console and proceeded to smear her face with coconut-scented SPF 90 sunscreen. Tiny golden Aztec calendars dangled from each earlobe. "With Bob gone, the Denver *nidus* chose me as its new leader."

I held my palms up for her to give me some of the sunscreen. "I thought that position went automatically to the most senior vampire in the community. That would be Mel."

"Under normal circumstances." Carmen squirted the lotion into my hands. "Because of these *vânători* attacks, the *nidus* wanted someone younger and more ruthless."

I dabbed the sunscreen on my cheeks. "And that would be . . . you?"

"Yes. Me." Carmen unzipped her jacket further and exposed breasts cupped within a black leather bra. She buttered the tops of her tits with sunscreen. "The first question from the *nidus* to me as the new leader was, what was I going to do about your investigation?"

She flicked her black hair over one shoulder and rubbed sunscreen onto her neck. "Before you answer, be aware that the question came directly from the Araneum."

My aura spiked defensively. "What's it to them?"

"The Araneum insists that we focus all our attention, at the expense of all other obligations, on finding and destroying the *vânätori*, on taking direct action."

"You mean killing humans outside of self-defense?"

"*Chalé.* This is self-defense." Carmen pursed her lips and applied blood-red lipstick. She flipped down the sunshade and looked at the vanity mirror. Laminated pictures of Frida Kahlo and the Virgin of Guadalupe were pinned next to the mirror. Of course Carmen wouldn't see anything in the mirror but the interior of the car.

"Do you know what I hate most about being a vampire? Fixing my makeup without a mirror." Carmen slapped the sunshade against the interior ceiling. "How many more vampires have to die before we do something?" She smoothed her hair.

"And the police?"

She polished the sunglass lenses with a tissue. "Subsisting on chalices and donated blood hasn't made us that complacent. We can cover our tracks."

"What does this have to do with my investigation?"

She put on her sunglasses and tugged at the corners to make sure they fit tight. "If things get . . . uh . . . sticky, I'll need you. These vampire hunters use guns. You have experience with firearms."

"And getting shot, too. Don't forget that part. Want to see my scars?"

Carmen peered over the tops of her sunglasses and gave me the once over. She zipped her jacket to cover most of her cleavage. "Some other time."

I put in my contacts. Now that I was unable to see auras, the world looked inert and unfinished.

She started the Audi and honked the horn. The station wagon honked back. Carmen pressed the gas pedal and her car darted off the shoulder of the road. Gravel pinged against the chassis. When the tires bit into the asphalt, the Audi lunged forward and we accelerated toward the highway.

Carmen cocked her thumb to the tiny backseat. "Gimme that portfolio, will you?"

The portfolio sat atop a pile consisting of cross trainers, a yoga mat, and a gym bag.

I placed the portfolio on my lap and stroked the cordovan leather. "Pretty nice. Expensive, no doubt."

"*Sí, un regalo.*" Carmen nodded simply. "A gift from one of my chalices."

"Like your leather outfit?"

"Like my leather outfit."

I tapped the instrument panel. "And the car?"

"What can I say? My chalices are generous people." Carmen gestured toward the latch on the portfolio's flap. "I asked the Araneum to send me what they had concerning vampire-hunter attacks in America."

I pulled out several manila folders and flipped open the first one, a document in a language I didn't recognize, followed by what appeared to be an English translation.

"What language is this?"

"Romanian," Carmen answered, "the native tongue of Transylvania. You'll need to become familiar with it."

I read the English translation. "It says that ten vampire deaths have been attributed to these *vânätori de vampir.* On a path that started in New York and ended in Denver."

I upended another envelope and a bunch of color photographs clipped together fell into my hand. A sticky note on the top photo read that these were photos of the *vânätori* pursuing us. On the back of each picture was the name of the man depicted.

The first picture. Mihail Vasile. A thin face, hungry eyes peering from under strands of hair, as if he were a shrew trying to hide in his own skin.

The second picture. Teodor Vlasov. A round, bearded

face, less a head than a hairy bowling ball perched upon a thick neck. I remembered him—he was the sniper who had killed Dr. Wong and was one of the two attackers who had dragged Bob out of the Buick.

Next. Petru Codreanu. A slightly lesser version of Vlasov, but with an equally fierce expression. Close-set eyes that seemed to flicker anxiously even in this frozen image.

Finally. Nicolae Dragan. An apt name for their leader. Eyes that burned at me from the paper. As I studied his image, his presence became so powerful that I expected an aura to radiate from the photo. In his beard and close-cropped, steely-gray scalp, he looked like a zealous mob boss, the kind who would incite a lynching and supply the rope. Dragan was the one who had come after me with a crucifix and an ax, and then more recently blasted Bob with a shotgun.

"Look familiar?" Carmen asked.

"Most definitely. All four of these scary bastards." I slid the photos back in the envelope, relieved at shutting the psychic connection.

I turned to a folder marked "History of Colorado Attacks." I read the first entry aloud. "Three vampires were allegedly killed by *vânători* in 1883, two around Leadville, the third at Central City."

"Wasn't our guys," Carmen said. "We're dealing with mortals. Those hunters would have died long ago."

I continued. "The next attack occurred in 1969." My thoughts froze on the date. I opened the folder labeled "Attacks in the 20th Century." "There were several vampire killings from 1910 through the mid-twenties. Then nothing until 1947."

I could feel my aura sparkle in alarm. Reaching into my pocket, I retrieved the paper Wendy had given me. I compared her list of nymphomania outbreaks with this record of vampire murders. "Roswell, New Mexico, 1947—nympho-mania and two vampires killed. Dayton, Ohio, 1952—nym-phomania and two vampires killed." I paused to control my quaking, excited voice. "Denver, 1969—nymphomania and *three* vampires killed. Now recently, another outbreak of nymphomania in Denver followed by the appearance of *vânâtori de vampir*. In every case, the vampire-hunter at-tacks followed the discovery of nymphomania by mere weeks, sometimes days."

We reached Highway 36. Carmen whipped the Audi around the corner. The tires squealed across the asphalt. I grabbed my shoulder harness. We cut in front of a semi. The driver blasted his air horn. Smiling, Carmen straightened the steering wheel and floored the gas pedal. The turbo-charger kicked in and the Audi zoomed west toward Denver.

"You keep driving like that," I said, looking back at the driver as he flipped us the bird, "and we won't need any vampire hunters to finish us off."

"Sorry," Carmen replied dryly. "I like to drive the way I like to have sex. You know, turbo-banging." She patted my knee. "You okay, grandpa?"

I clasped her wrist. "Don't test me."

Carmen grinned and tugged free. She raced the Audi around a minivan. "So the vampire attacks and the nym-phomania are related?"

"Have to be. There's too much coincidence. The question is, what happened in Roswell in 1947?"

"What's the date?"

"Of the nymphomania?" I perused Wendy's list. "July seventh, ninth, and sixteen."

Carmen reacted with a startled "No shit?" She pulled up the hem of her jacket and fumbled with the belt of her leather jeans. "I can tell you exactly what happened on July third of that year. The debris of a flying-saucer was found on the MacBrazel Ranch, near Roswell."

"How would you know that?" I asked, wondering why she struggled to undress.

As Carmen tilted her muscled abdomen toward me, she brushed her left hip against the bottom rim of the steering wheel. She displayed a *Star Trek* insignia tattooed below her navel. "As a Trekker, I'm up on all UFO lore."

I examined the tattoo. "Interesting way of remembering something. I would've just tied a string around my finger."

Carmen buckled her pants again. "Do any of those dates mean something to your investigation?"

I thought for a moment. "Rocky Flats started operations in 1952, the same year there was an outbreak of nymphomania in Ohio. I don't see a connection. Then in 1969, there was a plutonium fire at Rocky Flats, the so-called Mother's Day Fire."

Carmen took Wendy's list and flattened it across the spokes of the steering wheel. "That outbreak of nymphomania in Denver occurred shortly afterwards—in May, June, and July. When did the vampire-hunter attacks happen?"

I glanced into the folder. "August and September."

Carmen folded Wendy's list and handed it back to me. During a long moment of silence, she gradually tightened her fingers around the rim. Her knuckles turned white. She pressed harder on the gas pedal. "What is it about the nymphomania that draws the vampire hunters?"

I shrugged, embarrassed by my ignorance and inability to connect the facts. "I don't know."

Carmen passed a Corvette. "Let me check the dates. Maybe I can find something useful."

"Call when you do. In the meantime, I can do more than wait around Denver with my thumb up my butt." I tucked the folders back into the portfolio. "Give me twenty-four hours."

"Twenty-four hours for what?"

"I need twenty-four hours to complete my investigation.

At the end of that time I'll either be available for your direct action or I'll be dead."

Carmen eased off the gas. The speedometer needle arced down past a hundred miles an hour. "Dead? Killed by whom? Vampire hunters?"

I shook my head solemnly. "No, worse. The guards at Rocky Flats."

CHAPTER
25

I TURNED OFF HIGHWAY 93 for the entrance to Rocky Flats. At this time in the afternoon there was a line of cars heading in the opposite direction, going home. I was the only one coming in.

Low, dense clouds from an oncoming storm threatened the Front Range. The forecast called for an evening blizzard. Already, intermittent flakes of snow floated from the sky.

I continued past the administrative trailer complex where I worked and parked in the lot adjacent to the plant manager's office.

The Protected Area stood one hundred meters to the east. A Humvee with a machine gun mounted on the roof was parked outside the gate. Within the fence perimeter remained the white trailer, the same one Gilbert Odin suspected contained the cargo that had caused the nymphomania. Guards in sage-green parkas and armed with submachine guns walked the fence. A black semi-tractor truck backed up to the white trailer. Workers in heavy overalls and yellow safety helmets motioned to one another as they guided the truck into position. More Humvees and a row of white Suburbans were parked on the road leading from the Protected Area. It seemed that the trailer was going to move out tonight by convoy, regardless of the anticipated blizzard.

My plan was simple. I was going to get answers directly from Herbert Hoover Merriweather, the plant manager. If Merriweather wouldn't share what he knew with Gilbert Odin, Merriweather would have no choice but to cooperate with me once I put him under vampire hypnosis. Then I'd wait for the gloom of night to stalk and subdue the guards, hypnotizing them one by one until I could penetrate the Protected Area, break into the trailer, and expose the secret behind the conspiracy. Hopefully I wouldn't contaminate myself and the Denver metroplex in the process.

I no longer had the luxury of subtlety. Gilbert would have to deal with the consequences of my trampling over DOE's security rules. I'd tell him what I discovered, he would pay my fee, and I'd disappear into the vampire underground to lend my fangs in the fight against the *vânätori de vampir.*

Cracking my knuckles, I prepared myself for the unexpected. Nothing would surprise me tonight. To the attacker goes the initiative.

Flipping up the collar of my barn coat, I turned off the car motor and adjusted my knit cap. I clipped my ID badge to my coat, got out of my Dodge, and tread carefully across the icy sidewalk to the front door.

Past the second set of glass doors, a guard stood in the lobby. He wore full combat regalia, black webbed harness over a gray camouflaged uniform, a holstered pistol, extra ammo, and a gas mask strapped to his thigh. To his right, between the manager's office and myself, stood another guard. Besides a pistol, he was armed with an HK submachine gun slung over his shoulder.

Both guards stood taller and more alert when I came in and stamped snow from my boots. They glared at me, no doubt suspicious of why I wore sunglasses on a dark, snowy afternoon.

The first guard read my badge. "What's your business here?"

"Merriweather paged me."

The second guard stroked the forestock of his submachine gun. "You'll have to see him later. He isn't available."

The second guard took a position behind his comrade. Neither of them stood more than ten feet away from me, and their eyes stared into mine. Perfect.

"Then please give this message to him." Carefully, so as to not provoke the guards, I removed my sunglasses.

The closest guard's aura flared with alarm. His eyes opened wide and bugged out. "Holy—" He froze in mid-cry.

The second guard stepped back. His aura flashed bright. The two of them stood motionless like a pair of mannequins.

I didn't know how long I'd be with Merriweather, so I would have to fang the guards to keep them quiet. I bit them and dragged their limp bodies to an empty office and shut the door.

I put my sunglasses on again and approached the thick door to Merriweather's office. My vampire hearing caught him murmuring on the phone. He hung up.

Remembering that his desk was to the left, I opened the door, entered, and turned, locking the door before I released the knob.

Merriweather sat behind that wooden barricade he called a desk. His dark complexion matched the leather of his high-backed executive's chair. His squat, square-shaped head looked as if it had been screwed into the collar of his off-white turtleneck sweater.

He gasped when he saw me and immediately fumbled

with a drawer. I reached for my sunglasses to subdue him.

Merriweather pointed a SIG-Sauer 9mm pistol at me. "Don't move."

My hand stopped where it barely touched the glasses. "Careful now. That's not a stapler you're holding."

His thumb released the safety catch. "How'd you get in?"

"I walked." I wiggled my fingers to signal that I wanted to remove my sunglasses. "May I? It's dark in here."

"I said don't move, wise-ass." Merriweather shouted, "Security." He scowled and repeated, "Security."

When he realized that no one was coming, his expression tightened, and his finger curled on the trigger. "What did you do to my guards?"

"Sang them a lullaby."

The cell phone in my pocket buzzed and vibrated against my keys. Merriweather flinched but kept his gaze and the muzzle of the SIG-Sauer trained on me. "Don't answer."

"I don't intend to."

Merriweather glowered. After my cell phone stopped buzzing, he reached for the phone on his desk. In the instant he turned his eyes from me, I would fling off the sunglasses and zap him.

He hesitated from dialing his phone and squinted at me. "Step back. Keep your hands where they are."

My cell phone buzzed again.

"You're a popular man," he groused. Merriweather waited impassively until the buzzing stopped and diverted his eyes to his phone. I took my sunglasses off.

He flipped his gaze back to me. "I told you not to move. What the—"

The whites of his eyes looked like two enameled disks against his purple-black complexion. His shoulders jerked back, and his finger clutched the trigger. The SIG-Sauer fired. I ducked and broke focus with Merriweather's eyes before I could control him.

He dropped behind his desk, his aura so agitated with panic that it left a trail of sparks in the air.

I lay prone on the floor, supported by my fingertips and toes. I crawled toward the desk, quiet as a tarantula.

He groped for his phone, pulled it off his desk, and jabbed the buttons. The phone cord hung off the side of the desk close to me. I wrapped my hand around the cord and yanked. The phone jerked free, thumped against his side of the desk, and whipped over my head. The phone crashed into the floor, breaking into pieces.

Nervous gulps betrayed his location on the other side of the desk. I circled to the right.

My cell phone buzzed again. Now he knew where I was.

Merriweather's aura surged over the desk above my head, giving me enough of a warning to get ready. He lunged over me, leading with his pistol. He fired two wild shots into the carpet. I grabbed his hand and hooked my index finger behind his to block the trigger from moving again.

I stood and faced him. I twisted his arm. Our eyes met again. Merriweather froze in terror.

I grinned. "Boo."

He went, "Uh," and then relaxed, dazed, open-mouthed.

I grasped the SIG-Sauer by the barrel, unwrapped his fingers from the grip and took the pistol. His hand slowly dropped until it thumped against the desk. I slipped the gun into the pocket of my barn coat.

Holding his hand, I pushed him until he plopped back into his chair. I kept our gazes fixed and walked around the desk. His sleepy hooded eyes followed mine.

My fingers tingled. We were being watched. "Merriweather, is there a video camera?"

He pointed weakly to his right and whispered, "On the top shelf."

Security must have seen us. They were bound to come in here, guns blazing. I needed to plan an escape.

"Where's the video feed?"

"Over there." He gestured to a cabinet on his right.

A private system? "And the audio pickup?"

Merriweather touched the tape dispenser.

"None of this is hooked up to Central Security?" I asked.

"No."

"Why?"

He managed a tired chuckle. "The first rule of DOE. Cover your own ass well."

This was good news. The cavalry wasn't coming. Still, I had to destroy any evidence of my vampire persona. I held his hands and massaged the webs between his thumbs and forefingers.

"Close your eyes."

He did. After several deep breaths, Merriweather's head tipped to the left. His aura swirled slowly around him like the water in a smooth-running brook. I let go of his hands.

Plaques and photos from his navy career lined the top shelf. A black ball the size of an orange rested on the far end. I got up on my toes to examine the sphere of dark, translucent plastic. It sat on a round base. Barely discernible inside was a tiny video camera. A thin cable ran from the back of the ball to the gap between the shelf and the wall. I followed the cable down the wall to where it fit through a hole in the top of a cabinet. Kneeling, I pulled the cabinet doors. Locked.

I rested my knee against the cabinet for leverage and pulled hard, calling on preternatural strength. The handles dug into my fingers. I pulled harder. My strength didn't materialize. Frustrated, I examined my hands, wondering how much of my power I had lost.

I retrieved Merriweather's 9mm from my pocket and aimed at the lock. If no one had heard the previous three shots, then I should be okay. I fired. The bullet smashed into the lock, and the doors bounced open.

Inside the cabinet on the top shelf lay a Sony video recorder with a fresh bullet crease across the top of the case. The red recording light was still illuminated. Under the recorder stood rows of videotapes, each labeled with a date scribbled with a marking pen. I put the pistol back in my pocket, pressed the recorder's stop button, and ejected the tape.

A shredder rested over the top of Merriweather's garbage can. I yanked the tape from the cassette and fed the tape into the shredder, watching shiny black confetti dump into the garbage.

I turned to Merriweather. I studied his neck the way a chef would a cutlet. My fangs extended. After putting him in deep hypnosis, I was going to probe his mind and scrape out every detail he knew about the nymphomania and the cargo in the trailer.

My cell phone vibrated again. Annoyed, I pulled it out of my pocket and read the display.

It was Wendy. Had all the calls been hers? Four calls in less than ten minutes, what was the urgency?

Merriweather looked peaceful. I had time to answer Wendy and then fang him.

I put the phone to my ear. "Yeah, Wendy?"

A man's voice growled. "Felix Gomez, you shit from Satan, listen to this." His words carried a pronounced accent.

Vânători. My vampire senses went on alert.

Wendy screamed. "Felix, it's a trap. Don't—"

The phone bumped against something, and the man spoke again. "You want to save this witch? Then come get her, *vampir.* At the Soda Creek Wrecking Yard in Evergreen."

"Hold on. Where?"

"You heard me. You have two hours," he snapped and hung up.

CHAPTER
26

THE DILEMMA SQUEEZED MY head as if I were caught in a vise. Either stay and solve the conspiracy, while Wendy died a horrible death. Or, rescue her and lose the chance of finding out what remained hidden in the white trailer.

I was close to unraveling the conspiracy. The trailer waited a hundred meters away. A memo on Merriweather's desk stated that they would leave as soon as tonight's storm passed, which was forecast for three A.M. All I had to do was find out what was inside the trailer and this assignment was as good as over. Thankfully.

Except now the vampire hunters had Wendy. Why had they taken her? Because I had escaped from their trap twice and rather than chase me again, they offered her as the bait I couldn't refuse.

Time ticked past, as tangible as the air I breathed. Closing my eyes, I centered myself to stave off panic.

I massaged Merriweather's hands. His sluggish pulse quickened slightly.

"Merriweather, what's in the trailer?"

His eyelids fluttered as his mind struggled to rise through the subconscious state my hypnosis had put him in. "Red-light."

"Goddamn it, I know that." I fought the urge to shake him in frustration.

A vehicle rumbled to a halt outside on the parking lot. Two doors opened and slammed closed, followed by the crunching of heavy steps on the gravel around the building.

It was certainly more security guards. I held my breath and listened as two men entered the building and called out for Merriweather's sentries. They yelled frantically, clearly having found the guards I'd left asleep in another room.

I had run out of time to interrogate Merriweather. Dropping his hands, I clenched my fists in frustration. My hope was to escape before the guards charged in here. The safest way to flee was out the window next to the glass display case.

I stepped quietly to the window and unlocked the latch.

A guard tried the door and discovered it was locked.

I jerked the window open and pushed out the screen.

The guard kicked the door and called out, "Merri-weather—are you okay?" The guard yelled to his partner. "Call Central Security. We have an Amber Tango situation."

I sprang through the window and landed on the freshly fallen snow.

Behind me, the guard broke the door open and yelled, "I see him. He's going out to the side."

I sprinted along the wall and turned the corner. I lunged for my car's door and expected to feel a bullet claw into my back. Once inside I gunned the engine, spun the Dodge around, and headed for the plant exit. A guard ran out of the building and fired as the curtain of falling snow enveloped me.

I raced toward the plant exit, my head throbbing with anxiety. Everything about this case was one big snarl of trouble that grew more confused and desperate by the minute. Maybe I could get to Wendy and maybe I could get into the trailer, but first I had to lose these pesky guards.

Up ahead, a striped pole dropped across the exit lane along the right side of the guard shack. Red lights flashed on the pole. A guard came out of the shack and readied a submachine gun. He waved for me to stop.

Flooring the accelerator, I aimed for the pole. The guard brought the gun up to his shoulder. Just as I approached the guard shack, I veered to the left and shot out through the entrance lane on the other side of the shack. In the rearview mirror I could see the guard chasing after me, but by the time he had a clear shot I was out of range and lost in the snow. Nevertheless, I felt obliged to flip him off as I turned on the highway and headed to Evergreen.

My squeaking wipers arced through the flakes crusting my windshield. I called information for the address to the wrecking yard. Like any good private investigator, I kept local street maps under my car seat. I fished them out and alternated my attention between the icy road and searching for the address and directions to the wrecking yard.

Could I rescue Wendy and still solve this case? It was a little after five in the afternoon now. Wendy's captor had given me two hours, which meant they expected me around seven. I had ten hours at the most to drive to Evergreen through this blizzard, get Wendy, and return before the convoy left. The task seemed impossible.

The vampire hunters were waiting to ambush me, obviously. In turn, I knew where they were. And now so would all the vampires in Denver. I called Carmen.

She answered on the second ring. Her breath was labored

but relaxed. "Felix, it's you. I've just finished teaching my Butt and Gut class. Good thing you called. I found something else about the Roswell UFO."

"That can wait," I replied. "The *vânători* have captured Wendy Teagarden."

Carmen remained silent. She then spoke sharply. "When did this happen?" Anger slashed through her voice. "Where is she? How did you find out?"

"They called on her cell phone. They've got her at the Soda Creek Wrecking Yard in Evergreen."

"How could they have captured *her*?"

"I don't know."

"Where are you now?"

"Leaving Rocky Flats."

"Which means you're going after her alone?"

"Yes. Alone."

"Figures. You and that hero complex," Carmen said. "In this snow it'll be a while before the other vampires and I can meet you. We might be supernaturals but traffic makes us the equal of humans."

"I can't wait for you," I snapped.

"We'll get there as soon as we can. And, Felix, you were looking for a connection between nymphomania outbreaks and vampire-hunter attacks in New Mexico and Ohio?"

"And?"

"Do you remember that the recent outbreaks and attacks started after a UFO crashed in Roswell?"

I zoomed around a van. "Maybe we could go over this later."

"Give me a minute. The remains of the UFO and its crew were moved from Roswell to Wright-Patterson Air Force Base, just outside Dayton, Ohio, the second location of the nymphomania."

I eased off the accelerator. "What year?"

"Nineteen forty-seven. Then in 1952, the year when

nymphomania and vampire attacks surfaced in Ohio, that was when the UFO was moved again."

"Where to?"

"I don't know," she answered.

"You just said 1952."

"So what?"

"That's the year Rocky Flats became operational," I said. The image of the white trailer in the Protected Area flooded my mind. The disjointed details and facts about this case swirled about me like a cloud. Dr. Wong and his sudden trips to Area 51. The red mercury. The outbreaks of nymphomania. It all sounded too crazy to be true.

"Where did you get this info? And if you say the Internet, then you're wasting my time."

"No, it was from a vampire in Ohio. She worked as a civilian secretary for the air force back in the fifties. She claims that she heard about an extraterrestrial biological entity. An alien."

Alien? Was that the mysterious cargo in the trailer? A UFO? The infamous Roswell UFO?

"Felix, you there?"

"Yeah, I'm here." I accelerated again.

"You still going after Wendy?"

"Yes." My confusion coalesced into murderous determination. The vampire hunters would have to die. Then I would return to Rocky Flats and break into the trailer. I gave Carmen directions to the wrecking yard. "Get there as soon as you can."

"Be careful, Felix." She hung up.

By the time I had driven up the mountain on the interstate and taken the Evergreen exit, I had less than nine hours. Up here at altitude, the storm was a cascade of quarter-sized snowflakes. My vampire vision couldn't penetrate the blizzard much deeper than human eyesight. The vague shapes of buildings flanked the road. Ice caked my windshield-wiper blades. Hot air whooshed out the heater vents and kept my Dodge a warm metal cocoon.

My car crawled along at twenty miles an hour. Whenever I tried to speed up, the Dodge yawed across the road. Better to creep along at this pace than spin into a ravine.

A dim red traffic light hovered above the road. Lines of snow in the gray air outlined the pole holding the traffic light. A green rectangle smudged with snow hung from a cable. The sign said Byrant. I turned right, passing a NO OUTLET sign, and followed the road winding up the hillside.

To the left, behind a snow-encrusted chain-link fence, construction equipment looked like giant prehistoric beasts hunkered down for the winter. Down to the right, oblong cylinders of natural-gas tanks lay nestled together under a blanket of snow. A vacant two-story building loomed on the left. The road curved to the right, past rows of storage sheds.

Up ahead, a plywood sign rested against a telephone pole. Snow trickled down the spray-painted scrawl: Soda Creek Wrecking Yard.

My tires abruptly spun. The transmission whined. My Dodge slowed. I dropped into first and nudged the gas. The rear tires spun again. The car slid to the right and then backwards.

The hill was too steep. This was as far as I would get on wheels. I turned the steering to straighten the Dodge and let it settle with a thump against a pile of rocks marking the edge of the shoulder.

The heavy snowfall turned the glow of the street lamps into orbs of hazy luminescence. In the diffused light, a wire fence materialized in the haze of the snowfall. Scattered behind the fence were derelict cars and a tow truck. At the far perimeter of the yard stood a simple, prefab metal building with a pitched roof.

I searched for auras betraying the presence of humans lurking behind cover. Nothing. This place was lifeless as my refrigerator. And about as cold. I rubbed my hands in the hot air blasting from the vents and tried to absorb as much heat as I could.

My watch said 6:43. Time to move. I turned off the car's motor and tugged my knit cap low on my forehead. I pulled Merriweather's SIG-Sauer out of my pocket and checked the magazine. I had plenty left for the four vampire hunters. Those I didn't shoot and kill outright, I'd finish off with my fangs. My *kundalini noir* coiled expectantly, relishing the thrill of impending violence. Stepping out of the car, I stashed my keys and the pistol in the pocket of my barn coat. I cinched my gloves. My boots crunched into the snow. The sound sent a shiver up my back to remind me how much we vampires hated these frigid temperatures. A chilly dankness was okay, but this cold was bitter enough to freeze me into a big Popsicle.

The snow fell with a hiss. Halfway to the wrecking yard, I turned around to get my bearings. Snow an inch deep already covered my car's windshield.

My fingertips tingled. I sensed I was being detected but not watched, as if some force were tapping into the energy of my aura. Perhaps it was Wendy, there was much about her I didn't know.

How to sneak into the building? I could transform into a wolf. The fur would keep me warmer. But at some point I'd have to transform back into a vampire and then I'd be naked. The cold was barely tolerable in these garments. Without them, I'd frost over in minutes.

A strand of razor wire ran atop the fence. Hooking my gloved fingers into the fence, I swung my legs up. I balanced on top of the fence, then hopped between the spiraled strands of the razor wire and dropped to the ground. I should have floated but my vampire levitation powers were all but gone. Perfect.

My legs flexed to absorb the impact. The SIG-Sauer

sagged within my pocket. Now, inside the perimeter of the wire, my ears and fingertips tingled in alarm. This was the right place. The vampire hunters were here.

My fangs extended. My fingers curled in anticipation at clawing flesh and breaking bones. My vision turned red. I wanted more than to spill the blood of my enemies; I wanted to taste it even if I wouldn't drink it. So what if I had weakened powers—I also had the SIG-Sauer.

I crouched behind a Ford Galaxy resting on cinder blocks and examined the building's stained, corrugated metal surface. Piled against the back wall were jumbles of acetylene gas bottles, workbenches, a lathe, broken office chairs, and stacks of wheels. The relentless snowfall added to the bleakness of the yard. In the center of the building, a garage bay door faced me. Windows flanked the door. I hoped they had heat inside.

I hunched my shoulders and tightened my scarf. My fingers began to go numb. I hadn't expected to linger in the snow like this or I would've dressed in heavier clothes.

I zigzagged, creeping, through the yard to the bay door. My ears buzzed, warning of danger. Somehow I sensed that my aura was being probed. But how? Humans had no tools to detect the supernatural.

I halted next to the rusted hulk of a Studebaker. I scanned the roofline and telephone poles and tried to discern anything that looked like a video camera. Nothing.

I approached the bay door and pressed my ear to its surface. From inside drifted the soft murmur of a woman's whimper—Wendy.

I clasped the door handle to jerk it open and then stopped. This door wouldn't open quickly, if at all, and not without causing a racket. There was the window to my right. I'd break through that and rush in.

I looked through the dirty glass and scanned the interior. Anybody inside was tucked out of sight.

I lifted a car wheel from the snow and swung it toward the window. Grasping the SIG-Sauer, I leapt after the wheel as it smashed through the panes. I held my hands in front of my face to ward off the glass shards.

I skidded off a desk, knocked over a stack of notebook binders, and tumbled to the floor. It reeked of dust and grease. Two burning auras rushed from the gloom in opposite directions.

As I sprang to my hands and knees, a stiff heavy bar whacked my back. Pain blasted through my spine. Falling to my knees, I clawed the air and dropped the pistol. I barely managed to turn my head to the left to view that attacker.

An aura of hate outlined his beefy mass. He swung a length of rebar and hit me again along the small of my back. A lightning bolt of pain shot down my legs. I convulsed and choked.

From my right, a pole with a thick, open hoop on the end like a set of jaws reached toward my neck. My nostrils flared at the metallic smell. Silver. I grasped the pole but the shaft slid through my weakened grip until the hoop closed around my neck. The silver burned the bare skin of my throat. I gagged in pain.

A tall, bearded man twisted the pole so that the silver hoop singed and choked me. His scowling face matched the photograph of Nicolae Dragan, the *vânători* leader. The pain and panic kept me from focusing a vampire stare upon him. I fought to stop the agony by jamming my gloved hands under the silver hoop.

Dragan leaned over me and twisted the pole to keep the silver metal hoop pressed against my bare skin.

I writhed on the floor like a fish gaffed in the gills. I groped for the SIG-Sauer.

"Petru," Dragan yelled instructions to the other vampire hunter, who kicked the pistol from my reach. Petru grasped my right arm and kicked his heavy boot into my armpit. A spasm of excruciating pain shot across my torso and paralyzed me. My arm went limp. Petru looped a steel chain around my wrists and neck, then fastened me to a heavy metal pipe that he laid across my shoulders. He secured the chain to the ends of the pipe with steel padlocks.

Dragan pulled up on the pole, burning the bottom of my jaw, and forced me to get to my knees.

Petru grasped a steel cable and carabiner hanging from the ceiling. He snapped the cable to the pipe at a spot right behind my head.

The silver hoop around my neck opened, and Dragan pulled the pole away. I gasped in relief, light-headed with pain.

Dragan palmed a hand control at the end of an electrical cord dangling from the ceiling. He pressed a button. A winch whined from above and tightened the slack in the cable. The pipe lifted. The chain squeezed around my wrists. My shoulders were wrenched upward. Dragan kept raising the pipe until I danced on tiptoes, crucified. Sickened by waves of pain, I hung my head and retched, tasting bile and blood.

Dragan whisked the knit cap off my head. He grabbed my hair and slapped my face, hard enough to blur my vision. "Show your fangs now, spawn of Satan. Soon I'll have them in my hand and I'll be kicking your severed head out into the snow."

CHAPTER 27

I HUNG FROM THE steel bar. Rallying strength, I narrowed my eyes to focus my gaze and hypnotize Dragan.

He made a chopping motion. Petru whacked the rebar against my back. The blow was a thunderclap of pain. My legs gave out and I slumped against my restraints. The chain around my neck choked me.

Dragan waved Petru away. "I know about your hypnotic powers, *vampir*. Behave yourself or your last hours will be worse than any nightmare."

Petru stepped back into the edge of the musty shadows and picked up a sawed-off shotgun. His big hands caressed the wooden stock.

Gasping, I struggled to my feet. The haze of pain receded and my eyes looked to the other side of the garage bay.

Wendy lay on the floor where she had been gagged with

duct tape. Her hands were chained and locked together. The left sleeve of her purple scrubs had been torn loose and exposed a bloody bandage that clung to her arm. Her green aura radiated danger. Another of the *vânätori* in a plaid shirt and denim overalls held the loose end of another chain wound around her neck.

I strained against my steel yoke and motioned toward Wendy. "Let her go. You have me."

A dirty leer compressed the wrinkles on Dragan's bearded cheeks. His red aura pulsed with lust. "It's good to know that even vampires have this kind of weakness. You made it easy for us."

His leer turned into a scowl. "And what kind of a creature is *she*?" Dragan's hands grasped the chain around my neck and dug the steel links into my throat. "She's no vampire. Not like you, anyway."

I gasped to catch my breath, frustrated that I was unable to tear out his jugular with my teeth. "She's human. Of no threat to you."

"Human?" Dragan tightened the chain. "She has black powers. Before we subdued her with this"—he brandished a yellow plastic Taser gun—"she threw a liquid on Mihail, turned him into a frog, and then stepped on him." Dragan's voice hardened. "She stepped on him."

"Too bad it wasn't you," I said. "I'd love to scrape you off my shoe."

Dragan straightened up. His aura brightened and telegraphed violence. Anticipating the blow, I tensed my neck. He lashed out with the Taser. The plastic gun smashed my nose. Pain shot across my face, and blood seeped from my nostrils.

The blood trickled over my lip and dried. Dragan studied the blood and pinched the flakes between his fingers. The flakes crumbled into powder. He wiped his fingers on my coat lapel. "Even your blood is inhuman."

Dragan shoved the Taser into the pocket of his jacket. He snapped his fingers. "Teodor."

Wendy's guard yanked on her tether and kicked her in the side. I yelled and cursed at them to stop. Teodor snatched a police baton from his belt. He touched a switch on the handle and blue sparks crackled from the business end. He reached for Wendy's face and ripped off the tape covering her mouth. She winced in pain and cried out, "Felix, forget me. Save yourself."

Teodor tapped Wendy's bare arm with the baton. "Shut up, witch." The end of the baton sizzled against her skin. Wendy writhed and screamed. Her green aura flashed agony.

"Let her go," I screamed. "She's innocent."

"Innocent?" Dragan asked. "She's a demon like you, Felix."

Hearing Dragan say my name made this violation ever more personal. I lunged for him and managed just a few inches before the chain gouged deep into my throat.

Dragan grinned smugly. "Go ahead and struggle. You'll only die tired."

Though roiling with anger, I decided to save my strength for an opportunity to escape and rescue Wendy. I relented and let my body sag against the restraints as I took in the surroundings.

To my left, hot air radiated from the burner fixed atop the propane tank of a space heater. A plywood table flanked the space heater. On the table rested an ornate brass crucifix, a large leather-bound Bible, and a bowl filled with dark liquid, all surrounded by lit votive candles. At the far end of the table lay a heavy mallet and a thick wooden stake, both obviously meant for me.

Petru handed Dragan the SIG-Sauer automatic.

"A vampire with a gun?" Dragan asked. "Don't trust your fangs?"

"Come closer and find out."

"Let me show you a trick about your fangs." Dragan placed the pistol on the table. He picked up the bowl and held it before me. The thick liquid in the bowl smelled like human blood. In the blood floated two long pointed incisors. Vampire fangs. Wisps of my orange aura pulled toward the teeth, and I could feel the attraction.

"How did we know you were coming? *This* is how." Dragan swayed from side to side with the bowl. No matter how he turned, the sharp tips of the fangs followed me. I'd never seen this before. The fangs keyed on my aura.

Being human, Dragan couldn't see the effect on my aura. He gave me a quizzical look. "I don't understand how it works, only that it's based on legend. The teeth float aimlessly on the blood but as soon as one of you *vampir* approaches, they line up like these do." His gaze lifted from the bowl to me. "With this secret I have the means to pry all of you demons out of the shadows and into the light of God's justice. There will be no hole dark enough to hide you now."

His eyes sparkled malevolently. "It's ironic, what you vampires are most proud of is that which betrays you. These belonged to the accursed one I shot and pulled from your car."

"Bob." The name slipped from my mouth. I growled at Dragan and snarled until the chain around my neck gagged me.

Dragan remained safely out of reach. He gestured over his shoulder to the far side of the garage. "Your girlfriend donated the blood."

I fixed my gaze on the bandage over her arm. My *kundalini noir* thrashed within me. I whipped about in rage, heaving against the chains, struggling to bend the steel pipe fastened to my wrists and neck. Sweat sprayed from my face. My aura burned with a defiant radiance. I tugged and fought until I had barely enough strength to hang from the pipe and mutter, "You monsters."

"Us? Monsters?" Dragan chuckled. "You have a confused sense of morality. As for her," he tipped his head toward Wendy, "I guessed that her blood would make the attraction more powerful than human blood, and it did. I detected your presence as soon as you started up the hill. Your evil magic is your own undoing."

Dragan put the bowl aside and stepped close. "Now for the moment of truth. I'm going to examine your eyes. At the instant you try to hypnotize me, your girlfriend dies. Then you. Understood?"

Anything to keep him talking. I nodded.

Slowly, as if he were expecting me to explode, Dragan stepped closer. His breathing became shallow and nervous. His aura sizzled in near panic.

Petru tensed his grip on the shotgun. Teodor worked the switch of the baton, making it chatter and spark.

Dragan's eyes studied mine. The black orbs of his irises dilated in the center of his ice-blue pupils. I kept my hypnotic power in check. His breathing deepened and became confident. His aura smoothed as his irises shrank to pinpoints.

"You're the first that I've examined like this," he said in a muted, almost reverential tone.

"What about the other vampires you murdered?"

"Murdered? You can't murder the undead. I committed no crime. Besides, I never had time with them like I have now with you."

Dragan put his fingers on my face and spread my eyelids. He leaned close and studied my eyes. "Magnificent," he whispered. "These have transmutated completely into the eyes of a wolf. I'm going to enjoy studying them."

My fangs jutted from under my upper lip.

"Careful. Remember the girl," Dragan warned. He twisted my head toward the candles and crucifix. "You are proof that Satan exists."

"Really? *I've* never met him." I pulled my face away.

Dragan withdrew his hands. "You are cut from his cloth."

"You wanted time with me," I said. "Time for what?"

"Time to learn a few things. How many vampires are in Denver?"

"You didn't have to go to all this trouble for that answer. Hell, you could've called me and I would've told you." I made up a number. "Thirty-seven."

Dragan snapped his fingers. Teodor yanked on Wendy's chain leash, slipped the baton under the hem of her blouse and pressed it against her stomach. The baton emitted its evil cackle. Wendy gritted her teeth to keep from crying out as she convulsed and jerked on the floor.

"Stop it," I yelled.

Teodor grinned at me and raked the baton across Wendy's skin. She tensed her body to withstand the pain, then sputtered and cried out.

I yanked against the chains and hollered again.

Dragan grabbed my hair and shook my head. "Joke and your woman pays for your stupidity. We'll strip her naked, spread her legs, and jam the electric prod inside her. Understand?"

I choked down the bile welling in my throat. "Yes. Yes. Just leave her alone."

Teodor withdrew the baton. Wendy retched. She raised her head. Tears glistened on her cheeks. She avoided looking at me, and I knew that in this moment of anguish she couldn't help but blame me.

Dragan let go of my hair. "Who controls the vampires?"

"What are you talking about?"

"Who is the supreme authority?"

"No one. We're not like the army."

"Someone issues orders and you all obey. I've studied

your kind long enough to realize that vampires have resources too deep for an individual acting alone. When we
begin a campaign of cleansing, you vampires collectively
react and escape."

"Maybe in Romania, in Transylvania, vampires are more
organized than we are here. All that communism you lived
under."

"No. It's everywhere. A vampire disappears, his human
persona is listed as deceased, months later the vampire ma-
terializes in another country with a new human identity.
Documents are forged. Bribes paid. Bank accounts vanish
and reappear."

"If you're implying that there's a secret vampire society,
there is none."

Dragan tapped my forehead. "But you're wrong. I know
much about you. I even know about the spaceship."

These last words plowed through my desperation. "What
spaceship?"

"The one that crashed in Roswell and brought the sickness."

"Sickness?" I rose against the steel bar, alert and curious.

"The demonic lusting," Dragan said. "Women becoming
possessed with . . ."

I completed his thought. "Nymphomania?" Did the *vânători* hold the key to the secret behind the conspiracy at
Rocky Flats?

Dragan smiled agreeably. "Yes, you would know. The
crash of the spaceship, which your government rather clumsily tried to hush up, aroused our suspicions. What demonic
plague could come from space? Perhaps a new species of
vampires? Or something worse? The onset of the nymphomania confirmed our fears, and sure enough, we found you
bloodsuckers lurking to prey on the unfortunate victims."

"We don't need help seducing humans."

"It's more than mere seduction. At any time of human failure—war, revolution, and now this epidemic of nymphomania—you vampires circle about like vultures."

"And the spaceship?"

"We've kept vigil over the spaceship as your government moves it from place to place. Roswell . . . Ohio . . . then here. And everywhere it went, at one time or another, there was an outbreak of nymphomania."

"You said here. Where's here? Rocky Flats?"

"Of course here in Rocky Flats." Dragan's forehead wrinkled with suspicion. "Why would you ask? Don't you know?"

I just looked at him.

He grabbed my collar and repeated, "Don't you know?"

I shook my head and replied softly, "No."

"You know nothing about the spaceship?"

"Are you talking about the UFO from Roswell?"

Dragan nodded. He stared pensively at me and his eyebrows furrowed. "So you don't know about the connection between the spaceship and the nymphomania?"

"No."

He muttered something to Petru, who put the shotgun aside, turned around, and stooped into the shadows behind him. Petru picked up a shiny metal container the size of a shoe box. He cradled the container against his belly. The yellow and black warning symbol for radioactive material adorned the lid.

Dragan unsnapped the latches and opened the container. He carefully withdrew a thick glass bottle that was nestled in the black foam liner. A liquid in the bottle cast an exotic, shimmering glow, like that from a lava lamp.

Dragan held the bottle by the flange around the neck as if the contents made the glass barrel too hot to touch. He dangled the bottle before my face, close enough for me to feel the heat.

My aura turned yellow. Incredibly, every sensation was blanked out except for a pleasant warmth in my groin.

Dragan tapped my elbows. "Do you know what this is?"

"Only that it's probably radioactive."

"It's red mercury, the source of the nymphomania. This leaked from the spaceship. Dr. Wong took samples to that secret place near Las Vegas."

"You mean Area 51?"

"If that's what it's called."

Dr. Wong. The red mercury. A spaceship. Now all the clues meshed together and the conspiracy unraveled into one continuous thread. The nymphomania had been caused by the red mercury brought by the Roswell UFO. Red mercury supposedly produced by Rocky Flats. This was the mysterious material that contaminated the women.

Was this true? How could it be? Project Redlight painted the entire story as a hoax. Even Gilbert Odin dismissed the red mercury. I was energized by the need to confirm the truth. I tensed my arms against the chains but the steel links were too strong for my wrists.

Dragan returned the bottle to the box. Petru latched the cover and put the box back on the floor.

"This is all new to me," I said, feeling the warmth drain from my crotch. My aura returned to its orange color.

"Would any other vampires know?"

"No."

"Then what's your concern with Rocky Flats?"

"Because we vampires have questions of our own. Every time there's an outbreak of nymphomania you scumbags show up. None of us ever connected the outbreaks to the UFO. This news about the red mercury is a complete surprise."

Dragan crossed his arms. "Interesting." He shrugged. "And now that you finally know, too bad."

"What do you mean?"

"It means that I was planning for a long night interrogating you. But since I know more about this than you, why waste time? Petru, get the stake and mallet."

Petru grasped the items from the table.

"I thought you wanted to talk," I reminded Dragan.

"That was when I thought you had something important to share, which you don't. Now it's more useful for me to watch you die." He motioned to the table and the bowl of blood. "When I have more questions, we can easily catch another vampire."

Dragan unzipped my barn coat and took the stake from Petru. The wood reeked of buckthorn and I shrank back. The myth was that buckthorn resin burned us vampires like the most potent of acids.

Dragan cupped his hand behind my neck to hold me still while he dragged the pointed end of the stake across my shirt to the left of my sternum. He wiggled the tip into a gap in my ribs, directly over where my heart would've been. "It's time that I send you to Hell. Give my regards to Satan, you bloodsucking serpent."

CHAPTER
28

I HAD ONLY SECONDS before Dragan would hammer the stake through my rib cage. My mind clutched desperately for an opportunity to escape annihilation.

Dragan stood to my left and Petru to my right, both men even with the opposite ends of the pipe I was chained to. The slack in the overhead cable let me pivot with the pipe across my shoulders. My feet had enough purchase on the floor for me to get a strong swing. Certain that they were about to finish me, and that I had no choice but to die at their leisure, the *vânători* relaxed their guard.

Wendy and I made eye contact. Her big frightened eyes begged for help.

I'm trying, baby.

I swung the left end of the pipe toward Dragan and cracked it against his skull. His knees buckled, and he fell over the table, upending it. The candles tumbled to the floor and landed in the trash littering the room.

I immediately jabbed to the right and caught Petru across the nose. One hand came up to protect his face and the other readied the mallet to hit me. His eyebrows cinched angrily and his eyes narrowed. Our eyes locked long enough for me to hook him with vampire hypnosis.

Teodor yelled, "Don't look into his eyes"—but too late.

Teodor started for me, dragging Wendy by her chain tether. She pulled against him and kicked him across the back of one knee. His leg folded and he collapsed. The electric baton fell from his hand and clattered on the floor. She jumped on him and bashed him on the head with the steel links binding her wrists. Teodor writhed and bellowed in pain. He jerked his arm around wildly, backhanded Wendy and knocked her off him. He staggered to his feet.

I jangled my wrist chains and commanded Petru, "Undo these."

He clasped the key ring clipped to his belt loop. Blood dripped from his swollen nose. His obedient gaze remained fixed on mine. He groped for the lock on the chain and inserted the key.

"Hurry up," I said.

The chain rattled loose. My feet sank to the floor and my legs bore my entire weight. I was free. My wrists and neck ached where the links had pressed into my flesh. I snatched the mallet from Petru. "Hold still."

He did as I commanded and stood comatose before me. I walloped him on the forehead, leaving a circular imprint on the front of his skull. His face quivered, and his eyes rolled up into their sockets. He teetered like a plank and fell straight back.

Teodor was almost on me. Wendy picked herself up and lunged at him. Teodor spun about and grasped the chain around her neck. He shook her and cursed. "I'm going to kill you, demon witch."

"You first." Wendy flailed at him with kicks to his shins.

I flung the mallet at Teodor. Sharp pains zippered up my back where Petru had whaled on me with the rebar.

The mallet bounced off Teodor's skull. His head wobbled and he fell toward Wendy as if they were going to embrace.

Dragan lay next to my feet. I reached around him, picked up my pistol where it had fallen and took aim at Teodor's back.

I couldn't risk shooting him without endangering Wendy. At this range, the bullets would go straight through him and into her. Grasping Teodor by his collar, I smacked him on the temple with the butt of the SIG-Sauer. His eyes bugged out. He gasped and went slack. Wendy released her hold and backed away to let Teodor slam face first against to the floor.

I scrambled to find the keys on Teodor's belt and opened the locks on Wendy's chains.

She kicked the unconscious Teodor in the head. "*Sayonara*, you son of a bitch."

Fire burst from under the table and a wave of smoke rolled against the ceiling.

I pulled Wendy away. "Teodor will get his later." Together we moved for the front door and cupped our hands over our mouths to filter the smoke. The ache in my back cramped my right side and I limped beside Wendy.

A gunshot boomed, then again, and again. Dragan lay prone by the space heater. He jerked the trigger of a revolver and sprayed the air with bullets.

Shoving Wendy toward the door, I drew my pistol up and loosed one round at Dragan.

I missed.

But the bullet ruptured the propane tank of the space heater. A fiery blast knocked Wendy and me onto our backs. The SIG-Sauer bounced out of my grasp. Smoke swallowed us. Flames licked my skin. I didn't want to die. Not now.

Not roasted like a chicken. Both of us scrambled onto our bellies and crawled through the acrid smoke, bumping against the walls and furniture until we found the front door. We rose to our feet, staggered outside, and sucked in the clean, cold night air. Heavy snowflakes from the blizzard melted on our skin. The pain in my back ebbed and I hobbled alongside Wendy.

We scooted clumsily across the icy snow to the corner at the right and started down the hill. A mound of snow covered my Dodge.

Wendy folded her arms tight across her chest and hunched her shoulders to keep warm. A plume of vapor trailed from her mouth. Her flimsy scrubs didn't offer much protection from the chill.

I took the keys out of my pocket and peeled off my barn coat. I offered it to Wendy. Without breaking stride, she shoved her arms into the sleeves.

Behind us, flames and smoke poured out of the garage. The three *vânători* crawled, wheezing and coughing, out the back door and into the fenced lot behind the garage.

"Damn, these guys are as hard to kill as cockroaches," I said, feeling the threat of danger return. I wished I hadn't lost the SIG-Sauer.

We reached my car and both of us raked snow off the windshield.

"So what's the plan, Felix?" Wendy asked. "We lead Carmen and the other vampires here to finish these guys off, right?"

"No." I paused to catch my breath. The frigid night air scratched the inside of my throat. "We go to Rocky Flats."

Wendy stopped brushing the snow. "What?"

I dug ice from the door lock with my keys. "I need to confirm what Dragan said about the nymphomania."

"You mean his story about a spaceship?"

"Not just any spaceship—It's the UFO from Roswell.

Didn't you notice how my aura changed colors from the red mercury?"

"I thought it was a trick." Wendy resumed brushing away the snow. "What at Rocky Flats will prove that?"

"They're hiding something in the trailer bound for New Mexico."

She stopped again. "The UFO?"

"We'll see."

Dragan stumbled to the fence. He was a good hundred feet away, yet too close.

I yanked the driver's door open. Snow cascaded over the interior. "Hurry. Get in."

A shot rang out, a dull thud through the hiss of the snowfall.

Something stabbed me in the small of my back. An unbelievably fierce pain, followed by an overwhelming weakness, forced me to my knees.

Dragan clung to the fence with one hand, his other hand jerking the revolver. *Click, click, click.*

Wendy rushed around the front of the Dodge and cried out, "Felix."

Blood seeped down my skin against the inside of my shirt. I paused to gather strength to stand up and hand her the keys. "You'll have to drive."

"Where did you get hit?"

I took a baby step toward the car. "It's nothing a vampire can't handle. By the time we get down the mountain, I'll be fine."

She nudged me through the driver's door. I crawled over the center console and unfolded myself in the passenger's seat. Every movement was an exercise in agony. Turning my head to hide any expression of pain, I leaned against the door and hugged myself to fight the cold. Lucky shot on Dragan's part. And lousy luck on mine. I was hurt bad and getting worse. I should've felt my recuperative powers kick in—I'd been shot before—but this time I felt nothing but pain and a draining weakness.

Wendy let the Dodge coast backwards for a few feet then turned the front toward the bottom of the hill. She twisted the ignition key and the engine cranked over immediately. Good old DieHard battery.

Our breaths fogged the windows. Wendy rubbed her hand against the inside of the windshield to clear away the condensation. She flipped the heater switch to maximum.

I wiped the lower corner of the passenger window and peered at the exterior mirror. In the reflection, Dragan and the other two *vânätori* grew smaller and smaller.

Wendy drove faster. At the intersection at the bottom of the hill we slid through the traffic signal.

I motioned to the left. "That way."

Wendy skidded the Dodge through the turn. Suddenly, the streetlights went dark. It seemed as if doom had found us.

"Aw hell," Wendy said. "Ice must've snapped the power lines."

The swirling mush of snow swallowed the beams of our headlamps. The world around us was dark as ink. Wendy pulled tight against the steering wheel to bring her face close to the windshield. "Even with my vision I can't see where the road is."

The Dodge drifted to the right. Wendy turned the wheel but the car continued to veer off the road. She pumped the brakes. The tires bounced over the edge of the pavement. We rolled off the shoulder of the road, smacked against a guardrail, and stalled the engine.

I jostled against the inside of the door. Pain burned through me as if my guts had been set afire. For the first time in my existence, I welcomed the thought of death, if for nothing else than to free me of this agony.

She restarted the car but the rear wheels spun uselessly.

"Shit." Wendy rested her forehead against the top of the

steering wheel. "Well, at least no one's shooting at us." She turned to me. "You all right?"

Blood pooled under my hips. The touch of death felt cold. My teeth chattered uncontrollably.

"Oh, God. Felix, your aura."

I uncurled my fingers. The fading, trembling glow emanating from my hands resembled a match flame about to go out. I was too weak to panic as death embraced me.

Wendy unbuttoned my flannel shirt and slid her hand down along my torso. She withdrew her hand. The skin glistened with blood that turned into flakes. "Oh, Felix," she groaned, "it was only a bullet wound. Why aren't you healing?"

"I've been losing my powers."

"Why? How?"

"I don't know. Contamination from the nymphos? Something from the Iraq War?" I left the last option unspoken: Or maybe because I wouldn't drink human blood.

"We can't stay here all night." Wendy gripped the barn coat tight across her chest and hustled out of the car. She tramped through the snow and opened my door. "There's a building down the hill. We can take shelter there so we won't freeze to death."

I wouldn't live long enough to freeze to death.

She braced my arm over her shoulder and led me down the slope through the snowdrifts toward a shadowy rectangle, which, as we got closer, turned into a large shed.

Her efforts became futile. The feeling of hopelessness gave way to a new sensation, a sadness as I resigned myself to death.

We approached a door and peeked through the small window. Inside, saddles and other riding tack lay heaped about. Wendy tried the doorknob and discovered it was locked.

She turned away from the door. Snow fell across her

face. "There must be a house close by, but in this mess we could walk right past and never see it. Well, let's improvise." She balled the sleeve of the barn coat around her fist and smashed the window. Reaching through the broken glass, Wendy popped the door open. The place stank of horse sweat and manure. She pulled me along. My legs barely managed to carry me inside.

Wendy kicked over a stack of tarps and horse blankets and had me lie on top of the smelly mound. I held my side and stretched my legs while she draped a musty blanket over me.

My vision dimmed. My fingers and toes went numb. "Thanks for trying," I whispered, "but the end is close."

Wendy frowned. "Bullshit. Like I'm about to lose you. I know a little vampire first aid." She fetched a long sliver of broken glass from the floor. She pulled her left arm out of the coat sleeve and with the tip of the glass shard, flicked the bandage from her forearm. A slice in her skin marked where the *vânätori* had bled her.

Wendy bunched a corner of the blanket under my head and propped me up. She held her forearm over my face and twisted the glass shard into her wound. Tendrils snaked from her green aura yet her face remained placid. She withdrew the bloody shard.

Snapshots of what had brought me to this moment flashed before me. The war in Iraq. Our tragic ambush of the Iraqi civilians. Their bodies collapsing under the red hail of our bullets. The screams of the girl I had shot in the belly. My drowning in remorse. The Iraqi vampire condemning me to this fate of wandering the earth as one of the undead. Adding to my misery, there was the guilt that made me abhor the nourishment of human blood. If there was anything I could do before I died, it would be to ask the little Iraqi girl for forgiveness.

Wendy's hot, fresh blood dripped onto my lips. Though

she was more than human, I couldn't drink her blood. I tried to nudge her arm away.

Wendy cupped my head and forced the wound on her forearm into my mouth. Tears glistened in her eyes. "Drink." Her whispering voice quavered as she stroked my head. "Please, this could be the only thing that can save you."

The blood flowed over my tongue and down my throat. A great current of energy rushed through my spine, a jolt so strong that I passed out.

CHAPTER
29

I WAS STANDING IN the mist beside a dark canal. The pungent odor of burnt ammunition stung my nose. Curious and a bit afraid, I took one step forward. A metallic clink sounded from under my feet. I looked down. Spent brass cartridges surrounded my military boots. Desert camouflage fatigues covered my body. An M4 carbine weighed down my arms. A sudden familiarity overwhelmed me, a sensation that yielded to a great terror. I was back at the exact place where my fellow soldiers and I had ambushed and murdered the Iraqi civilians.

In the gloom before me lay four figures. Slowly they pushed up from the ground. In the meager light, I recognized them as the Iraqi family we had mistakenly gunned down.

Shouting in fright, I retreated several steps and readied my weapon to defend myself. But the carbine was gone. I lifted my empty hands to shield my face and glanced about for a way to escape.

The four figures advanced haltingly, as if struggling to balance themselves on bones shattered by bullets and grenades. A diminutive female in a pale dress led them. She was the girl I had shot. A dark blotch stained her belly, over the spot of her terrible wound.

A wave of paralysis froze my legs, and my lungs seized, damming the breath in my throat.

Coming closer, the Iraqis gave awkward smiles from faces ragged with torn flesh. The two women raised their arms, one of them offering just stumps, as our weapons had hacked off those limbs.

The little girl fixed her gaze upon me. Her eyes looked as big as they were the night I had shot her.

"Where are we?" My voice trembled.

Her tiny voice blossomed inside my head. "In the place between life and death. We've been waiting for you."

"Waiting? Why?"

"Because our hatred for you is as strong as the guilt that torments you. If we are to proceed into Heaven, we must forgive."

"Forgive me?"

"You are not responsible for what happened. Those sins belong to those who started the war. We forgive you."

A red aura grew from each of them. My skin tingled. The envelope of an orange aura surrounded my body.

I held up my hands. My fingernails extended into talons. I started toward the Iraqis. "But I'm still a vampire."

The little girl managed a smile. "We've done our part."

All of our auras blazed, becoming brighter and brighter until I was engulfed in a blinding light like the center of the sun itself.

Then all went dark, and I was alone.

Deep within me, my *kundalini noir* stirred. This black serpent of vampire energy uncoiled, pumping strength and vitality into my undead flesh.

My eyes popped opened. The cool air swelled my lungs. Every detail in the shed seemed crisp and new. I smelled mare's sweat on the blankets and tack. A hidden mouse nibbled from behind a sack of feed.

I clenched my fists and marveled at the intensity of my aura sizzling around me. The other vampires had been wrong. Human blood alone wouldn't restore my powers. I had needed to expunge the curse of guilt from the carcass of my mortal soul. Wendy's supernatural dryad blood had sent me to the edge of the afterlife, where I found absolution. I felt new and refreshed, like a reptile that had shed its old skin.

Wendy scooted away from me. Her green aura radiated distress. "Felix, are you okay?"

I straightened my legs and rotated upwards on my heels until I stood. "I feel better than okay, I feel like murder."

"But your wound . . ."

I lifted the back of my shirt and touched the fresh scar that had formed over the bullet hole. "It's just a souvenir now."

Tucking the shirt into my trousers, I peered out the broken window at the frigid calm night. A layer of new snow covered everything. "How long was I out?"

"More than an hour."

I read my watch. "It's three-thirty in the morning. We've got time." I pulled the blanket off the floor and draped it over my shoulders.

"Time for what?"

I grabbed a broom leaning in the near corner. "To highjack a convoy from the Department of Energy."

Wendy followed me outside. "Don't suppose I could talk you out of it? Maybe get help from the other vampires?"

"This is my investigation."

The snowfall had turned our footsteps from the Dodge into a trail of shallow depressions. My feet sank into the snow. I levitated until the soles of my shoes barely scraped over the iced surface and then I started up the incline to my car.

A square hulk of an orange snowplow with flashing amber lights rumbled above on the road.

"If the state highway trucks are out," I said, "then the roads must be clear."

My Dodge Polara sat wedged against the guardrail. With the broom, I whisked snow off the car. "Wendy, get in and start the engine."

She cranked the V-8 over. I discarded the broom and blanket, grasped the rear bumper, and lifted. I pulled backwards until the tires touched the pavement. Moving to the front of the Dodge, I gave the grill a hearty push. Wendy gunned the engine, and the car lurched back onto the highway.

I jerked open the driver's door. "Let me drive."

Though my vampire powers couldn't enchant the Dodge, I drove as if they could. I kept the gas pedal flat against the floor and let the rear end of the car swing across the icy pavement and ricochet off the guardrails.

Wendy tightened her seat belt and braced her arms against the dashboard. "I thought this was a collectors' item."

Pieces of my car tore loose and clanged on the road. "Was," I replied.

Her aura bristled with alarm. "And just how are you going to get into the trailer?"

"I'm not sure. But it shouldn't be very complicated."

"Just foolish and dangerous?"

"Wouldn't be any fun if it wasn't. I can drop you off someplace safe if you like."

Wendy shook her head and grinned. "I haven't been tagging after you all this time just to wimp out now."

"Good. I could use a copilot on this kamikaze mission." I turned off the interstate and proceeded to Highway 93.

The road curved and rose up the hill and then straightened on the plain leading to Rocky Flats.

Far ahead, a confusion of flashing lights collected alongside the road.

"We're just in time," I said. "There're marshaling the convoy. Wendy, unfasten the convertible top."

She reached up and unsnapped the latches holding the convertible top to the windshield. The front end of the convertible top frame vibrated for a second against the windshield. The cold wind blasted in and ballooned the fabric. With a great rip, the frame collapsed backwards and banged against the trunk lid.

The oncoming lights grew brighter.

I willed my fingernails to lengthen into talons. Clenching the steering wheel, I pressed on the accelerator. The wind whirled into the driver's compartment. The broken frame flailed violently, and one by one the metal struts broke apart. With a final rip, what was left of the convertible top tore free and fell behind us on the highway.

An unmarked white Suburban streaked past. Then a Humvee, with a bar of flashing lights fixed to the roof.

The next vehicle was as imposing as a locomotive, certainly a semi pulling the white trailer.

"Scoot your foot over and step on the gas pedal," I shouted to Wendy.

She turned her body at an angle and her shoe nudged my foot off the accelerator.

With my hands remaining on the steering wheel, I drew my legs up and squatted on the driver's seat. "Give it more gas."

"Like this?" She flexed her leg. The engine grunted and the Dodge surged forward.

I held tight. "Yeah, like that." I peeked over the windshield. Frigid night air blasted my face and hands. The headlights of the semi tractor fused into one brilliant comet flying at us. Adrenaline flooded my body. My nerves felt raw, as if my skin had been peeled back and sensations shot directly into my brain.

"Now take the wheel. Keep going straight, and as fast as you can."

Wendy grasped the steering wheel. "Felix, you're a god-damn menace."

"At least I'm not boring." With my left hand on the door and my right against the edge of the windshield, I cocked my body. The massive grill of the semi rushed at me.

"Don't look back. Don't slow down," I shouted to Wendy. "The guards will be too busy with me to chase after you. Take care. I'll see you later."

Shoving back against the seat, I sprang through the air. For an instant I glided free and then smashed against the radiator grill, hitting hard with as much grace as a squirrel about to become roadkill. My brains rattled inside my skull. My feet scrambled to catch the lip of the front bumper. The truck swerved from side to side as if the driver had sensed my impact.

The Humvee preceding us slowed and closed the gap. Gravel kicked up by its tires pelted me. A roof hatch opened and a helmeted guard in combat gear appeared. He trained a spotlight on me. The circle of white illumination caught me splayed across the radiator grill. I was the center circle of a bull's-eye. I clung to the radiator, glowing in the glare of the spotlight, my clothes rustling in the wind whistling past.

The guard in the Humvee took aim with a submachine gun. The red thread of a laser beam shot from beneath the gun and quivered on my face, like death's finger tracing against my cheek.

I clambered over the hood just as a spray of bullets stitched into the radiator, venting jets of steam.

The driver of the truck and his guard became pie-eyed with shock at seeing me. The guard leaned to one side and flipped open a gun port in the right side of the windshield. I grasped the windshield wipers and hauled myself tight against the windshield, out of his line of fire.

The guard on the Humvee fired again. His bullets scratched the armored glass about me. I snaked over the windshield and lay atop the roof.

Two bullets punched from inside the roof and exited inches from my face. I stabbed my claws through the roof, tearing the metal, and peeled the roof back. A long burst of automatic fire shot through the void.

A pause. The guard had to be reloading. I looked into the hole I had made. The guard shrank away in terror and whimpered like a puppy. His hands clutched at a fresh magazine. I seized the guard by his collar, lifted him out of the cab, and tossed him screaming over my shoulder.

I slithered into the cab and bared my fangs to the driver.

He hollered into his radio microphone and groped for his holster. With my right hand, I grabbed him by the throat while my left hand twisted his wrist until he yelped in pain. The truck weaved across the road, left and right.

I reached around him, popped the door open, and shoved him out. Grasping the rim of the big steering wheel, I straightened the truck's path. Waves of steam curled from the punctured radiator.

The guard in the Humvee let fly another burst that pinged harmlessly against the thick windshield.

Chortling with glee, I accelerated and rammed the rear of the Humvee. The Humvee careened back and forth across the highway. The guard flopped in the hatch like a sock puppet before dropping inside. I rammed the Humvee again. It swerved, tipped on two wheels, and rolled over.

The temperature gauge on the instrument panel sprang into the red zone. I had perhaps a minute before the engine seized.

Up ahead, the Suburban spun around. In my rearview mirrors, another Humvee raced closer to box me in.

I flicked off the headlamps and running lights. I veered to the right and smashed the darkened semi and trailer through a barbed-wire fence bordering the road.

Using vampire vision, I navigated around the largest of the big rocks littering the plain. The truck bellowed as it crashed over the treacherous ground. The trailer groaned on the fifth wheel. I dropped into low gear and flogged the engine, dragging us through the snow.

The transmission started to grind. The engine whined. The tachometer redlined. The truck bogged down and stopped with a wheeze and a grunt of steam.

I kicked open the door and stood on the running board. The Humvees were a half-mile away, picking their way around the stones that had pummeled my truck. Searchlights washed over the glistening snow.

I had but a few short minutes to find out what was hidden in the trailer. Unfastening a pick ax lashed to the back of the cab, I dropped to the snow and hustled to the trailer. A padlock the size of a clay brick held the rear doors. I jammed the thin end of the pick head between the lock and the hasp. I twisted the pick and turned until the handle broke.

A gentle tap—like the tripping of a bomb fuse—whispered from behind the doors. The stink of polyurethane and isopropanol farted into the air. I sprang upward and landed on top of the trailer roof. From under the rear of the truck, out shot streams of foam the size of railroad ties. The streams snaked on the ground and melted a swath through the snow. The foam set and hardened. To anyone caught in it, it would be like getting doused with instant-setting concrete.

Just to make sure that no more surprises waited, I stamped my foot on the roof of the trailer. Nothing happened. I jumped up and down once. Again, nothing happened.

Certain that this booby trap had run its course, I dropped from the roof and balanced on the knots of hardened foam. I grabbed the pick head with my bare hands and twisted again, grunting, and flexed my legs to get better leverage.

The padlock cracked apart. I flung the pieces aside and unbarred the doors.

A second metal door protected the cargo. The seal of the Department of Energy warned me not to proceed.

Stop me.

This door I grasped by the hinges and tore it loose. I stepped over the threshold and into the deepest secrets of Rocky Flats.

CHAPTER
30

I ENTERED AN ARMORED VAULT. Six black boxes the size and shape of coffins were lashed with cargo straps to platforms on the floor trunnions. Along the left and right walls stood black metal drums marked with radiation symbols and placards announcing Hg-209, red mercury. Were these the boxes and drums the RCTs discovered just before they first became contaminated and then went sex crazy?

I stepped between the first two of the black boxes. A pair of metal shipping bands secured each of the lids. I chose a box and plucked at the bands with my talons until each band snapped apart with a twang.

Poised on the edge of my destination in this mystery, I hesitated, out of apprehension that what lay in the box was either nothing but disappointment, a hoax perhaps, or the kernel at the heart of the darkest of conspiracies. Could this be proof of the spaceship, the Roswell UFO, as the *vânători* had claimed?

In the distance, the flashing lights and headlamps of the convoy escort flicked across the snow. I didn't have much time before the security force closed upon me.

Breathless, as if reaching into a lion's cage, I raised the lid. The aura about my hands changed from orange to yellow, exactly as it had earlier in the presence of Dragan's red mercury. Startled and suddenly afraid, I closed the lid. Thankfully, my aura returned to orange.

The effect seemed temporary. In any case, since I might already be contaminated, there was no point in stopping. I raised the lid again, and again my aura turned yellow. And the more I opened the lid, the farther the color change progressed down my arms.

The auras of the contaminated RCTs had turned an identical hue when the nymphomania took hold. Just as before, when Dragan had brought the vial of red mercury close to me, an electric twinge now shot along my spine and down to my crotch, filling my groin with a pleasant warmth. I couldn't help but smile despite my apprehension.

I pushed the lid up until it locked in the vertical position. Inside the box rested a large transparent tube filled with a viscous liquid. Floating in this liquid was a wizened, blackened corpse the size of a German shepherd. The corpse had an unusually large head, a plain oval face, a tiny slit of a mouth, two even tinier slits on the bump of a nose, and a pair of enormous almond-shaped eyes.

A gasp escaping my throat startled me, and I realized that I was so stupefied by what I'd seen that I had forgotten to breathe.

Dark cloth overalls covered most of the body, but whether the suit was extraterrestrial in origin or had been provided by humans to protect any modesty, I couldn't tell. The body emitted no aura. This creature was long dead. An inventory tag dangled from the collar. The liquid had bleached the writing but I could still read "509th Bombardment Group, Roswell Air Force Base," and the scrawl of a long-forgotten colonel together with the date, "7 July 1947." This thing in the tube could only be an alien. An EBE. An extraterrestrial biological entity.

Holy shit.

I withdrew my hands and the yellow aura effervesced for a moment. I closed the lid. The aura around my hands and arms changed back to its usual orange. The warmth in my crotch dissipated.

So everything was true. A chill made me shudder. Earth's creatures weren't alone in the universe. I craned my head back to stare at the trailer ceiling and wonder about the cosmos beyond. We were but dots on a miserable speck of a rock tucked into an insignificant corner of the galaxy.

Disgust with humanity overwhelmed me. We had finally made contact with an alien civilization and this was the best reception provided, to hide the visitors? Why the secrecy?

Angrily, I turned to the second box, broke apart the shipping bands, and opened the lid. Inside rested metallic forms in fantastic shapes, all of a uniform pale color like the dull side of aluminum foil. There was nothing whose function I could recognize, though every piece had this attribute in common, thin conduits about the diameter of a pencil running through them. I grasped one long shape the size of my arm. The surface was hard and unyielding. The shape felt warm, as if heated, and was surprisingly lightweight. The glow of my hand's aura changed from orange to yellow. I dropped the piece and in reflex wiped my hand on the edge of the box, once again relieved when my aura returned to its normal color.

On the inside of the lid I read a warning label. All the conduits had been purged of Hg-209 with high-pressure steam.

The red mercury in the drums had come from the UFO, which the federal government had no doubt dismantled to learn the aliens' technology. By now I was convinced that exposure to the radiation from these aliens and their spaceship was what had caused the nymphomania.

I was about to close the lid when I noticed an object of a darker color buried in the tangle of aluminum-hued metal. Risking more exposure to the yellow glow, I reached back into the container and pushed aside the other pieces.

The object had what looked like two handles jutting from opposite sides of an open-ended square box, its width about the size of my two fists held together.

I grasped one of the handles and lifted. The object was also made of metal but of a heavier density and cool to the touch. The dark color was like the blued steel of a gun. The glow around the object was faint and didn't affect me as had the other piece.

I held the object by both handles and looked through the box. Inside were layers of clear glass or crystal in assorted shapes, stacked together to form a display of some kind. The object didn't look like a weapon. Perhaps it was a gun sight or a camera. I turned the object over and saw a round notch on the bottom, the logical place for an attachment point. The object had no buttons or switches, so I couldn't guess how it worked.

I put the object back in the container and closed the lid.

Turning my attention back to the interior of the trailer vault, I inventoried the containers. They contained enough volume to hold the wreckage of a small airplane. How large was the original ship? Was there more debris somewhere else?

What a tragedy. The government had proof of intergalactic visitors and was going to dispose of the evidence as if it were yesterday's trash. It was like a chimp finding a telescope and, not knowing what to do with it, burying the telescope in the dirt.

Could this secret go even deeper? Were there more alien bodies? Perhaps a survivor kept prisoner, much as a vampire like myself would be if captured by the humans. And had there been more alien contacts after this crash?

A helicopter roared overhead. A searchlight scanned around the back end of the trailer. I retreated behind the boxes and waited to see what happened. The helicopter sounded as if it was landing nearby. Rotor-wash blasted snow into the trailer, then settled, then blasted again as if the helicopter had landed and taken off right away.

Someone approached. A yellow glow illuminated the open end of the trailer.

My *kundalini noir* buzzed with energy. A second yellow glow? From whom? From what? I glanced to the boxes around me. I was aware of the three nymphomaniacs initially contaminated and the material in this vault. Who else would glow?

"Felix," called the intruder. The voice I instantly recognized as that of my friend Gilbert Odin. "You're safe for now. It's just you and me."

Gilbert? What was he doing here?

His tall frame came into view behind the trailer. Large eyeglasses sat on the bridge of his nose.

Incredibly, a brilliant yellow aura surrounded him.

I had to repeat the astonishing discovery to myself.

A brilliant yellow aura surrounded him.

I realized this was the first time I'd ever seen him without my contacts.

I waited for him, confused and stunned by his yellow aura. My own aura grew more intense, and the hairs on my neck and arms stood up in alarm.

Swaddled in a puffy down parka, Gilbert strode in his

overboots across the muddy tracks the semi had plowed through the snow. The cackle of radio traffic came from a receiver strapped to his shoulder. "Come out," he reassured me. "It's over."

"What's over?" I shouted. Anger displaced my confusion. Did he mean I was caught? If so, he was mistaken. I pressed against the steel wall of the trailer vault. Gilbert's yellow aura wouldn't make a difference—like any cornered beast I'd kill anyone or anything blocking my escape.

"I'm supposed to negotiate your surrender," he said.

Gilbert had better have another plan if that was the case.

"Come out," he repeated.

"Like hell," I yelled back. I wasn't about to get into the open and let a sniper measure my skull with the crosshairs of a rifle telescope. "You want to talk, you come in here."

"All right," Gilbert said. He climbed over the back end of the trailer. His aura looked like a boiling froth, signaling anxiety and fear. Good, he had much to fear from me.

I searched beyond him and looked for the telltale auras of any companions lurking in the darkness. He was alone. Easy prey for vampire hypnosis.

Gilbert stood and his large body filled most of the doorway. The thick, almost overpowering, odor of cabbage seeped from him. As he straightened up, he turned down the volume of the radio he carried. His right arm suddenly extended and in his hand he held a device that looked like a pistol—bronze-colored, open sights, and a pointed muzzle with rings around the barrel. The way he aimed it at me was proof enough that it was a weapon, something futuristic. Buck Rogers meets Dirty Harry.

His aura tightened close around his form. An occasional spike of heated emotion lashed out, like a flame shooting from a bed of coals. By reading his aura I could tell that he was trying to remain calm and keep panic from overwhelming him. Gilbert may have had this strange yellow aura but he still reacted emotionally like a human.

But not a human. Every nerve of mine pulsed and readied me for the attack. Not yet comprehending what I suspected, I waited for a moment before daring to say, "You're one of them. An alien."

CHAPTER
31

"FELIX, WHY WOULD YOU say that?" Gilbert tilted his weapon. "It's the blaster, isn't it? Well, I knew better than to use bullets against you." He leveled the gun. "Step out here where I can get a good look at you."

"Nothing doing," I replied. "You want a look, you come back here." When he came close, I would hypnotize him.

A wave of brash determination pulsed through his aura. He stepped into the trailer vault. His finger started to compress the trigger.

With vampire quickness, I jumped to the right.

A bolt of blue light shot from the muzzle of the blaster. The bolt struck the armored wall behind me and splattered white droplets of molten steel.

I had Gilbert by the throat while his blaster still pointed uselessly at where I had been. His eyeglasses clattered to the floor.

"What—? How?" he stammered as he sank to his knees.

His aura blazed with fear and emitted spikes of terror that writhed like tentacles. The cabbage odor spewed from him. "Okay. Stay calm." He lowered the blaster and pulled his finger from the trigger. "Let's talk."

I motioned to the glowing spot on the wall where his blaster had struck. "You call that talking? Drop the gun."

The blaster fell from his hand. "I don't mean to cause trouble."

"A little late for that. Is that weapon proof of peaceful intentions?" I tightened my claws around his windpipe.

"Self-protection. Every species has that right."

I kicked the blaster and sent it skidding into the far end of the vault.

"Careful." He spoke in a rasped whisper. "That thing's expensive, and I'm signed for it."

"The only reason I won't kill you is that I need questions answered." I stared into his eyes. No effect. He was definitely not human.

This imposter had said nothing about his yellow aura. Or my orange one. He couldn't see them. He didn't know. I kept this advantage to myself. I knelt over him and cradled his neck in my talons as I read his aura. I loosened my grip slightly, but he knew that I could decapitate him in an instant.

"What happened to the real Gilbert Odin?"

The muscles in the imposter's throat convulsed as he tried gulping. Finally he managed to say, "He was abducted years ago."

"Then why are you here? To abduct me? To abduct others?"

"No. To safeguard the surveillance vessel, the UFO."

"Safeguard from whom?"

The radio clipped to his shoulder suddenly cackled with traffic. "Hawk Vanguard. Hawk Vanguard. This is Eagle Team. What's your situation? Over."

The imposter raised his hand and motioned to the radio. "Please, they're calling me. I don't answer, they'll assume the worst and open fire."

I released my grip and let the imposter go. He withdrew, coughed and clutched his throat. After a moment, he unsnapped his microphone and spoke. "Eagle Team, Hawk Vanguard here." The imposter gave me a conspiratorial glance. "Negative on the intruder."

"Why are you here alone?" I asked.

"Believe it or not, I'm playing the hero. It pays extra." He clipped the microphone back on his shoulder harness and massaged his neck. He found his glasses and put them back on.

"You asked who I safeguard the UFO from?" The alien imposter motioned out the trailer, back toward the security force. "From the humans. Normally when there is an incident like this, rescue teams retrieve the ship and cleanse the crash site. In Roswell, your government seized the surveillance vessel and occupants before we could react."

"We?"

The imposter pointed toward the sky. "The Galactic Union."

"There are more of you?"

The imposter rose to his feet and leaned against the wall. "Many more. It's a *galactic* union."

"Where is Gilbert?"

The imposter's aura flashed nervously. "Your friend Gilbert Odin didn't take the zero-point flux well."

"I don't know what the hell you're talking about. You mean Gilbert's dead?"

The imposter sighed. "It happens. He passed away soon after the, uh, abduction. Really, we meant him no harm."

"If you're an alien, how come you don't look like the stiff in the box?"

The imposter laughed. He sounded like Gilbert. "One of

those stiffs—good way to put it. Careless assholes would be more accurate. They knew Earth was off-limits. No, I'm not one of them. I'm from a different species, one closer to yours. Human."

"I'm not human. Not anymore."

"My apologies, Felix. I'd resent the slur, too. Humanoid, then."

"You swear pretty good for an extraterrestrial," I said.

"I watch a lot of cable television."

The imposter's radio cackled again. A wave of anxiety pulsed through his aura. "We don't have a lot of time."

"Let me worry about that," I replied. "You were chosen to replace Gilbert because you most resembled him?"

"Not completely. It took some minor cosmetic surgery, replacing my stalk eyes with these," he touched his eye sockets, "removing my sucker toes, rearranging my genitals, that sort of thing."

"Sounds painful."

"It's a living."

"You might want to work on that cabbage stink," I said.

"Huh?" He lifted an arm and sniffed. "My genome profile could need tweaking. That bad?"

"Trust me. You got a name—beside Gilbert Odin, I mean?"

"My original name is hard to pronounce unless you have a trifurcated speaking passage."

I remembered Gilbert Odin's, rather the imposter's, denials when I first brought proof that it was the red mercury that had caused the nymphomania. My jaw tightened and the bitterness of my anger rose into my throat. "You lied to me."

The imposter's aura lowered into a sizzle. "Sorry."

I splayed my fingers so that he could better appreciate my talons. "You knew all along. About the nymphomania. The UFO. I brought you Dr. Wong's diary and you said it was a hoax. Why?"

He looked over his shoulder. The lights of the security force became brighter as they neared us. The imposter's aura sizzled with nervousness. "We don't have time for long discussions. The Eagle Team gets here and finds us like this, then my cover is blown."

"They don't know you're an alien?"

"As far as DOE is concerned, I'm Gilbert Odin, GS-15."

"Why the lie?"

"Like I said, to safeguard the UFO."

"Safeguard how? The government's torn apart the UFO. They've certainly dissected the crew."

"I keep tabs on what's learned."

"Why not announce your presence to the planet?"

His radio called again. He answered, "Eagle Team, still negative on the intruder. What's your ETA?"

"Hawk Vanguard, give us five mikes."

The imposter rubbed the microphone nervously. "You got five minutes, Felix."

"Keep talking."

"We can't announce ourselves because we're not supposed to be here," he said. "That's the complication. Otherwise we would've intervened a long time ago. Earth is under quarantine. Humans are much too violent and dangerous of a species."

"Why would our government keep the UFO a secret?"

"Fear mostly. Of us. Of mass panic. They used Project Redlight to spread disinformation and debunk the existence of UFOs, aliens"—the imposter made quotation marks in the air—"creatures like me. It then became more expedient to stick to the lie than admit the truth. That's what all governments do best."

"Even the Galactic Union?"

"Even the Union."

"If you knew about the UFO and the conspiracy to cover it up, why hire me? Why press me to investigate?"

"To prove that DOE's security precautions weren't good enough to stop a determined intruder. Which you've done, in spades."

"And you've been involved with this since the Roswell crash in 1947?"

"Me?" the alien asked. "Hell no—do I *look* that old? I hope not. I was assigned about ten years ago. You see, after your government moved the surveillance vessel from Roswell, we lost track of it. I have to hand it to the humans, they can be sneaky. That's one reason they are so dangerous."

"You knew nothing of moving the UFO from Roswell to Hangar 18 at Wright-Patterson Air Force Base?" I asked. "Then from Wright-Patterson to Rocky Flats?"

"No. I swear."

"How does Rocky Flats fit into this?"

"Your government needed better facilities for its studies. All the security surrounding plutonium at Rocky Flats was a sham to cover the real secret."

"The study of this UFO?"

The helicopter passed overhead. Its rotor blades drummed the air.

The imposter followed the noise. "Yes," he answered simply.

"And the use of rare, radioactive materials for weapons manufacture was a cover to hide this isotope of red mercury?"

"Another yes."

"And the nymphomania?" I asked.

"An unexpected consequence," he answered. "It only happened to human females. Earth women are surprisingly complicated."

"Tell me about it."

The imposter's gaze shifted to the containers behind me. His aura grew barbed points, indicating deceit and anxiety.

"There's more to this, isn't there?" I moved toward him, my fangs and talons growing to maximum length.

The alien cringed against the wall of the vault. His eyes grew so wide with fear they looked ready to pop from their sockets.

"Was getting me to break into this trailer part of your alien plan? What did you really want?"

His aura burned hotter and went from distress to outright terror.

I pressed a talon into the soft flesh under his chin. "Talk or I'll do more cosmetic surgery."

The imposter turned his gaze back to the containers. He remained silent.

I pushed my talon in a little harder. "Did the Union send you here to die?"

The imposter shook his head. "No."

"Then what are you here for?"

"The Psychotronic Device."

I withdrew my hand and pointed over my shoulder. "In those?"

He nodded.

"What does this Psychotronic Device look like?"

Gilbert's imposter pantomimed with his hands. "Maybe this big."

The dimensions were about the same as the object I had found.

"What color is it?"

"I'm not sure. It should look like a box with handles."

I grasped the alien by his arm and led him to the container where I'd seen the object. I opened the lid—the yellow glow spilled out—and pulled out the box with handles.

The imposter's aura lit up with swirls of delight. He reached for the device.

I pulled it away. "This is the reason you wanted me to get into the trailer?"

He didn't have to say anything. The way his aura blazed was enough to signal a yes.

"Why didn't you get it yourself?"

"Felix, this is the *blackest* of the top-secret programs. The Roswell crash happened when the humans' atomic bomb program was in full swing. It didn't occur to us until years later that the United States would hide the surveillance vessel under the security umbrella of its nuclear weapons program." The imposter panned his hands over the containers in the vault. "How could I ask to inspect something that supposedly didn't exist?"

"And once the UFO was buried deep in Carlsbad Caverns . . ."

The alien finished my sentence. "I'd never get to it."

"And you hired me to do your dirty work."

"Isn't that what private detectives are for?"

He had me there, the intergalactic weasel.

I held the device by both handles and raised it toward Gilbert's imposter. He shirked back.

"What does this Psychotronic Device do? Why was the Roswell UFO carrying it?"

"To test"—the alien cleared his throat sheepishly, as if embarrassed—"the existence of psychic energy. According to the theory, every living creature emits an aura of psychic energy."

The imposter stood within his sheath of a yellow glowing aura. Psychic energy was no theory, it was as real as electricity.

"You have living creatures where you're from. Why come to Earth to test this?"

"Actually, the test involved a little more than proving the existence of psychic energy," he replied.

We vampires used our knowledge of psychic auras to manipulate humans. His use of the words "a little more" implied a sinister motive. The device was no toy.

"How *much* more?"

"I don't know. My job was to safeguard the surveillance vessel and recover the Psychotronic Device."

"Now that you've found this, what are you going to do?"

"Report to my superiors in the Union."

My grip tightened angrily on the handles. Earth's vampires didn't need competition from extraterrestrials. No one else would pluck our pigeons.

"Then here." I pressed the handles together and crushed the box. The glass panes inside shattered and sprayed out the opposite end toward him.

The alien covered his face and crouched. His aura flared in despair. "What are you doing?"

I smashed the device against the container until I held a piece of battered junk. I offered it to him. "Here. Proof that you found it. Happy?"

The imposter took the device. A glass shard tinkled to the floor. He stared at the misshapen, broken mass and slumped his shoulders as if his luck had the weight of concrete. "Not really."

"It's been more than fifty years since the crash," I said. "Why haven't you made another one?"

"The inventor was on the vessel. His secrets died with him."

The alien's aura dimmed to the color of a rotten yolk. He bore the expression of a man who had let diamonds flush down the toilet. The alien tossed the device back into the container and closed the lid.

I could kill him out of spite but the alien imposter was only doing his job, like any other schmuck. Right now I felt sorry for him.

His aura lightened and swirled with renewed curiosity. "You are an amazing creature, Felix Gomez." His gaze moved to my talons and then right into my eyes.

Vampire hypnosis should've flattened him by now but there was still nothing.

"You have such powers. Such strength." He squinted. "Those fangs. Those claws. You . . . are a vampire? Humans are so superstitious. Interesting, I didn't think you actually existed."

"Same goes for you."

A searchlight illuminated the trailer's doors.

"The security force is almost here, Felix. You better leave."

"Not yet. Before we kiss and say goodbye, there's one more thing."

"What?"

"You owe me thirty thousand dollars. I didn't do this as a hobby. You wanted confirmation of what was in the trailer and here it is." I stepped on the broken glass and made it crunch.

The alien tightened his lips in frustration. Carefully, he unzipped his parka and from an inside pocket produced a large manila envelope folded over into a thick packet. "I'd hoped you'd take this money and scram before asking too many questions. When I hired you, I got more than I bargained for."

"That's a common complaint from my clients."

The alien handed me the packet. "In cash, to keep bookkeeping simple. I'll keep your secrets if you keep mine."

I opened the envelope and ran my thumb across a stack of hundred-dollar bills. "That's a promise. What about Merriweather, the plant manager?"

"He's made his navy rank by believing two plus two equals five if that's what his superiors tell him. He's no different from any other civil servant."

"And the damage?" I asked. "The wrecked vehicles? The injured?"

"This administration is used to hiding expensive catastrophes. Let the White House worry about it."

"And the agent that I killed? The assassin?"

"A rogue. According to the federal government, the man died doing freelance covert work in Ecuador."

I waved my hand at the containers. "Now you know. What happens next?"

"I have a Q-clearance. That means I forget whatever DOE tells me to forget. Now beat it before the security force gets here. If I need you again, I hope you'll be available."

"If?" I asked.

The alien winked at me. "Make that when."

The glare of dozens of searchlights focused on the rear of the trailer. Excited radio traffic blared from the imposter's receiver.

"Hawk Vanguard, we've got the trailer surrounded. What's your situation? Over."

"Felix, you're trapped." The imposter pulled the microphone loose. "Eagle Team, this is Hawk Vanguard. Negative on the intruder."

"Roger," the radio answered. "We're securing the area to make sure the intruder doesn't slip away."

The imposter rubbed his face. His aura became a low burn of worry. "It's too late. You won't escape."

I pulled my wallet, cell phone, and everything else from my pockets, and dumped it all into the manila envelope. I shoved the envelope into the imposter's hands.

"What are you doing?" he asked.

"Escaping," I answered and stepped back into the vault. I pointed to the blaster on the floor. "Don't try anything. So far tonight you're batting zero against me."

I undid my shirt and trousers, crouched on the steel floor, and summoned the wolf transformation.

My body tensed to accept the shock of pain. My heartbeat accelerated. Every inch of my skin burned where animal fur poked from flesh. I couldn't withstand the agony and dropped to my side. My limbs twitched as my bones twisted from vampire to wolf shape. A long muzzle extended from my face.

I lay on the cold floor, panting, gathering my strength. My ears perked up to take in the delicate sounds from outside. I sniffed the air and deciphered the many smells. Sage. Mineral lubricants. Buffalo grass. The reek of cabbage from the imposter. Anxious, sweaty men crept around the trailer.

I sat up and shook loose the man garments draped around my neck. Standing on all four paws and wagging my tail, I stepped free of the pile of man things and advanced on the alien imposter.

His aura blazed around him with awe and terror. With my jaws I snatched the envelope from his hands and bounded for the door.

Two men in black appeared at the end of the trailer. They pointed weapons.

I lunged forward, knocked them aside, and landed in the snow.

The humans brayed like donkeys.

"Holy shit. What was that? A coyote?"

"Coyote—hell—that was a wolf."

"Get it. Open fire."

Weapons barked and bit the ground to my left and right. The flying machine thundered above. A bright circle of light swept over the rocks and snow. I dodged the many men converging on the trailer. Their auras lit up with confusion and fright.

I choose a crooked path through the deepest of night's shadows. Running uphill, I cut into a ravine between the scrub pines. My legs pushed beneath me in a gallop. My breath surged past the envelope in my snout. The stupid humans fell farther and farther behind. If I had lips, I would have smiled.

CHAPTER
32

I PARKED MY CADILLAC against the curb. Wendy reached over the console between our seats and took the bag of blood from my hand. A plastic drinking straw jutted from the top of the bag. I was getting used to human blood and looked forward to feeding on succulent necks.

Wendy interlaced her warm fingers with mine. For the last three days we hadn't done much except stay locked up in my apartment and screw, and yet we still yearned for each other's touch. A scarf hid the fang marks on her neck.

A black van marked Federal Taskforce/Homeland Security, swerved around us and halted in front of a fleabag hotel on the opposite side of South Santa Fe Street. The doors of the van sprang open and out bounded five officers in black SWAT gear, masks, helmets, and shotguns at the ready. They queued in a tactical stack at the lobby door and, on the leader's signal, scrambled in.

Another officer climbed out of the van's cab and came

our way. The torso narrowed from the healthy swell around the bosom to a trim waistline, then filled out again to a nice set of hips. Obviously a woman. Her leather overalls were cinched with a belt that held a small holster and pistol. She bent down toward my window and tapped the glass.

I depressed the switch and lowered the window.

She raised her mirrored sunglasses to the rim of her black helmet and showed me vampire eyes. "Hi, Felix. Wendy," Carmen said. "We're acting on a tip that the *vânätori* are here in the U.S. as illegal terrorists."

"As opposed to legal terrorists?" I asked. "The van is a nice prop."

"It's no prop. The new local district coordinator for federal counterterrorism is family." Carmen unsnapped the chin-strap and removed her helmet. Shiny black hair cascaded loose. She ran her tongue over her fangs. "We'll be interrogating, then disposing of, the *vânätori*."

The five officers emerged from the lobby, dragging Dragan, Petru, and Teodor, who were cuffed and blindfolded. Dragan shouted for help. One of the officers pulled the blindfold up and Maced him in the eyes. Dragan howled in pain. With his mouth agape, another officer jammed a rag down his throat. The officers shoved the *vânätori* into the van and climbed in. There was scuffling and the whack of batons on flesh. I smiled at the sounds. *Give those human bastards a whack for me.*

Carmen replaced her sunglasses. "Care to join us? Felix? Wendy? Get your last licks in?"

"I'll pass, though give Dragan my regards. I'm sure that you'll have fun without me." I raised my hand, Wendy's fingers still clasped to mine. "Besides, we're in the middle of our own fun."

Carmen smiled and creased the dimples in her cheeks. "Hmmm, I could join you later."

Wendy said, "Three's a crowd, Carmen."

"Crowds can be fun."

Wendy replied, "We'll take a rain check."

Pushing away from the door, Carmen laughed. "I'm not used to brush-offs. Take care, Felix. Wendy. *Adiós.*" She walked toward the van and wiggled her tight, leather-clad buns.

Carmen slammed shut the rear doors of the van and got in the cab. The van rolled away, roof lights flashing.

I started the Cadillac and cruised north.

Wendy squeezed my hand. "I'm going to miss you."

"What do you mean? I'm planning to stay here in Denver . . . with you."

Wendy sighed. "I've lived long enough to know that nothing's ever permanent."

"So what gives?"

"The Araneum's sending me to Indianapolis."

"Oh." I let go of her hand.

Wendy kissed my neck. "Don't act so glum. We're not apart yet. I've got a month before I go, and that's plenty of time for lots and lots of goodbye sex."

Flip the page to check out
the next declassified installment
from Mario Acevedo,

THE UNDEAD KAMA SUTRA

CARMEN PULLED ME into the alley. A vampire scent trailed her, an aroma of damp moss and dried roses.

She stopped and faced me. Triangles of a neon-green bikini top barely covered her breasts. Gold and coral earrings dangled alongside her neck. She raised her sunglasses and revealed the reflective red disks of her *tapetum lucidum.* Her smile parted and showed the tips of her fangs. "Felix, it's a good thing we came to your rescue."

Like I needed rescuing from that fatso inside. I smiled back. "What are you doing here?"

She spread her arms. "Isn't it obvious?"

I took in all that taut, sienna-colored skin. Her tan looked perfect, too perfect even for an expert undead application of makeup. I sniffed and detected no trace of cosmetics. This tan was real? Impossible.

"I give. What's your secret?"

Carmen poked me in the stomach. "Geez, Felix, aren't you first going to ask me how I've been? Whadda ya think?" She put an arm out for me to inspect.

I dragged my finger across her wrist, still amazed at how authentic her tan looked. "This can't be real."

"As real as these." Carmen shimmied and her breasts wobbled.

Anyone else, and I would've been all over them. But Carmen's sexual manner was as subtle as a bear trap and she had the reputation of wringing even male vampires dry.

But a vampire with a tan? Pigs flying. Cats doing geometry. Dogs playing poker. All those would've amazed me less. "And you're not even wearing sun block?"

Carmen shook her head. "Nothing between me and the sun but this beautiful bronzed skin. And what brings you to Key West?"

"I heard you're working on *The Undead Kama Sutra*."

The ends of her smile pointed to the dimples in her cheeks. "You naughty boy."

A bar stool crashed through the window of the saloon and landed on the street.

My hands curled into claws and my talons grew. "We better go inside and help your friend."

Carmen laughed. "Jolie can handle a battalion of Marines. Public brawling is her hobby."

Shouts and the smashing of wooden furniture boomed out the broken window.

"Sounds like Jolie's having lots of fun." I started for the door, hoping that she'd left some of Mr. Fish Fear Me for me to thump around the floor.

Carmen grasped my wrist and led me out of the alley toward the two choppers. "Don't spoil it for her."

The thin, almost-nothing strap of Carmen's bikini bisected a sleek, muscular back. Her ponytail pointed to a trim waist. Denim shorts rode low on her hips. Her toned legs glistened like copper in the electric light of the salon marquee.

Carmen looked over her shoulder. "You checkin' me out?"

Maybe I should risk getting wrung dry. I put on my best smirk.

She winked. "Thanks. Otherwise there's no point in dressing like this."

"Where we headed?"

Carmen unclipped the keys hooked to a belt loop on her shorts. "You asked about *The Undead Kama Sutra* and how I got my tan. It's time to show you." She grasped the handlebars of the green chopper, arced her leg over the frame, and settled onto the seat.

I asked, "Did you get my messages?"

"I did."

"Why didn't you reply?"

Carmen inserted the ignition key. "You asked what gives? I wanted you to come and find out. Show me how bad you want to know." She cocked her thumb to the pinion seat of the motorcycle. "Climb on. We're going to the dock."

"I can drive. You ride on the back."

Carmen shook her head. "Like hell. It's my bike. You can either walk or ride bitch."

"I'll follow in my car."

Carmen started the engine. She shouted above the roar from the exhaust pipes. "Quit being such a macho *caga palo*." Take the stick out of your ass. "Forget your goddamn car. It's not going anywhere. Just get on."

You couldn't argue with Carmen. I swung a leg over the rear seat. Carmen reached with her left hand and groped for my arm. She pulled it around her waist. My right arm reached around so that I clasped both arms around her very trim and firm middle. For a vampire she was surprisingly warm, or was that my imagination?

I had barely planted my feet on the rear pegs when the

chopper jumped from the curb. The front wheel tucked to the left, Carmen barely straightened it before we flipped to the side. We swerved past a yellow Porsche Carrera, missing the rear fender by millimeters.

We skimmed close to a row of parked cars. I had to jerk my shoulders aside to avoid getting slapped by the mirrors.

"There's no rule that says you can't drive down the middle of the road," I shouted.

"You want to obey the rules," she shouted back, "then stay away from me. Shut up and enjoy the scenery."

Carmen took Duvall Street and merged into traffic. We approached the harbor and parked alongside a steel-pipe barricade.

I got off the bike first, thankful that we'd made it without being flung against the asphalt. Carmen took a tightly wrapped paper bag out of one of the leather panniers. The quart-sized bag bore a crude inked stamp: *Yerbas de Botánica Oshún. Miami, Florida.*

Herbs of Oshún Apothecary. My mother and aunts used to shop in Mexican *botánicas* for folk remedies, some which worked and others were merely superstitions—and a waste of money. "Does what's in that bag have anything to do with your tan?" Maybe some of the superstitious recipes did work.

Carmen squeezed the bag and crinkled the paper wrapping. "I didn't buy this to make bread."

Typical Carmen answer. "Who's Oshún?"

"She's an *orisha*, a Santeria goddess."

"Santeria? So this is about voodoo? You're going to stick pins in a doll of me?"

"I don't need pins or Santeria. I can kick your ass on my own."

I stepped out of her reach, just in case she wanted to prove something. "How did you get involved with Santeria?"

"I'm Cuban." Carmen crouched to fit a lock on her front

brake disk. "It's part of my heritage. The African slaves brought their beliefs to the Caribbean. You don't know much about Santeria, do you?"

"I know some. There's that song *Babalu*, by Ricky Ricardo. That's about Santeria, right?"

"He was Desi Arnaz when he recorded it," Carmen said. "And yes, the song is about Santeria."

"So who is Oshún?"

"The queen of beauty and sensuality. We call upon her magic."

"For what?"

"To make us better lovers, of course."

"How come Desi Arnaz didn't write a song about her?"

"I don't know, Felix. If Desi was alive you could ask him."

Dozens of sailboats and yachts were moored to the pier and their lights twinkled festively over the water. Carmen walked down the ramp to a thirty-foot Bayliner cruiser and hailed someone onboard.

I removed my sunglasses.

A man stepped out of the cabin. A red aura surrounded him. Human.

Carmen stepped off the dock and into the cockpit of the boat. She and the man clasped hands, and he kissed her on the cheek. Her orange aura glistened with affection. Vampires only show that kind of attraction to *chalices*, humans who willingly offer themselves, and their blood, to their vampire masters.

Carmen waved me aboard and I joined her in the cockpit. She introduced me to Thorne, a ropey-muscled man in his mid-twenties. The word strapping came to mind; someone who could satisfy her sexual appetite. Was he her research partner for *The Undead Kama Sutra*? A bandana covered his neck, advertising his status as a chalice to those in the undead family. He didn't say much and smiled politely.

Carmen carried the botanica bag and stooped to enter the boat's cabin. She came out empty-handed and ordered that we shove off.

Moving athletically on his sturdy hairy legs, Thorne cast loose from the moorings. Her hungry gaze followed him.

Thorne took the helm. He flipped switches across the instrument panel. The navigation lights flicked on. The engine coughed to life. Above the cabin, the radar antenna on the mast began to spin. He adjusted the volume of the radio so the squawks of harbor traffic faded into the background. The Bayliner cruised slowly away from the dock.

A woman's shriek—sounding like a cross between a drunken sorority girl and a hyena on fire—echoed from the pier. An orange glow streaked toward us. Jolie.

She bounded from the edge of the pier toward us. Our boat was a good hundred feet away. Jolie sailed through the air and pumped her arms to keep the momentum. She used vampire levitation to land softly beside Carmen and me.

Jolie raised both her arms in a triumphant salute. "Ta-da."

"Yeah, great," Carmen chided. "Where's your motorcycle?"

Jolie's aura dimmed. "Shit. I knew I forgot something."

"How was the fight?" I asked.

"Totally awesome. One of those assholes got the drop on me and nailed me good." She pointed to shiner on the right eye. "I'll bet it's a beaut."

"Looks . . . wonderful," I said. "Hurt?"

"Stupid question." Jolie touched the swollen tissue around her eye. "Course it hurts. Too bad it'll heal by the time we get home."

"Which is where?" I turned to Carmen.

She loosened the braid of her ponytail. She closed her eyes in a blissful trance as she raked her fingers to untangle the tresses. Leaning against the railing of the gunwale,

Carmen silhouetted herself against the lights of Key West. Her hair shimmered like a lacy halo. "Houghton Island. It's in the Snipe Keys northeast of here."

Once in open water, Thorne opened the throttle and the Bayliner rocked on its wake. Jolie yanked off her boots and socks and scrambled barefoot to the prow, where she sat on the foredeck and sang—more or less—tunes from the '80s. Thorne played with the GPS on the instrument panel and adjusted our course. In the far darkness, red, green, and white lights marked the other boats floating by.

I took a seat on the fantail. "Aren't the Snipe Keys government islands?" I asked.

Carmen's aura sparkled with assurance. "That's what makes our resort so exclusive."

"A resort? How did you manage that?"

Carmen gave a dimpled smile. "We have chalices in high places."

"We?"

"There's a bunch of investors, a few select vampires and chalices. It was my idea . . . and Antoine's. You'll meet him."

"A few select vampires and chalices? High rollers, I'll bet. Fun and games on a private island. Must be paradise."

Carmen's aura prickled with worry. "It was. That's why I'm glad you came here."

"Sounds like someone's found a turd floating in the punch bowl, and I'm supposed to fish it out." Trouble followed me everywhere.

"Lovely visual, Felix. Yeah, I could use your help."

"Doesn't sound like research for *The Undead Kama Sutra.*"

"It's not." Carmen paused for a beat and then explained in a monotone. "A chalice has been missing for two days."

A missing chalice? I already had plenty to keep me busy, thanks to Gilbert Odin and the Araneum. But Carmen as an experienced vampire wouldn't have asked for help unless she needed it.

"You got a name?"

"Marissa Albert. She arrived at the Key West airport and disappeared. Too bad you didn't have a chance to meet her, you might have had a lot in common."

"How so?"

"She's a private investigator."

"Was Marissa here on a case?"

Carmen looked flustered. "She didn't mention it. She called last week and asked for a reservation to the resort. It was kinda sudden, but not too unusual."

"And you know her from where?"

"We met when I was traveling through Minneapolis." Carmen smiled at the memory. "She's a wonderful chalice. It'll be a shame if anything happened to her."

"Why would you suspect that? Maybe she ran into a friend and changed plans."

Carmen lost the smile. "She wasn't the type to not let me know. I wouldn't describe Marissa as flighty."

A missing chalice and an alien threat? Was there a connection? I wanted to share what the Araneum had offered but they had ordered that I keep the information secret.

A series of black humps appeared on the horizon. Thorne pointed the Bayliner toward the largest one.

"Houghton Island," he said.

As we approached, the island and its crown of trees looked like spiked teeth jutting from the water. The word paradise hardly came to mind—it looked like my ass was about to get bit.

LEGENDS OF THE RIFTWAR

HONORED ENEMY 978-0-06-079284-8

by Raymond E. Feist & William R. Forstchen

In the frozen northlands of the embattled realm of Midkemia, Dennis Hartraft's Marauders must band together with their bitter enemy, the Tsurani, to battle *moredhel,* a migrating horde of deadly dark elves.

MURDER IN LAMUT 978-0-06-079291-6

by Raymond E. Feist & Joel Rosenberg

For twenty years the mercenaries Durine, Kethol, and Pirojil have fought other people's battles, defeating numerous deadly enemies. Now the Three Swords find themselves trapped by a winter's storm inside a castle teeming with ambitious, plotting lords and ladies, and it falls on the mercenaries to solve a series of cold-blooded murders.

JIMMY THE HAND 978-0-06-079299-2

by Raymond E. Feist & S.M. Stirling

Forced to flee the only home he's ever known, Jimmy the Hand, boy thief of Krondor finds himself among the rural villagers of Land's End. But Land's End is home to a dark, dangerous presence even the local smugglers don't recognize. And suddenly Jimmy's youthful bravado is leading him into the maw of chaos . . . and, quite possibly, his doom.